WHISKEY KILLS

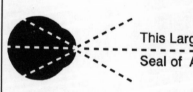

This Large Print Book carries the
Seal of Approval of N.A.V.H.

WHISKEY KILLS

A KILLSTRAIGHT STORY

W3.

JOHNNY D. BOGGS

THORNDIKE PRESS
A part of Gale, Cengage Learning

GALE
CENGAGE Learning™

Detroit • New York • San Francisco • New Haven, Conn • Waterville, Maine • London

GALE
CENGAGE Learning

Copyright © 2010 by Johnny D. Boggs.
Thorndike Press, a part of Gale, Cengage Learning.

LIBRARY OF CONGRESS CATALOGING-IN-PUBLICATION DATA

Boggs, Johnny D.
    Whiskey kills : a Killstraight story / by Johnny D. Boggs.
        p. cm. — (Thorndike Press large print western)
    ISBN-13: 978-1-4104-2963-6
    ISBN-10: 1-4104-2963-6
    1. Indians of North America—Fiction. 2. Murder—Investigation—
Fiction. 3. Large type books. I. Title.
PS3552.O4375W47 2010b
813'.54—dc22   2010016574

Published in 2010 by arrangement with Golden West Literary Agency.

Printed in the United States of America
1 2 3 4 5 6 7 14 13 12 11 10

In memory of, and with many thanks
to, Tony Hillerman

CHAPTER ONE

The wind . . . biting, cold, unrelenting.

The sky . . . gunmetal gray, ugly, ominous.

The ground . . . barren, frozen, hard.

All matched Daniel Killstraight's mood.

For three days, he had been riding, hardly eating, barely sleeping, searching, freezing, swearing. Three days without seeing anyone, or anything except ravens, a red-tailed hawk, and a few scrawny, ticky Texas longhorns. Three days without any lessening of his anger. Three days of bitter memories. Three days since they had buried Sehebi, who the Pale Eyes knew as Willow. The four-year-old daughter of Toyarocho. Grand-daughter of Teepee That Stands Alone.

He had crossed the North Fork of the Red River, knew he was beyond the reservation of the Kiowas, Comanches, and Apaches, knew he was out of his jurisdiction, that he had no authority for what he had been hoping to do for three days now. Daniel had ridden into disputed Greer County, which the Texians had claimed since before Daniel was born, even before his father had been born, ignoring the United States government that designated this land as part of Indian Territory. He knew what those Texians would likely do to him if they caught him.

Daniel Killstraight did not care.

Catching the scent of wood smoke, he tugged on the braided-leather hackamore, and swung off the buckskin mare. For the past three or four miles, he had been riding in a narrow gully, partly to escape the wind, mostly to escape detection. Not many white settlers had dared to try to make a home in Greer County, but those that did remained far from friendly to any stranger, especially a Comanche Indian wearing a badge. A post office had been established recently, one post office covering 1.5 million acres, but he was nowhere near that post office.

A moment after he climbed out of the gully, he spotted the smoke.

His coat was gray, too small for him, stained, full of holes, surviving the years after the Centennial Exposition in some forgotten crate before being handed down to the tribal police. Although the wool pricked like goat heads, the coat did offer some protection from the wind. Pinned beneath a missing button was a shield badge, stamped with a bow with two crossed arrows, and the words *Indian Police.* Dropping his head, Daniel stared momentarily at the piece of tin, before scanning the countryside again. His trousers were made of deerskin, and he wore Comanche moccasins, a sutler's red shirt, bear-claw necklace, and a stiff-brimmed, high-crowned black hat with a hawk feather stuck in the band. His clothes revealed part white man, part Indian, and that's how Daniel often felt himself, even if he had not one drop of *taibo* blood in his veins. Yes, his mother had been Mescalero, but Daniel was Nermernuh. The People. Comanche.

He dropped back into the gully, grabbed the hackamore, and led the mare through the winding ditch, their feet crunching the ice, then sloshing through water, an inch deep at first, growing deeper, until it reached Daniel's ankles, and he stopped, hearing the wind moan through the blackjacks. Before climbing out of the gully, he drew the Remington as the buckskin lowered her head to drink.

Out of the gully, Daniel lay on his belly, staring ahead at the stand of blackjacks. He could hear the voices, smell not only wood smoke, but the aroma of salt pork frying in a skillet, and his stomach growled. He pulled the revolver's hammer until it clicked, then carefully rotated the cylinder, checking the percussion caps on the rusty relic the agency gave the Indian policemen.

For an instant, he hesitated, wondering if he should ride back for help. *Are you afraid?* he asked himself with bitterness. A raucous laugh roared out of the blackjacks, and Daniel remembered again, blood and anger rushing to his head. He lowered the hammer, and crawled on his belly toward the trees, hearing but no longer feeling the wind, seeing those blackjacks transform into the Wichita Mountains, fifty or sixty miles northeast.

The smoke turned into images of Sehebi, Toyarocho, and Teepee That Stands Alone, and the wind became cries of mourning. He thought of Sehebi, and why he had traveled so far.

The sky remained a perfect blue except for one small white cloud standing over the Wichitas, as the winter-worn grass waved in the cold wind. Daniel and Ben Buffalo Bone were the first to arrive at the Toyarocho's camp, having left Leviticus Ellenbogen and Grace Morning Star behind. The new Indian agent showed himself to be a mighty poor rider, and Grace Morning Star was in no hurry to see Toyarocho's daughter again.

In front of the lone teepee, Toyarocho's wife — the one wife the agents had let him keep — sat on her knees, blood running in rivulets down both arms, her long, black hair chopped short, singing a wailing song, while other women stood around her, crying their songs of grief.

Off to the right, Toyarocho sat on a lichen-covered chunk of granite. He, too, sang, although he had not slashed his arms or hair, and his song was not one of pain. His arm waved with the music, an empty bottle tight in his hand.

"Whiskey," he sang in the little English he knew. "Whiskey. Whiskey. Whiskey. Me good Comanch'. Whiskey. Whiskey. Whiskey."

He stank of it.

Like most men of The People, Toyarocho was short, chubby, with a round, fat face, thick arms, and glistening, black hair that fell in two long braids. He was slightly shorter, and somewhat heavier than Daniel, beaten by the reservation, beaten by whiskey. He still dressed like a Kwahadi of old, but his bloodshot eyes looked dead. Beside him, Daniel saw a mountain of broken glass. Despite the chill, Toyarocho was shirtless, his sides raked with scratches along his rib cage. Most of the wounds had clotted, but one had reopened, sending blood dripping down his side, staining his deerskin. Toyarocho was too drunk to notice, or care.

In front of Toyarocho's lodge, like an ancient cottonwood tree, waited Teepee That Stands Alone. Daniel turned to Ben Buffalo Bone, and signaled his friend to take care of Toyarocho. The tribal policeman reached behind his gun belt, and found the iron handcuffs, but Daniel shook his head, and walked to the teepee.

At six-foot-one, Teepee That Stands Alone towered over most of The People. He was a Kwahadi *puhakat,* a healer of much importance, of great power, for The People. Medicine man, the Pale Eyes called them, but the *taibos* knew little of The People. In the old days, before a continuous war with the Texians and bluecoats began, *puhakats* had been the real leaders of The People. The ones who could talk to the Great Spirit, who helped the younger men and boys on their vision quests, who could heal the sick, solve problems, point The People down the right path to follow. War changed that, bringing the war leaders to power, pushing back the healers. Yet Teepee That Stands Alone had never lost his standing. Before

12

the Kwahadi band had surrendered when Daniel was just a boy, Quanah Parker had always sought the counsel of the great *puhakat,* Teepee That Stands Alone. Even after the Pale Eyes had made Quanah Parker the chief of all The People, men — bluecoats, black robes, Texians, and The People — continued to seek out Teepee That Stands Alone for his wisdom.

Nothing from the Pale Eyes could be found on him. He wore a full-feathered bonnet, deerskin leggings, shirt, and moccasins. Even his lance was made the old way, its wooden point sharpened, and hardened by fire. Most of The People used steel points, acquired from the Pale Eyes by raid or trade. All of The People knew that if Teepee That Stands Alone ever wore something not made by The People, his *puha* would vanish, and he would become a worthless old man, powerless, forgotten.

He looked older, but no less forceful, than Daniel remembered. Even the tears streaming down his face could not lessen his presence. Yet when he spoke, his voice quavered — "I could . . . do . . . nothing." — he spoke in Comanche, and, limping aside from the opening, using his lance as a crutch, joined the women in song.

Swallowing, trying to steel himself for

what he knew he would find in the lodge, Daniel ducked inside.

Inside, he knelt, sighing heavily, as he reached out and touched the cold body of the four-year-old. Gently he lifted her hands, saw the blood under her fingernails. Outside, Toyarocho sang his drunken song, and Daniel pictured the scratches on his sides, recalling what Grace Morning Star had told them at the agency near Fort Sill. The sound of cantering horses rose above the songs of mourning, and he knew Grace Morning Star and Leviticus Ellenbogen had arrived. Before leaving the teepee, he covered Sehebi's face with an ancient buffalo robe.

He moved past the mourners, glancing over his shoulder at Ben Buffalo Bone and Sehebi's drunken father, and walked directly to the agent. Grace Morning Star ran past him, tears streaming down her face. It had been the silver-haired Grace Morning Star, the last surviving wife of Teepee That Stands Alone, who had found Sehebi, tried to revive her, then ridden all the way to the agency in hopes of returning with a Pale Eyes doctor who could stop Sehebi from taking the journey to The Land Beyond The Sun.

No luck. There was no doctor at the

agency, never had been, and the major at Fort Sill said, with measured regret, that he had to operate on a bluecoat soldier, and that his assistant surgeon was in the field, that neither could make it to the Wichitas to check on some Comanche kid until the next day at the earliest. It didn't matter.

Leviticus Ellenbogen dropped the reins to his bay gelding, raising a gloved right hand to cover his mouth. He had arrived from Buffalo, New York, the latest appointment to the post, and so far had seldom traveled more than a couple of miles from the agency. He had witnessed ration day, but had never seen, probably never even imagined, how The People would react to the death of a child, or any loved one. Self-mutilation. Wailing. Now Teepee That Stands Alone had removed his beautiful bonnet, and had sawed off one of his long braids, tossing it onto the fire. As he worked to cut off the other braid, Grace Morning Star took a knife from Toyarocho's wife, laid her own hand against a rock, and chopped off the tip of her little finger.

Ellenbogen's dark eyes stared, uncomprehending, unprepared, and, when he finally lowered his hand, he said in an ugly whisper: "That's. . . ."

Daniel finished the sentence for him. "Barbaric?"

The agent's mouth closed sharply, and he looked sternly at Daniel. He was a gangly man in black broadcloth and a blue greatcoat, dark hair turning gray, with eyes almost as dark as Daniel's. He spoke with a German accent Daniel had often heard during his years east at the Carlisle Industrial School as well as in the Pennsylvania mines, and a thin, six-pointed star, instead of a cross, dangled from a gold necklace that hung over his puffy navy tie.

The Pale Eyes in Washington City had sent many agents to oversee the Comanches, Kiowas, and Apaches: Quakers and Methodists, ex-soldiers and Texians. Most did not last long. They either couldn't handle their "wards" or they were forced to resign after being caught cheating their Indian subjects, and filling their own pockets with money. Grafters. Frauds. Hypocrites. Bastards. Daniel had had the last agent, Ephraim Rueben, taken into custody by federal officers — Comanche policemen weren't allowed to arrest white men — and Rueben was now imprisoned in the federal penitentiary at Fort Leavenworth, Kansas. Daniel didn't really know Leviticus Ellenbogen, but considered him to be as useless, as corrupt as all of his predecessors.

Ellenbogen's eyelids knotted, and he started to speak, decided against it, and took a deep breath, slowly exhaling and then tugging on his thick graying beard.

"Make your report, Sergeant Killstraight."

"It's like Grace Morning Star said. Sehebi is dead. Killed by her father." Daniel tilted his head toward Toyarocho, who had stopped singing as Ben Buffalo Bone led him to the horses.

"She put up a fight," Ellenbogen said. He had seen the scratches on Toyarocho's bare chest. "Was his intent . . . ?"

"The People do not beat our children," Daniel said. "We aren't as barbaric as some races." Frowning harder, Ellenbogen clenched both fists, but said nothing. "Toyarocho is a drunk," Daniel continued. "He has been one for years. He returned to his lodge this morning, drunk, and passed out on top of Sehebi. She clawed him, but Toyarocho would not waken, would not roll over. She suffocated."

"His wife was in that teepee!" Ellenbogen yelled.

Daniel blinked, staring, not believing the tears in the agent's eyes.

"Didn't she hear the noise?" the agent cried. "Couldn't she feel her child kicking, fighting for her life?"

Daniel looked down. "Likely," he said softly, "she was drunk, too."

"My God!" Ellenbogen roared. He bowed his head into hands too large for the rest of his body.

Daniel left the grieving agent alone, found Ben Buffalo Bone, and helped get Toyarocho into the saddle.

"Where do I take him?" Ben Buffalo Bone asked in Comanche.

"Narawekwi," he answered. The jail at Fort Sill would have to hold Toyarocho for now.

"What will become of Toyarocho?"

"I don't know," Daniel said wearily in English. "It will be up to Quanah."

"No!" Daniel turned to the voice. Agent Leviticus Ellenbogen strode toward them, stopped, his face red underneath that wide-brimmed black hat. "A father killing his daughter will not be heard at your Court of Indian Offenses. No, by thunder. Never. Yes, Mister Buffalo Bone, you take that . . . that. . . ." The tall agent tried to steady himself. "You take him to Fort Sill . . . you tell the colonel that this murderer is to be arraigned in Wichita Falls. You tell. . . ."

Toyarocho started singing again. The agent blinked, his mouth open. Finally Ellenbogen swallowed, and, turning in revulsion, barked a final order: "Get that drunkard out of my sight!" Ellenbogen walked toward Teepee That Stands Alone, and Daniel looked up at Ben Buffalo Bone.

"You heard him," Daniel said.

"Yes." Ben Buffalo Bone's head fell. "She was a sweet little girl. It does not seem fair."

"It isn't." Daniel turned, and followed Agent Ellenbogen.

The burial had been simple. Such was the way of The People. Leviticus Ellenbogen could not understand that, either, but he withheld comment, even shook Teepee That Stands Alone's hand after what would pass as a funeral. For the first hour, he did not speak as they rode east toward Fort Sill.

"You think I'm too tough, don't you?" Ellenbogen asked.

The question came as a surprise. Daniel didn't know how to answer.

"You'd turn over that drunk to Quanah Parker," the agent said. "What would he do? Slap his wrist?"

Daniel wet his lips. Leviticus Ellenbogen, who had arrived at the agency barely a month ago, had much to learn. The People would have dealt much harsher with Toyarocho than some *Tejano* judge across the river.

"He killed his own daughter," the agent said again.

"He had help," Daniel said.

Both men reined in their horses. The agent stared. Daniel waited.

"What do you mean?" Ellenbogen asked.

"Toyarocho did not make that whiskey himself."

The agent considered that for a moment. "I have heard about those Creek whiskey runners. They have been a blight on this reservation."

"This wasn't Creek," Daniel said.

"How can you tell?"

"The bottles. The smell. *Taibo* whiskey."

"*Taibo?*"

"White man." He pointed south. "Texas."

Ellenbogen kicked his gelding into a walk. Daniel followed. Five minutes later, the agent stopped his horse again. Turning to Daniel, he tugged on his thick beard with gloved fingers.

"Do you think you can find those whiskey runners?"

Daniel didn't answer. He turned his horse quickly, and kicked the mare into a lope, riding back toward the Wichitas. He was thinking of Sehebi as he rode.

He was thinking of her again as he crawled

in the biting wind toward the stand of blackjacks where the whiskey peddlers waited.

CHAPTER TWO

"Blake," said the man kneeling over a cast iron skillet, "we got company."

Daniel rose out of the brush, and stepped into the clearing. Until then, he had kept under cover, crawling and crouching until he reached the edge of camp, then not moving until he knew exactly what he was up against. Two men. That's all.

The one by the fire set the skillet next to an equally blackened coffee pot, and slowly rose, pushing back his tan coat. He was a tall man, sporting a fuzzy mustache and hazel eyes. Didn't appear to be much older than Daniel, but you could never really tell about a *taibo*. No belt gun that Daniel could see, and his knife, a store-bought butcher's, rested in the skillet atop grease and salt pork. The tall man hooked his thumbs inside his trousers, and glanced at the battered buckboard parked in the shade. Although a Henry rifle leaned against the rear wheel, he made no move for it.

"What the hell," snapped the man named Blake as he bulled his way through the brush, pulling his suspenders over his shoulders, then stuffing a muslin shirt in patched britches. He jerked to a standstill, as if he had slammed into an invisible wall, staring at Daniel for a moment before he started forward again, cautiously now, wiping his hands on his legs, not halting until he found himself beside the tall man.

"Some kind of sentry you is, Uvalde," Blake said.

Older. Much older. A dirty white beard formed a point at the V in his shirt. The beard looked dirtier than the battered hat, which also formed a point, aiming toward the gray sky. The rest of his face looked as if it had been run over by a farmer's plow, and dried in the sun. Blake wasn't as tall as his partner, but likely weighed twice as much.

Gnarly fingers groped his beard. "You hear what I said?" he barked again.

"You told me to fry up some supper, Blake. Didn't put me on guard duty. Said we didn't need no guard."

"We don't." With a quick smile, Blake walked around the fire. "You're off the rez, buck," he told Daniel, still grinning. His

23

front teeth reminded Daniel of a quilt of sorts. One gold. One black. One yellow. One missing. One brown. "Long way from the agency, I say." Blake frowned at Daniel's silence. He raised his voice. "I say you're off the reservation, boy." He stretched a big arm out, pointing east. "Reservation. That way. T'uther side of the river. Best run back there, buck. Else the Army'll get you. Or Texicans who ain't as friendly as me and Uvalde. Ain't that right, pard?"

"That's right." The young one lacked the old man's confidence.

Daniel held his tongue.

The man called Blake lowered his arm suddenly, and swore. "You speak English?" Nothing. *"¿Habla usted inglés?"*

"He ain't a greaser, Blake. He's an Injun. Kiowa, I warrant."

Blake turned to glare at his partner. "I know what he is, and he ain't Kiowa, neither. Bunch of them bucks know Spanish better than a Mex. He's Comanch'."

"Jesus!" Ulvade's eyes widened.

"Don't piss your pants. He ain't after our scalps." Blake winked at Daniel, and stretched his grin. *"Rekwaru taibo? Huh? Rekwaru taibo?"*

His syntax was wrong, and, like most Pale Eyes, his tongue tripped over the words of

24

The People, but Daniel had heard worse attempts from white men. This one, at least, tried.

"Speak English? *Rekwaru taibo? Rekwaru taibo?* Speak American, boy? You deaf?"

"He's wearing a badge, Blake," Uvalde said.

"I ain't blind." Blake snapped his fingers, and his big head bobbed. "Oh, now I savvy. It's whiskey that you want. *Posa baa?*"

Blake shot a quick look at his partner, explaining: "Injun lawdogs got the biggest thirst there is, whether they's civilized like Creeks, or savages like Comanch'."

Facing Daniel again, Blake said: "That it, buck? *Posa baa?*" He pretended as if he held a jug, brought his hand to his mouth, swallowing, then staggering a crazy man's dance. When he stopped, he looked at Daniel. "That's it, ain't it, buck? *Posa baa?* It's *posa baa* that you want. Well, come on in, Mister Comanch', we got whiskey to warm you up."

The old man moved with surprising litheness for a man his size, reached the wagon, and leaped onto the bed. He threw back a stained canvas tarp. As Daniel walked toward the fire, he heard the clinking of glass against glass. *"Taa-daaaaaa!"* Blake, sounding like a magician at some dog and pony show, raised a bottle over his head. He uncorked it with his teeth, spit the cork into his free hand, and took a long pull, then started to toss the bottle at Daniel, only stopped, bringing the bottle back to his big gut, laughing.

"Money," he said. "*Puhihwi? Ekapuhihwi?* This good whiskey. Ain't free. Costs money. You got any, buck? *Puhihwi? Ekapuhihwi?* Or we can work out a trade, maybe so."

"I have money," Daniel said, and the laughter died. With his left hand, Daniel reached into his coat pocket, fingered a gold piece, pulled it out, holding it in the sunlight, then tossing it onto the ground, halfway between the fire and the wagon. "How much would that buy me?" he asked.

Blake's Adam's apple bobbed. "You been holdin' out on me, Comanch'. Speak real good English, don't you? Not an honest way of doin' business." He corked the bottle and flipped it, sending it sailing toward Daniel as he climbed not so sprightly off the wagon. Slowly, wily now, the whiskey peddler made his way toward the Henry rifle.

Instead of reaching to catch the bottle, Daniel let it drop, clunking on the ground, and rested his right hand on the butt of the big Remington in his holster. "That's close enough to that rifle."

Blake stopped. The young one whispered something, and moved back a few steps from the fire.

Watching them, Daniel retrieved the heavy bottle, thumbed the cork onto the dirt, and held the whiskey under his nose. His eyes burned, and he drew the pint back. It was ceramic stoneware, fairly heavy, made for beer. Daniel had seen similar bottles back in the grog shops of Pennsylvania where the miners would go after their shifts, bringing Daniel, who worked alongside them, even though Daniel did not drink. Deep under the surface of the earth, Daniel had been a fellow worker, breathing the same bad air, working the same grueling shift, sharing jokes with those husky Irish and German workers. In the beer gardens, however, those burly Pennsylvania men treated him more like the mine's mascot.

He shook away the memories, and thought back to Toyarocho's camp, the mountain of broken glass shining in the sun. Daniel examined the bottle closely. True, Toyarocho had held a bottle like this one in his hand, but most of the shattered glass seemed different. Not the tough stoneware, but more recent, lighter bottles, some cobalt, but mostly clear glass. Daniel could also picture shattered pieces of brown clay jugs in that pile of rubble. Slowly Daniel tilted the bottle, letting the whiskey puddle at his moccasins.

"The hell are you doin'?" Blake roared.

"I paid for it," Daniel said. When the bottle was empty, he tossed it, letting it thud near the coin he had thrown. "That's a twenty-dollar gold piece," Daniel said. "Should buy more than one pint. Let's see what else you have."

Nobody moved, until Daniel drew his revolver. Blake started for the rifle, but a sharp word from Daniel stopped the man as Daniel thumbed back the hammer. He started to point the .44 at the old man, then decided the other man would be more pliable.

"Show me some more bottles," he said.

Uvalde hesitated.

"You ain't got no right!" Blake thundered. The old man kept looking through the brush, searching, Daniel guessed, for deputy marshals — white men. The runner couldn't quite figure out what was going on, not comprehending yet that Daniel was here alone. Likely trying to guess what Daniel wanted. Whiskey? Money? Scalps?

Daniel steadied the revolver. "Now," he spoke harshly, and the young one, Uvalde, made a beeline for the wagon, climbed into the back, and brought up a bottle in each hand.

Ceramic stoneware, just like the one Daniel had examined.

"Are they all like that?" he asked.

The question perplexed the tall man.

"That kind of bottle?" Daniel explained. "Big, old, heavy ones. Not like the newer bottles they're making."

"Yeah." Uvalde sounded uncertain.

"No jugs? No canning jars? On the reservation, I've seen whiskey in ink reservoirs, coffee cans, gourds. Are yours all in bottles like those?"

"Yeah. Beer bottles. From the. . . ."

"Shut up!" Blake snapped.

"I haven't seen bottles like this around here," Daniel said.

Blake's bronzed face reddened. "Who the hell are you? What do you want?"

"You," answered Daniel, surprised he could hold his temper, which raged behind his façade. He tapped his badge.

"Metal shirt." The big man snorted. "Comanch' lawdog. Well, you ain't shit to me. You got no jurisdiction, Comanch', no matter how good you savvy and speak English. This here is Greer County, for one. For another, red niggers ain't got the right to arrest no white man. No place. Never!"

29

"Maybe he wants . . . you know . . . ," Uvalde started, and Blake rediscovered his ugly grin.

"Yeah. Is that it, buck? What's your name, by the way? I'm Blake Browne. This here is my new pard, Uvalde. Ted Smith's what he calls hisself, but I don't think Smith is his truthful name. You got a name, don't you? You can share your name with old Blake Browne. Hell, boy, I likely sold your grandpa whiskey on the Arkansas River back in the good days, when you Comanch' was lords of these southern plains, back when this was nothin' but a kingdom of Comanch', and old Blake Browne . . . wasn't so old back then . . . made a fine livin' treatin' with your chiefs." Another wink. "And your squaws."

"Sergeant Daniel Killstraight."

"Sergeant." Blake tried to whistle, but didn't quite succeed. "Sergeant. I see. What you get paid, boy? Eight dollars a month? Maybe ten?" A fat finger stabbed at the gold piece. "Not enough to be carryin' no Liberty coin, that's certain sure. So you want a little, how do you say it, a token of our appreciation? Tribute? A little payment for helpin' out old Blake Browne and Uvalde Ted Smith by lookin' elsewhere when we's in your neck of the woods. Is that it, Sergeant Dan'l?"

30

"I want your two hides," Daniel said.

"You're 'bout to get a come-uppance, buck," Blake snarled. "No uppity Injun speaks to me like. . . ." He stopped, shook his head.

"No, you ain't after no bribe. You's here for Dakota. Dakota paid you. That's it. Hell, I should have knowed it all along. Well, you tell Dakota to go to hell. Courtesy of me and Uvalde. Blake Browne's got a claim on this territory. It's always been Blake Browne's territory. I made that one deal with your boss, but that's all, and never again. Wouldn't have done it then had I known what a burr under my saddle. . . ." He stopped just long enough to snort and spit. "No, I ain't interested in partnerin' with your crooked boss."

"I am here for Sehebi." A taboo among The People, speaking the name of the dead, but Daniel didn't care. He wanted these two louts to remember her name. Ice tinged his words. Uvalde and Blake barely heard him.

"Don't know the gent," Blake said.

"She's dead. She was four years old. Whiskey killed her."

Whirling, Blake demanded a bottle from his partner, and started guzzling. Despite the cold, sweat damped both men's faces.

Daniel moved to the fire. The smell of the

salt pork, now cool, pained him. He had to fight the urge to snatch up the meat, and devour it. He was famished, but he controlled those emotions, that one, anyway, but he knew he couldn't contain the fury boiling inside him, not much longer.

"See," said Blake Browne, lowering the bottle, and wiping his mouth with a dingy shirt sleeve. "I don't know what your beef is, but Blake Browne is a businessman. I don't sell no whiskey that I wouldn't drink myself, not even to a whiskey-rotted Comanch'. You ask any of your savage pals. You ask anybody from Teepee City to Huupi and Riverland to Fort Cobb, and they'll tell you that Blake Browne's an honest dealer of fine spirits."

"Whiskey's illegal on the reservation. You two are bound for Judge Parker, I warrant, in Fort Smith."

"Like hell." Savagely Blake Browne grabbed for the Henry.

The Remington roared, shattering the bottle in the old man's left hand, spraying him with shards and whiskey. His right hand jerked back as if burned by a brand.

"You killed her!" Only later, after he could remember what happened, did Daniel realize he had spoken those three words in Comanche. He fired again, destroying the bottle in Uvalde's hand. "She was four years old," he said, speaking English now, "and you killed her."

"We ain't killed nobody . . . ," Blake Browne started. Then he was screaming as Daniel ran, unable to restrain his rage. Daniel saw Uvalde leap off the buckboard. He fired, high over the running man's head, heard Uvalde crashing through the brush, yelling as he fell into the gully.

The mules struggled against the rope pickets.

The wind rustled in the blackjacks.

Blake Browne recovered to grab the Henry, but Daniel was on him, pounding him with the heavy barrel of the Remington.

"You can't touch me!" Blake Browne bellowed. "By God . . . I'm . . . white. . . ."

It felt like a dream.

Uvalde Ted Smith screaming from somewhere in the gully, the mules braying, stamping, finally pulling free, bolting through the blackjacks, and the sound of tearing flesh, metal against bone, the cries and grunts of Blake Browne. Daniel saw none of this. He only saw Sehebi's lifeless body, and her drunken father, holding a pint of whiskey.

Daniel held the empty bottle now. He

didn't remember picking it up, using it for a club. His Remington was back in the holster, and Blake Browne lay on the ground at his feet, crawling toward the fire, still alive. Daniel raised the bottle. Heavy. Had to weigh more than one pound, and empty at that. He hammered the bottle downward, aiming at Blake's white head, but, at the last second, he changed course, and the bottle struck the whiskey runner's shoulder.

He stopped, exhausted, reason returning to him. The only sound, Blake Browne's whimpering.

Sweating, Daniel dropped the bottle, wet his lips, and picked up the gold coin. He shoved it into his coat pocket, and drew the Remington as he walked to the rear of the wagon. The .44 roared. He kept pulling the trigger until the hammer snapped empty. Amber whiskey spilled from the crate, spreading across the floor, soaking into the tarp.

Moving with a purpose, Daniel holstered the empty revolver, and stooped over the fire, grabbed the end of a burning chunk of oak, and lifted it like a torch, moving back to the wagon. Without a word, he pitched the firebrand onto the canvas, and watched the flames, hearing the bottles softly explode, fueling the inferno, smelling smoke, feeling heat that almost singed his eyebrows.

Later — how long he wasn't certain — he stood over Blake Browne's body. The man lay face down, arms stretched out, fingers dug in the ground.

After that, Daniel remembered nothing, until he was riding away on the buckskin mare the next morning, watching the Wichita Mountains rise from out of the plains, feeling the first flakes of snow sting his face.

CHAPTER THREE

He answered to Daniel Killstraight, a name the Pale Eyes had given him. As a child, when the Kwahadi band of The People roamed El Llano Estacado as free people, he had been called Oá, meaning Horn. Later, still a boy, probably no older than seven or eight, Daniel had earned a new name, His Arrows Fly Straight Into The Hearts Of His Enemies. His father's name. Given to him by his father, who had taken a new name, Marsh Hawk.

They were Nermernuh. What was it the white-haired whiskey runner had said? *The good old days . . . when Comanch' was lords of these southern plains . . . when this was nothin' but a kingdom of Comanch'.*

Good old days? Maybe. Yet Daniel couldn't remember much about those times. Mostly what he recalled was starving, especially after the white hunters had destroyed *chutz,* buffalo, the lifeblood of

The People. Especially after bluecoats had attacked their camp in the cañon the Pale Eyes called the Palo Duro. Had destroyed their food. Killed their horses, perhaps a thousand fine animals, pushed The People into the relentless Staked Plains, hunted them as The People had once hunted and crushed their enemies.

Without mercy.

They ate their dogs until there were no more dogs left in camp. They survived on turkey, breaking the taboo of The People by eating such things, when they could find the birds, grasshoppers when they could not. Holding out as long as they could.

In the hot months of his ninth year, he was with his father, mother, his friends, all weakened by the lack of food, by the blistering sun, when the bluecoat chief known as Bad Hand sent a messenger — a Pale Eyes doctor called Sturms — into the Kwahadi camp on the White River. Bad Hand sent a message. The Kwahadi could surrender, to live in peace, where they would be protected from the *Tejanos,* or they would be hunted down. Killed.

He was there, after Sturms returned to Bad Hand, watching Quanah talk to Teepee That Stands Alone, Isa Nanaka, and Daniel's father, Marsh Hawk, and then watching Quanah ride off to seek a vision to tell him what he should do. He was there, broiling in the sun, when Quanah returned, his face gaunt, eyes strained, cheeks wet with tears.

He was with Quanah when the last of the Kwahadis — one hundred warriors, maybe another three hundred Kwahadi — rode or walked to Fort Sill, the bluecoat fort built in the heart of what had once had been that kingdom of The People.

He remembered Bad Hand's Long Knives taking their rifles, their pistols, their horses.

Oh, yes, Daniel remembered all that.

"You have an education," Ellenbogen had told him shortly after the new agent had arrived in Indian Territory. "You are blessed with that education. You should use that education to help your people. You know the ways of the white man. You know the ways of your tribe. You could be a tremendous help. You could be as powerful as Quanah Parker. You shouldn't be so bitter. Remember your education, son."

Education? Oh, yes, Daniel remembered that, too.

First, they sent him to the mission school near the agency. Trying to translate His Arrows Fly Straight Into The Hearts Of His Enemies was a challenge the Pale Eyes could not master, so he became Killstraight. When he was thirteen years old, two Pale Eyes in black broadcloth suits took him by the arms, led him to a spring wagon with several Arapahoes — one of them singing his death song — and told him he must go to the Carlisle Industrial School. He didn't get to say good bye to his mother. His father had already been sent to some place called Fort Marion in some place known as Florida. Only his father refused to endure such shame, had broken free, jumped off the train, and had been shot down by blue-coats.

A blessing, perhaps. His father had died fighting for freedom. Many of The People who would return from dark, damp Fort Marion three years later came with the lung sickness, which left them gasping for breath or coughing up blood. Eventually this sickness, which the Pale Eyes called consumption, would send many warriors to The Land Beyond The Sun. Isa Nanaka would be one of those, although, tough as he was, he lived longer than most. Long enough to see Daniel return from his exile in Pennsylvania.

Carlisle, Pennsylvania.

One Kwahadi boy, just as frightened as the other Indians — one hundred and thirty-six in all — Lakotas, mostly, with Cheyennes, Arapahoes, Kiowas, and a few Pawnees, enemies of The People, enemies of just about every tribe on the plains. A bluecoat soldier oversaw the school. A tall man. A good man, really, though Daniel knew he, like most of his kind, was misguided. Daniel had been forced to point to white letters scratched onto a blackboard. After he had made his choice, School Father Pratt told him that he had a new name, Daniel. He must never refer to himself as His Arrows Fly Straight Into The Hearts Of His Enemies. He was Daniel. A good name. A strong name. An Old Testament name. A fine choice.

Later, one of the Pale Eyes women said Killstraight was not a Christian surname, that it conjured images of depredations, of rapine, of the barbarous nature of these savage fiends. His name should become Daniel Strait. "A noble Anglo-Saxon name," she said. "I knew many Straits in Hertshire."

School Father Pratt had smiled, and said: "Perhaps, but having taught this lad for these past few years, I think Killstraight fits him like a glove. Leave it Killstraight, Missus Hall. Daniel has earned that much, I warrant."

Earned it? Yes.

At Carlisle, they had shorn his hair like he was some Navajo sheep, cutting off his long braids, and the men of The People cherished their hair. They had whipped him whenever he spoke his true tongue, made him pray to the Pale Eyes' god, made him forget, or tried to make him forget, who he was, who his people were.

"Kill the Indian," School Father Pratt had often said, "not the man."

They taught him the English tongue, taught him how to be a carpenter — the Indian boys had to help repair, even build some of the buildings they would use to learn the ways of the Pale Eyes. After four years in Carlisle, they sent him to work for some hard-rock farmer in Franklin County, and, later, he spent an eternity hidden from the sun in those damp coal mines.

After seven years, they let him come home. Back to the reservation. Home.

Or was it home? Had he ever had a home?

That had troubled him for the first year back on the reservation. He remembered his mother, long dead, a Mescalero Apache woman who sang so lovely. He remembered that, as a boy, some of his friends would tease him, telling him that he did not truly belong to The People, and that he was only half a boy, the other half Apache.

After seven years traveling the white man's road, he found himself a stranger among The People, wondering who he was, where he was going, what he should do.

So he had taken a job — something School Father Pratt and his fellow educators had chiseled into their students. Find employment. Work hard. It is good for your soul, will build your self-esteem, will help you better yourselves. Work. It is the way of the white men. Show enterprise. Improve your standing. Buy things. Own things. Follow the white man's road. It is the only way to better yourselves, to improve your position, to survive in this world.

Ben Buffalo Bone, his friend, had introduced Daniel to the agent Ephraim Rueben, had bragged that Daniel would make a fine Metal Shirt. Ben Buffalo Bone was of the Kotsoteka band. As children, they had attended the missionary school together, but Ben had not been snatched away and spirited to Pennsylvania.

So Daniel had become a Metal Shirt, drawing $8 a month, which he seldom saw, getting a badge, a revolver, and an itchy, moth-eaten blouse.

Ben Buffalo Bone had brought Daniel to his lodge, given Daniel the cabin that the Pale Eyes had built for Ben's father. The old peace chief never found much use for the cabin, hated the damned thing, really, not understanding how Pale Eyes could live in a dark structure of squares when a teepee represented the circle of life, the way of The People. The old man had lived in his teepee, and let his horses stay in the cabin. After Ben's father had died, his uncle took Ben's mother as his wife, but kept the cabin as a stable.

Daniel didn't mind the cabin. Didn't mind the horses who shared his home. He enjoyed the scent of horsehair, even horse apples. *If only School Father Pratt had let us share our quarters with horses,* he thought. But that would not be following the white man's road.

In his first year as a Comanche Tribal Policeman, Daniel had slowly found his way. Perhaps his seven years living among the Pale Eyes had helped him send the crooked agent Ephraim Rueben to prison, and a few others, including another Comanche Metal Shirt. After that, the new agent had promoted Daniel to the rank of sergeant, not so much because of Daniel's prowess as a lawman or detective. No, Daniel knew he had stumbled his way through that investigation, and the *Police Gazette* probably wouldn't have labeled all those missteps, guesses, and bumbles as investigation.

There had also been a girl involved. She was in prison somewhere. A girl who worked at the mission. A Pale Eyes girl. A girl he had grown to like. Daniel didn't like to think about her.

Instead, he thought of Rain Shower, Ben Buffalo Bone's sister.

Tried to, at least. His thoughts kept leaving the lovely Rain Shower, his past, always coming back to Uvalde Ted Smith and Blake Browne. Always pointing to Toyarocho, and four-year-old Sehebi.

"Best way to know if the Creeks are running whiskey on the reservation is if you have a bunch of drunk Metal Shirts."

Hugh Gunter had told him that, a long time ago, and it often proved true. Gunter was a tall, forceful Cherokee, an officer of the United States Indian Police with jurisdiction over the Five Civilized Tribes. Gunter had become a good friend, a mentor, along with another tall peace officer, a Pale Eyes gent with a weather-beaten face, furrowed brow, and whopper of a mustache, a man named Harvey P. Noble, a deputy United States marshal riding for Judge Isaac Parker's court in Fort Smith, Arkansas.

Both men had taught Daniel a lot about being a lawman, being a detective, although

Daniel still didn't think of himself as either.

Best way to know if the Creeks are running whiskey. . . .

During that first year as a policeman, he had learned a lot about Creek whiskey runners.

Yet it wasn't just the Creeks. Choctaws had been arrested, and federal marshals had sent scores of Pale Eyes — from Kansas, Arkansas, and Texas — to prison for selling intoxicating spirits on the reservation. Every one of them was a bigger scavenger than a raven. They'd use anything they could find to keep their whiskey in: bottles, jugs, buckets, coal-oil cans, clay jugs, oaken kegs, usually a hodge-podge of containers, and, sure, maybe, a pint-sized beer bottle made of ceramic stoneware.

Yet every bottle in the back of Blake Browne's wagon had been the same. Cases of the stuff, all stamped:

Cox & Coursey Bottling Works
Home Brewed
GINGER BEER
Dallas, Texas

So what? Daniel thought. It was over now. He didn't know what was bothering him. Uvalde had been running so fast, he most likely had reached Dallas by now. Blake Browne had taken a vicious beating. Daniel had taught them a lesson. They wouldn't be back in Comanche country again. They wouldn't be selling whiskey to Toyarocho. They wouldn't be responsible for another four-year-old girl's death. They wouldn't leave The People in mourning again.

It was over.

Yet something kept eating at Daniel's stomach. Festering away. He had no regrets over what he had done to Blake Browne.

He heard Blake Browne's voice: *You's here for Dakota.*

That's what the old man had said. What else?

Dakota paid you.

Who was Dakota? What had Browne meant? What did it mean? Anything?

Tell Dakota to go to hell.

What else? He tried to hear the old whiskey runner's voice.

Blake Browne's got a claim on this territory.

And: *I made that one deal with your boss, but . . . never again.*

There was something else.

I ain't interested in partnerin' with your crooked boss.

Important? He wasn't sure, but it kept bothering him. He tried to forget it, tried to

46

convince himself the job was finished, that Blake Browne was finished. Yet it gnawed at him as he tried to sleep, and then he opened his eyes, seeing the marsh hawk, perched before him, singing his song.

Dakota. Dakota. Dakota.

CHAPTER FOUR

He heard her voice, softly calling his name.

Daniel tossed off the blanket, and sat up, rubbing the sleep out of his eyes while recognizing the pungent aroma of his home. A horse snorted. After he found his hat, he pulled himself to his feet, and detected another scent before he saw her.

With a gentle, perhaps even bashful smile, Rain Shower held out the tin cup.

"Ura," Daniel thanked her as he took the steaming cup. She said nothing as Daniel took the first sip of coffee. Sweeter than usual, almost like candy. Ah, Daniel remembered, ration day had come while he had been chasing those two whiskey runners. Using sugar at this rate, Rain Shower and her family would be out long before the next rations were handed out, but that was fine.

"I did not hear you return home," she said in Comanche.

"It was late," he answered, and the silence

returned.

The bay stallion, which had been the pride of Ben Buffalo Bone's father, began spraying the floor with urine, so Daniel suggested they step aside. With a quick nod, Rain Shower led the way.

Despite the morning's chill, the sun began to warm Daniel. The snow, what little had stuck to the earth, had already melted. He saw his buckskin in the round corral, smelled the wood smoke, and watched Ben Buffalo Bone's mother sitting under the brush arbor, cooking breakfast.

"You still look tired," Rain Shower said.

"I feel tired," he answered. Daniel noticed the badge on his blouse. He had slept in his clothes. He must have been exhausted, couldn't remember even putting his horse in the corral. Couldn't remember hardly anything. He lifted the cup, stopped.

Now he remembered.

Beating the hell out of the whiskey runner. Burning the whiskey wagon.

A frown hardened his face.

Said Rain Shower: "I should have let you sleep."

"Kee." He shook his head. "I must work. Report to the agent."

"Did you find the men you sought?"

He stared at her, thinking: *Your brother*

49

has a big mouth.

Mr. Leviticus Ellenbogen must have told Ben Buffalo Bone where Daniel had gone, and Ben, as was his nature, had told his sister. Probably anyone else he had seen. Daniel sipped his coffee, but it had a bitter taste now.

"Were those men Creek?" she asked.

"Taibo," he replied, barely audible.

"Did you . . . ?" she asked, her voice much sterner now.

What else did Ben tell you? he thought, only to correct himself. *No, it isn't Ben Buffalo Bone. She sees it in my face.*

He noticed her face, too.

Round and lovely, even with her full lips lined in a scowl. Her black hair, parted in the middle, shone in the morning sun, and fell past her shoulders. She wore a dress of gray wool — Daniel pictured her picking up the bolt of cloth at ration day last autumn — that she had decorated with beads and shells. A bone necklace adorned with crosses of German silver hung from her neck. Ben Buffalo Bone's oldest sister was probably two or three years younger than Daniel, but she looked older this morning. Daniel glanced at her hands, worn, dried from the sun and wind, and he remembered one of the school mothers back at Carlisle, how she always lamented how her hands made her look ten years older, no matter how much cream she rubbed on. Rain Shower didn't have the liver spots like Mrs. Thornton, but her hands looked twenty years older than her face.

Life had always been hard on the women of The People. Women had few rights. They were property from the time of their birth, belonging to their fathers, and, once they married, they were owned by their husbands. When they became old, they had no place of honor or respect. They were ignored, cast aside, the same as any old Nermernuh man. Some tribes took care of the elders, but not The People. They let them die. "Do not grow old," a fellow Metal Shirt named Twice Bent Nose constantly advised Daniel.

"Those men will not bring whiskey to the land of The People again," Daniel said. Her face registered no emotion. "I burned their wagon, and the whiskey they had not sold." She didn't even blink. "No, I did not kill them. I could not kill them," he said, and his head dropped.

That was a lie. He could easily have killed Blake Browne had he not summoned enough strength to control his temper after it had been unleashed. He had killed a white man before, maybe not directly, but he certainly had caused that thief and killer's violent death, and he didn't regret it, didn't lose any sleep over it, rarely even thought about it. When Daniel raised his eyes, he saw Rain Shower smile softly, with relief. She no longer looked older than her years.

"I am glad," she said.

"I am, too," he said, which, he found surprising, was true. He wondered if Teepee That Stands Alone would be pleased. No, that was unlikely. Teepee That Stands Alone would have truly avenged the death of his granddaughter, the corruption of his son. He would have burned the wagon of whiskey, true, but only after he had tied Blake Browne and Uvalde Ted Smith to the wheels, and roasted them alive.

"My brother!" Ben Buffalo Bone shouted, and slapped Daniel's back, dumping the rest of Daniel's coffee onto the ground, and prompting a giggle from the girl. "When did you return home?"

"Last night," Daniel said. "Very late."

"*Tsaa!*" He took the tin cup from Daniel's hand and pitched it to his sister. "Agent Elbow wants to see you. This he told me, has been telling me for days. I do not know how many days. But he has said that as soon as you return, you must see him. Let us ride, my brother. It is good that you are home. I was afraid you would miss the celebration."

"What celebration?" Daniel asked.

"In three suns, my sister becomes a woman."

Daniel shot a quick look at Rain Shower, and Ben Buffalo Bone's hammer-like strike bruised his shoulder blade again.

"Not her. We celebrate the passage of Oajuicauojué!"

Nodding, Daniel understood. Oajuicauojué was Rain Shower's younger sister. She had reached puberty. The rite would be anything but fancy, but the feast afterward would be enormous.

"You will be there?" Rain Shower asked.

"I would be honored," he said.

"Come, brother!" Ben Buffalo Bone yelled again. "I must take you to see Agent Elbow."

He spent the next few days at Huupi, in the southwestern corner of the reservation, trying to negotiate a treaty between two old men, one of the Yamparika band, and the other a Penateka.

Long ago, the Yamparika had been the northernmost band of The People, rarely, if ever, venturing farther south than the Canadian River. Indeed, old Isa Nanaka had once told Daniel that the Yamparika had been the last of The People to leave the great mountains of the northwest, where The People had once lived with their brothers the Shoshones.

So, it was natural that the Yamparika thought they were superior to any other band, and, in Huupi, a Penateka had taken the brunt of a Yap Eater's wrath. Try as he might, Daniel could never really figure out what the disagreement was all about, and, when he tried asking the Penateka, it was Daniel who took a blow to the back of his head, delivered by the old Yap Eater's walking stick.

"Do not believe Freckles!" the Yamparika said.

"I am as Comanche as you!" the Penateka snapped back after the insult.

The Yamparika laughed. "You," he said to the silver-haired Penateka. "You are not truly of The People. Your clan has copulated with so many *taibos,* and Saretika, even Nashonit and Dokana. You would even wed a Tonkawa if you were not afraid they would eat you." He spit on the ground.

"At least I do not marry my sister," the Penateka said. "Or my mother."

Daniel stepped aside, and watched the fight.

He was glad to see the Penateka win, although both men were gasping and bleeding, and too tired to carry on any further. The Yamparika had angered Daniel, for he could remember hearing similar insults during his childhood, listening to boys his age, or even older men, accuse him of not being Kwahadi because his mother was a Mescalero Apache.

With the help of the old men's wives, Daniel got them underneath a brush arbor, and let the old women bathe their cuts, wipe the mud off their faces, and the dirt out of their hair, before he spoke to the two old men.

"I have more important things to do than watch old fools beat themselves bloody." Daniel tapped his badge. "This makes me a chief." He showed the sergeant's chevrons Rain Shower had sewn onto his blouse. "And this . . . this gives me great *puha*. Power to take you before Quanah Parker. Our chief is not as merciful as I am. If I have to come back here, old men, I will bring you back to Quanah, and he will send you to the dark place. The damp place. The stone prison either at the soldier fort or, maybe, in the jail of the *Tejanos*."

When he had given the words time to sink inside two incredibly thick skulls, Daniel knelt beside the Yamparika. "Do you understand my words, Coyote Chaser?"

The old man flinched when his wife dragged a coarse rag over a large scrape on his cheek. "Yes," he snapped.

Daniel turned to the Penateka. "Do you hear what I have spoken, Seven Beavers?"

"There will be no trouble," the old man managed.

"Good."

Daniel spoke briefly to Coyote Chaser's wife, then mounted his buckskin, and rode north. He kept the horse in a good lope, wanting to reach home in a hurry, not daring to miss the puberty ceremony of Rain Shower's sister. Likely the agent would demand a report. Ellenbogen had Daniel spending more time writing papers than riding, but at least he didn't force Daniel to rake the grounds, hoe his garden, burn trash, and handle other jobs meant for women, the way the previous agent had worked most of his policemen. Besides, Ellenbogen, who had been so anxious to see Daniel after his encounter with the whiskey runners, had not wanted to hear much about what had happened in Greer County. Actually Daniel had not even mentioned that he had left the reservation.

"Are they dead?" he had merely asked.

"No," Daniel had said, watching relief sweep across the agent's brow.

"Did you chase them off the federal reserve?"

"Yes."

"Good."

"Do you want me to write a report?"

"Not this time," Ellenbogen had answered. "I think it is best to keep this matter between you and myself. I should never have encouraged you to pursue those men. They were white, right? Not Creek?"

"Yes."

Ellenbogen had looked up, wetting his dried lips. "I don't know what I was thinking, sending you off like that. Could lose my appointment if Washington found out. I don't know what I was thinking."

"You were thinking of the girl," Daniel had reminded him, and Ellenbogen, relief replaced by anger, immediately had ordered him south to Huupi.

"You should take my sister for your wife," Ben Buffalo Bone said, whacking Daniel's back.

"Oajuicauojué would not have me," Daniel said.

"Not her." Ben chuckled. "The old one."

Daniel looked across the camp, glad to

find Rain Shower's attention on her younger sister, too far away, he hoped, even to hear Ben's booming voice.

"I do not have enough horses to pay your uncle," Daniel said, thinking: *And for what I am paid as a policeman, am unlikely ever to have enough.*

Ben muttered something under his breath, then wrapped his arm over Daniel's shoulder, and pulled him close. "I am glad you are here. It is right that you are here. You are family. You are my brother. This is an important day."

The People were never much for ceremony. Daniel had heard the chaplain at Fort Sill say Comanches, compared to other tribes, were like atheists. Such sentiment might be a little harsh, Daniel thought, but he could see how a *taibo,* or even another Indian, might think that.

Cuhtz Bávi, Ben's uncle, led his great bay stallion, a giant at some seventeen hands, out of the house, and Oajuicauojué grabbed the tail. With a shout from the aging Kotsoteka, the stallion took off at a trot, pulling Oajuicauojué along, the girl singing as they ran across the prairie, praying that the big horse would pass on to her his strength, his power, his speed, beauty, and lissomeness.

No, Daniel thought, moved as he watched

the young girl follow the horse. *We are not atheists.*

"Do you remember your celebration?" Ben Buffalo Bone asked.

"Yes," Daniel said with a smile. "I was young. Too young, really. We went on a buffalo hunt. And my father gave me his name, then took another. I remember. I remember that well. And you? Do you remember your passage?"

Ben's arm left Daniel's shoulder, and dropped by his side.

"The People were free during the time of your journey, but not in my time," he said. "A buffalo hunt. That would have been a great ceremony. There was no buffalo for my feast. Still, my father let me kill the *Tejano* cow at ration day." He nodded, and resurrected his grin. "It was good enough. To be with family, it is always good. Is that not so?"

Ben's uncle was waving them over. "Yes," Daniel answered. "It is always good."

After offering the pipe to the six directions, Cuhtz Bávi passed it to Ben Buffalo Bone, who smoked first, then handed the pipe to Daniel. Ben's uncle spoke softly, smoked, and laughed, pointing at his niece. Daniel turned, but his eyes fell on Rain Shower first, and stayed there until Ben tugged his shoulder.

"Come," Ben said, "let us eat."

"Haa," Cuhtz Bávi said, more grunt than word, and set the pipe aside, and rubbed his belly.

They ate from copper pots stewed and boiled beef, rabbit, dried antelope, pecans, pemmican, and airtights of corn that Ben had collected on ration day. Cuhtz Bávi had invited many families to celebrate Oajuicauojué's becoming a woman, and The People began arriving, bringing more food. Rain Shower stood under the brush arbor with her younger sister, sharing the blend of mesquite beans and bone marrow that tasted sweeter than *taibo* sugar.

They gorged until Daniel thought he might explode. No wonder so many of The People were fat, he thought, but still accepted a piece of fry bread from Ben's mother. He wanted to take a nap, wondered if he could sneak away now in the crowd, hide in the cabin with the horses. Failing to stifle a yawn, he stepped toward the cabin, but Ben Buffalo Bone stopped him.

"Bávi," he said, his tone serious.

"Yes?"

Face hardened, eyes becoming slits, Ben tilted his jaw toward the brush arbor. "My brother, there is why I wish you would bring my uncle ponies. There are many reasons I would like for you to take my sister for your wife. But he is another reason." Ben spit, and hurled a beef rib across the yard, sending a horde of dogs chasing it.

The man's name was Nácutsi. Pale Eyes called him Gunpowder, and he was just as explosive. Like Daniel, he was Kwahadi, although he was a good deal older than Daniel, and had been one of The People who had been imprisoned at Fort Marion when Daniel was just a boy. He was angry, bitter, and Daniel had arrested him at least twice — no, three times — since he had become a policeman. Ben Buffalo Bone had arrested him another time. Maybe more.

"Nácutsi?" Daniel said incredulously. His stomach soured when Nácutsi forced Rain Shower's hand in his big right paw. "Nácutsi courts your sister?"

Ben didn't answer. The dogs began fighting over the rib bone. Nácutsi turned toward the animals, dropping Rain Shower's hand, and laughed. He reached into the back pocket of his Long Knives britches.

"Son-of-a-bitch," Daniel swore in English. Both hands tightened into fists, and he bulled his way toward the brush arbor as Nácutsi raised a ceramic stoneware bottle,

stamped *GINGER BEER* in big blue letters,
and drank.

CHAPTER FIVE

"Who stitched up your head?"

"Rain Shower," Daniel answered, "and her mother."

Outside, the wind must have been blowing toward Medicine Bluff Creek, because, even inside the post hospital, with the windows closed tightly against the cold, Daniel could smell the Fort Sill stables. It reminded him of home. He sat on a narrow cot, near a window, the morning sun providing plenty of light for the post surgeon's examination.

Major Chad Becker's smooth fingertips traced the outline of the deep cut that stretched about an inch above Daniel's left eye. Daniel kept cringing, expecting him to press the tender spot with *taibo* spite, but the surgeon had the soft touch of a woman. His hand dropped by his side, and Major Becker stepped back, nodding.

"They did a nice job, Sergeant Killstraight. What did they use, horse hair?"

His head bobbed slightly. "Cuhtz Bávi's giant bay. His pride and joy. A great honor for me."

"During the late rebellion, probably before you were born, I once used a fiddle string to sew up a saber cut." The doctor produced a small bottle. "I'm going to put a little carbolic acid on it, just to protect against infection. After the stellar operation performed by your two women friends, it would be a shame to have gangrene set in and force me to cut off your head in order to save your life." With a wink, the doctor splashed liquid onto a white cloth.

"It might burn a little," Major Becker warned.

It did.

The hospital was crowded, typical for Fort Sill. Bluecoat soldiers always thought of some malady to keep them away from work, although from the looks of some of them, they really were sick or injured. A few snored, some coughed, four sat on a cot playing cards, but most kept quiet. The ones closest stared at Dr. Becker's treatment. One grunted about the stink of Indian, prompting a chuckle from another spectator, but the major shut them up.

"I can easily treat your croup, Corporal

Thomas, with skunk grease, and send you back to the guardhouse, O'Malley, broken fingers and all."

The sick bluecoats fell silent.

"Listen, Sergeant," Major Becker said, "I'm sorry I could not make it to see that little girl. Agent Ellenbogen told me what happened. But Lieutenant Nesbitt's appendix burst. It required immediate surgery. . . ."

"There was nothing you could have done," Daniel said.

A door opened and closed quickly, and Daniel heard Leviticus Ellenbogen's shoes pound across the wooden floor. The agent sounded like a Pale Eyes mule walking no matter where he was.

"Mein Gott," Ellenbogen spoke in a hoarse whisper, removing his tall silk hat, shaking his head, then clucking his tongue. He wore the same suit of ill-fitting black broadcloth.

"Bloody savages," the Irish trooper with the busted right hand said. "What do you expect from Comanch'?"

"You're one to talk, O'Malley," the major said. "The sergeant here was doing his duty, arresting a drunk. You know all about drunks, don't you, O'Malley? Want to tell Sergeant Killstraight and Mister Ellenbogen how you busted that hand of yours?"

Brooding but silent, the soldier rose from his bunk, and crossed the hospital to join the poker game.

"How is he, Doctor?" Ellenbogen asked.

"He's fine, sir. The Comanche women did a grand job patching him up. I give all due credit to those women, but more to the thick head of your policeman. No fractured skull, although he might have a headache for a day or two. When he first arrived, I gave him a tincture of laudanum to help ease the pain. Bring him back in a week, and I'll remove that horse hair."

"Horse hair?" Ellenbogen waited as if expecting to be informed that the post surgeon was only joking.

Instead, Major Becker grinned at Daniel. "Or you can let one of your women take it out."

"You're gentler than they were," Daniel said, and the doctor laughed.

"Then," the agent said, uncomfortable and unsure, "the sergeant is fit for duty, *Herr* Doctor?"

"Fit and able, Mister Ellenbogen." Major Becker was already crossing the room, shouting: "Let me examine that hand of yours, O'Malley!"

Daniel grabbed his hat and blouse, and gently put them on as he led the new agent toward the front door. Masking his satisfaction upon hearing Trooper O'Malley's scream and explosion of profanity proved impossible.

Daniel rode and Ellenbogen walked from the Fort Sill hospital to the headquarters for the Comanche, Kiowa, and Apache reservation, a small cabin spitting distance from Cache Creek. Leviticus Ellenbogen had made several changes in the cabin from the previous agent, although his desk remained covered with papers and ledgers, a cigar case, can of pipe tobacco, a porcelain inkwell that appeared to have been hand-painted, and a Bible, although Ellenbogen's Testament looked larger than the previous agent's, the leather and paper worn and stained, as if he had actually read the book numerous times. He saw no tintypes of Ellenbogen's family — Daniel didn't know if the agent even had a family — but several items now hung from the wall to give the agency a touch of civilization: a couple of lithographs that appeared very old, a colorful sampler, a newspaper clipping, but what caught Daniel's eye was a portrait of President Cleveland.

Noticing Daniel's attention on the portrait, Leviticus Ellenbogen said: "I campaigned for Grover when he ran for the mayor's office in Buffalo. A man of strong principle. A man of strong character. Believe me, Sergeant, it took a lot for me, an Israelite and a staunch Republican, to laud and even cast a ballot for a Presbyterian Democrat."

Thought Daniel: *And now you have been rewarded for it.*

He took off his hat, and wiped his brow. The cabin was stifling. It always was, no matter the season. Outside was probably forty degrees, dark and overcast, but the agency door remained open to let in relief. Dark, cramped, hot, with the air always filled with dust. Daniel preferred his own cabin, even with the horses. A mouse scurried across the floor, unnoticed by the agent, and out the door. *Well,* Daniel thought, *maybe this isn't such a reward.*

Ellenbogen was talking about the reforms the President had accomplished as mayor and governor, and reforms he was pushing for in Washington. Seeing that he had lost Daniel's interest, he pointed at a chair, and told Daniel to sit down.

"The Comanche brave called Gunpowder is in the stockade at Fort Sill," Ellenbogen said. "He should have been sent to Major Becker for an examination, also, but refused.

You beat him soundly, Sergeant."

The grin made Daniel flinch. The Pale Eyes doctor was right. His head had begun to throb. He wished he had some more of that tincture Major Becker had given him when he first arrived at the hospital. He didn't care any for the taste of laudanum, but it sure killed his headache in a hurry.

"Not me." Daniel pointed to his head wound. "Nácutsi laid me out with the bottle. Ben Buffalo Bone, his uncle, and Teepee That Stands Alone beat him soundly."

From what Daniel had heard, most of the thrashing should be credited to Teepee That Stands Alone, who had arrived for the feast moments after Daniel had started the fight with Nácutsi.

"Ben Buffalo Bone says Na—" Ellenbogen's tongue tripped over the name, so he gave up. "He says Gunpowder was in a state of inebriation."

Daniel nodded.

"At a religious ceremony to honor one of Ben's sisters?"

Another nod, even though Daniel wouldn't have called it religious.

"Where is Ben Buffalo Bone?" Daniel asked.

"From what Frank Striker tells me, you

sent Ben Buffalo Bone to Gunpowder's camp at Big Wichita Valley while those women. . . ." Ellenbogen shuddered as his eyes fixed on the stitched cut on Daniel's head.

Frank Striker was the agency interpreter, a giant Texian who had married a Kiowa woman. Daniel stared at his moccasins.

Ellenbogen asked: "Do you not remember giving such orders to Ben Buffalo Bone?"

Daniel shook his head. "Nácutsi hit me pretty hard."

"You are sure you are well enough for duty, Sergeant?"

"Yes," Daniel said.

"Why did you order Ben to Gunpowder's camp?"

"I'm . . . well. . . ." He shrugged.

With a heavy sigh, Ellenbogen absently reached into his coat pocket and withdrew a pipe. As he filled the bowl with tobacco, he shook his head, saying: "I had hoped we had put an end to the whiskey runners on the reservation. I had hoped the federal marshals and increased patrols by the Army, and with you Indian policemen, of course, would stop this nefarious activity. Perhaps we should hire more Comanche policemen." He struck a match on the desk top, and held the flame to the carved ivory bowl.

"It is hard to find men among The People who wish to become a Metal Shirt," Daniel said. "Not for eight dollars a month, and no rations."

Ellenbogen ignored the bitterness.

"Whiskey is a pestilence on this reservation," Ellenbogen said. "Are you still convinced these runners are not Creek Indians?"

"Not the ones I found. The Creeks usually bring in whiskey from the north, maybe the northeast. The ones I followed from Toyarocho's camp traveled into the disputed country. Creeks would never travel that far south or west. These new whiskey traders are crossing the Red River from Texas."

"White men," Ellenbogen said with disgust, setting his pipe on top of his Bible. "The Creeks I perhaps could understand, but these white men. . . ." He shook his head.

"Not white men," Daniel said. "*Tejanos.* Texians. I don't think they will return, though."

Ellenbogen grinned slightly, uneasily, and tugged his beard. "Just in case, I will ask the colonel at Fort Sill to increase patrols along the Red River. I will also write the United States marshal in Fort Smith, and the Texas Rangers in Wichita Falls to please

71

assist us in putting an end to this malady."
He removed his hand from his beard, staring hard at Daniel. "Is there anything else I should do?"

Daniel stared back, wondering. The previous agent never would have asked Daniel for advice. What did this Ellenbogen really want? He wet his lips, tried to see behind those black eyes, but found nothing.

"There are two other people I would ask you to write," Daniel said. "One is Hugh Gunter. He is a United States Indian Policeman."

"I am not altogether familiar with that organization."

"Union Agency in Muskogee," Daniel continued. "Jurisdiction over all Five Civilized Tribes."

"Yes, but you said these new runners are not Creeks. Why would we need help from this branch?"

"I wouldn't want the Creeks to start up their whiskey trade again in full force."

After a few puffs of his pipe, Ellenbogen nodded.

"Also," Daniel said, "write Deputy Marshal Harvey P. Noble. He works at Judge Parker's court."

"I have already said I would write the marshal in Fort Smith."

"Write Deputy Noble, too."

"What on earth for?"

"Because I know him," Daniel said. "I trust him."

Ellenbogen considered that, and agreed. "Very well. Let us understand each other, Sergeant. This agency is not where I desire to end my days. This is my chance, though, to prove to President Cleveland and Secretary Lamar that my ability matches my loyalty. My career faces a mighty mountain because of my tribe, just as you, being Comanche, face your own obstacles because of your tribe. We have much in common, you know. So we must work together. You are my ears and eyes, Sergeant. You are educated, unlike most of your fellow policemen. I have trouble communicating with many of your people. You and I can work together. We must work together."

Daniel did not answer. He wasn't sure what to say. So, he waited.

The agent started to speak again, but footfalls froze his lips, and he looked past Daniel at the door. Daniel turned to see the broad-shouldered, black-mustached interpreter framing the doorway in buckskin britches and a porkpie hat.

"Beggin' your pardon," the interpreter drawled. "Didn't know you had comp'ny."

Daniel looked back at the agent.

"It's all right, Mister Striker," Ellenbogen said. "What is it?"

"Well, this Penateka squaw run up after ridin' her hoss to death. She's beggin' us to send Teepee That Stands Alone to heal her papa, only she don't know where his camp is. Says her papa took bad sick, and the Penateka medicine man can't do nothin' for him."

"Teepee That Stands Alone." After testing the name, trying to jar his memory, Ellenbogen looked at Daniel. "Isn't he . . . ?"

"Yes," Daniel said. "He's Kwahadi. His camp is in the heart of the Wichitas."

"That's a right far piece," Frank Striker said. "Want me to ask that Yankee sawbones at the fort if he feels like ridin' all the way to Huupi?"

"Huupi?" Daniel pushed out of his chair. He headed out the door, sliding past Frank Striker with a half-hearted pardon, looking at the corral, at the lean-to, asking the interpreter where he could find the Penateka woman. Before Striker could answer, he saw her leaning against the trunk of a large elm tree. Forgetting his headache, Daniel dashed to her. She looked up. Yes, he knew her.

"Your father is sick?" he asked in Comanche.

74

"Yes." Tears streamed down her face. "A sickness in his belly. He spits blood. Do you know Teepee That Stands Alone?"

"Yes," Daniel said. "I will send for him."

He turned, now running for the corral, asking Ellenbogen and Striker to send a runner to the camp of Teepee That Stands Alone, telling them that he would ride to Huupi to investigate. His head hurt even more.

"Should I ask for Major Becker's assistance, as well?" Ellenbogen asked.

"Yes," Daniel said, although, after hearing the daughter's words, after seeing the fear etched across her face, Daniel believed that there was nothing any doctor, be it a blue-coat surgeon or a revered Kwahadi *puhakat,* could do for the old Penateka warrior named Seven Beavers.

CHAPTER SIX

As The People prepared Seven Beavers's body for the journey to The Land Beyond The Sun, Daniel ducked inside the old Penateka's lodge. A harsh wind battered the canvas teepee as he knelt, the piercing screams of the dead man's daughter drowning out the songs of mourning. The stench inside soured his stomach. A good thing the wind blew so hard, he thought, else he might lose his breakfast. Squatting, swallowing down the bile, he touched the spots of dried blood on the blanket, saw where Seven Beavers had thrown up, saw where his hands had clawed into the hard ground, fighting the pain in his belly, fighting off death.

Outside, a man's voice boomed in guttural Comanche: "Metal Shirt! Leave this place. We must burn the lodge of the warrior who is no more."

That was the way of The People. They

would burn most of what Seven Beavers had acquired in his life, although anything of value — his shield, perhaps, his favorite pipe, maybe a knife — would be buried with him. His medicine would be tossed away, and a good horse would be killed over his grave so he would not have to walk. Even in death, The People despised walking.

"Hurry, Metal Shirt!" the man demanded. "There is nothing of value for you to steal."

True enough, Daniel thought. He wasn't sure what he was looking for anyway. An old Comanche was dead. There was no mystery. He had gotten sick, died an agonizing death. What did he expect to find? No mystery. No crime. Why had he ridden so hard from the agency?

His head hurt.

Daniel knew what brought him here. He thought he had failed these people, failed Seven Beavers. He thought that arrogant Yamparika, Coyote Chaser, had ended his feud with the Penateka by poisoning him. So he came here hoping to find some evidence to prove Coyote Chaser had committed murder.

"Metal Shirt! We will burn you with this lodge!"

No crime has been committed here. Daniel sighed, and then he saw it.

"Metal Shirt!"

"Shut up," Daniel barked back as he moved across the teepee, softly fingering the dead kitten. Calico-colored, stiff as a board, lying next to something Daniel had never dreamed he would find in Huupi. As he turned the cold piece of ceramic stoneware over, he recognized those blue stamped letters:

Cox & Coursey Bottling Works
Home Brewed
GINGER BEER
Dallas, Texas

He lifted the bottle, shaking it, hearing some liquid, and raised it to his nose, sniffing. Whiskey. A lot had spilled out. Daniel could make out the dampness on the ground, and the kitten must have entered the teepee, and lapped it up. Blood had pooled under the calico's head, the baby's teeth protruding as if the skin had been pulled back tightly, leaving a snarl frozen in death.

Outside, Daniel showed the bottle to the big-mouthed Penateka brave, who waved a torch in his right hand.

"Was Seven Beavers drinking this whiskey?" he asked in Comanche.

"You cannot arrest him now, Metal Shirt," the man said. "Unless you wish to follow him on his journey." His left hand gripped the bone handle of a knife.

"Was Seven Beavers drinking from this bottle?" Daniel demanded. He had seen the Penateka around on his last trip south, but didn't know the warrior's name. A big bull of a man, with arms like oak limbs, and a brutally pockmarked face.

"You should not speak his name, Metal Shirt. Have you no respect? Did your years among the Pale Eyes make you forget the ways of The People?"

The Penateka was right, of course, but Daniel didn't care. He was about to reach for his Remington, when Coyote Chaser spoke softly as he rounded the corner. "It is all right, Turuhani. Take your hand off your knife, my son. Tell this Kwahadi warrior what he wants to know."

"Warrior?" Turuhani scoffed, turned his head, and spit on the ground. "He is nothing but. . . ."

Coyote Chaser silenced him with a sharp rebuke.

Turuhani pointed toward Seven Beavers's daughter. "Yes, Ohapia found her father in his lodge. He complained that he had a fire in his belly . . . that the whiskey must have started it. Ohapia threw the bottle across the lodge. I tried to make the demon leave his stomach, but the blood poured from his mouth as he coughed. I could not put out the fire inside."

"You are a *puhakat*," Daniel said. *A little young,* Daniel thought, *to be a medicine man.*

The man straightened. "I am. I have not abandoned the ways of The People."

"Unlike the man who must make the journey to The Land Beyond The Sun," Coyote Chaser said.

The two spoke briefly, and Coyote Chaser asked Daniel: "Is it all right if Turuhani burns this lodge?"

With a nod, Daniel stepped away from the teepee, holding the bottle at his side. Coyote Chaser motioned him to follow, and they walked toward the brush arbor to get out of the cold wind.

"Have you seen this bottle?" Daniel asked.

"I have seen ones like it," the Yamparika answered.

Coyote Chaser looked beyond Daniel as the flames devoured Seven Beavers's home, and snorted. "Look at that. Made of the ugly cloth the bluecoats use for their tents. Not of buffalo hide." He shook his head. "A Yamparika would never live in such a place. It is good that we burn it. It is good that I never have to mention his name again."

"You hated him," Daniel said.

Coyote Chaser shook his head. "I hate what he had become. I hate what many of The People have become."

He sounded a lot like Teepee That Stands Alone.

"The place where I dwell would offend you, too," Daniel said.

"You, I can understand," Coyote Chaser said. "The Pale Eyes took you from your father and mother. They sent you to live with their kind for a long time. You are not to blame for all you have forgotten, all you have lost. But that Penateka." He grunted, and said nothing more.

Daniel lifted the bottle. "I found this in his lodge. A baby cat lay beside it. It was dead."

"Good. A cat is a Pale Eyes pest, good for nothing except feeding coyotes and hawks. The Penateka of whom we speak" — Coyote Chaser was careful not to speak the name of the dead — "he had many such pests to play with. What good is a cat? Dogs have much purpose. Not as valuable as a horse, but good animals to have in a camp. But cats? Worthless. As worthless as the man who is no more."

"I think that the whiskey in the bottle

killed both that man and the baby cat."

Coyote Chaser stared in silence, his black eyes not blinking until the burning teepee collapsed, and he looked back at the flames.

"I think the whiskey in this bottle was bad. Poison."

Another grunt came from the old man. "Pale Eyes whiskey kills," he said at last.

An image of Sehebi appeared in Daniel's mind. His head dropped. "In many ways," he said, but Coyote Chaser did not hear.

"Do you know where the old Penateka got this whiskey?" he asked after a minute.

Coyote Chaser remained silent for a long while. "Perhaps it is better this way," he finally said. "To die now. Before he was too old to be useful. So old he would be abandoned by The People, cast out to die. Yes," said the Yap Eater as he walked away. "Yes, this was better."

He would make his report to Agent Ellenbogen, then take the whiskey bottle to Major Becker at Fort Sill. Perhaps Becker could examine the remnants of the liquid, tell Daniel what had killed Seven Beavers and the kitten. Bad whiskey wasn't new to Indian Territory. Daniel had heard of such things. Traders often doctored the liquor they sold to Indians with chewing tobacco or turpentine, ammonia or gunpowder, cut-off snake heads or strychnine — sometimes all of those. Creek whiskey wasn't high-grade, but, as far as Daniel knew, no Comanche had ever died from it, at least not as Seven Beavers had died. Creek whiskey had never killed a kitten.

Agent Ellenbogen would file a complaint, and the federal marshals would track down Blake Browne and Uvalde Ted Smith and arrest them. Maybe they would be charged with manslaughter. Probably not. That would be hoping for too much. But the Pale Eyes law would put those two vermin behind bars for a long time.

Maybe.

It was a plan, at least, a start, a way to avenge not only Sehebi, but also Seven Beavers, and that's why Daniel almost dropped the ceramic stoneware bottle on the floor of the agency when he saw Blake Browne standing in front of Agent Ellenbogen's desk.

"That's him!" said Browne, equally startled. "That's the red nigger that burned my wagon. And all my tradin' supplies. That's him, damn it!"

Browne's face remained puffy, bruised, with a bandage wrapped around his head. His lips were split, swollen, so misshapen that Daniel could barely understand his words, and Browne grimaced upon completion of his outburst, and lifted a finger to his mouth.

"Reckon I'll just arrest the son-of-a-bitch now." A big man stepped from the corner, out of the shadows, putting a gloved right hand on the butt of a revolver while his left withdrew heavy iron bracelets that must have been tucked behind his back.

"Now, hold on here, just one minute, Ranger," Ellenbogen said.

"Red nigger," Blake Browne added. "Damned Comanche butcher."

"And, you, too, Mister Browne. You will watch your filthy language in my office, sir."

Daniel focused on the Ranger. A *Tejano,* duck trousers stuffed in brown stovepipe boots, a badge made of a Mexican *peso* pinned to the lapel of his striped vest. A giant of a man with red hair that touched his shoulders, and a slightly darker mustache and underlip beard, and several days of beard covering the rest of his sun-beaten face. His eyes were blue, the cold blue of a killer, and Daniel knew this Texas Ranger hated his guts.

"Daniel." Ellenbogen cleared his throat. "Daniel." He wet his lips, pulled on his beard, tried to think of what to say, how to explain.

Daniel didn't wait. "Seven Beavers is dead," he reported, and held out the bottle. "This is what killed him." He stared across the room at Blake Browne.

"I don't know no Seven Beavers," the whiskey runner said.

"Do you know this?" Daniel shook the bottle.

"Never seen it before." Above and below the bandage on Blake Browne's head beads of sweat popped out.

"Your wagon was full of these," Daniel said.

"My wagon was full of trade goods." Browne had turned to look at Ellenbogen, telling the agent, defending himself, not daring to look at Daniel again: "I had beads and blankets, and I got a permit to trade to the Injuns, sell them quality merchandise they can't find on this side of the Red River. And that's what I was doin'. I done showed you my permit. I been treatin' with Injuns since 'Forty-Four, back when Texas was still a Republic. I was comin' back from my latest trading, and this buck comes up and ambushes us. Ran off my damned partner. Uvalde up and quit me. Too scared to hire on with me no more. Reckon I can't rightly blame him at all, but I got my rights, and I swore out a complaint in Wichita Falls."

"Which is where we're taking him," the Texas Ranger said.

"You have no jurisdiction here, sir," Ellenbogen said.

"I got enough," the Ranger replied.

"Jurisdiction." Without turning away from Ellenbogen, Browne pointed at Daniel. "What jurisdiction did this buck have when he burned my supplies, my wagon? No thievin' Comanch' can arrest no white man. That's the law. You know it's the law."

He stopped, rubbed his jaw, swallowed, and continued, but without the force. "He burned my wagon. Destroyed all my blankets and beads and such. And Ranger Quantrell is haulin' him back to Wichita Falls to stand trial." He paused. "Lessen you want to make things right by me here. Else, I might have to report you to the Department of the Interior."

"Mister Browne," Ellenbogen said. "Ranger Quantrell." He stopped again, started massaging both temples. He wasn't used to confrontation, Daniel decided, didn't know what to do, how to act, what authority he had.

Yet the agent surprised him, lowering his hands, trying to stand a little straighter. "Do not threaten me, Mister Browne, because I

can easily have your so-called permit re-
voked, sir. And you speak of jurisdiction,
well, let me remind you that, when you took
the ferry across the Red River, you left
Texas."

"I got a right," Browne said, "to get paid
for what I lost."

"And if, Mister Browne, we rode to the
site of your burned wagons, I am sure we
would find not the charred remnants of
beads and blankets, but bottles that once
contained contraband liquor. Bottles such
as the one Daniel holds in his hand."

The Ranger sniggered. "How does that
whiskey taste, boy?"

He lost his temper. Sent the bottle flying.
Catching, for just a moment, the frightened
look in the Ranger's face as he ducked.
Then Daniel was charging across the room,
lowering his shoulder, hearing first Browne's
shriek, then a grunt as Daniel slammed into
Browne, wrapping his arms around the
whiskey runner's waist and sending them
both sailing over Ellenbogen's desk.

He didn't remember anything else until
cold water fell across his face, and his eyes
opened to reveal Leviticus Ellenbogen
kneeling over him.

When he tried to seek out the burning,

pounding spot behind his left ear, Daniel's arms felt heavy. Iron manacles bit into his wrists, tight, almost cutting off the flow of blood.

"Are you all right?" Ellenbogen said. He held a rag, dripping water, in his right hand. The Ranger, the big man named Quantrell, shoved the agent aside, and jerked Daniel to his feet.

"Come on, boy," he said, "it's time to light a shuck for Texas. You're under arrest."

Fighting off dizziness and nausea, Daniel turned toward Ellenbogen.

"You didn't tell me you went beyond the reservation," Ellenbogen said. He lifted the arrest warrant. "This says you were in Texas when you burned that wagon." A heavy sigh followed. "I have been told to comply. . . ."

The Ranger pushed Daniel toward his horse. "We're hauling your hide to Wichita Falls, buck," the Ranger said. "And I just pray to the Almighty that you try to escape."

CHAPTER SEVEN

They would kill him long before they ever reached Wichita Falls. Daniel wondered if he should start singing his death song, wondered if he had a death song. No. That was not the way of The People. He wouldn't let the red-headed Ranger and miserable Blake Browne shoot him. He'd fight. Like his father had fought, and died, for freedom. Die as a man. Die *really* trying to escape rather than be shot in the back and have the Ranger say he had been killed trying to escape. Die like Nermernuh!

The Ranger rode alongside him, pointing the huge barrels of a Greener shotgun at Daniel. Up ahead rode Blake Browne. Grinning, the Ranger thumbed back one of the hammers, as if he had read Daniel's mind.

Suddenly the Ranger turned, looking down the trail. A ploy, Daniel figured. Trying to coax Daniel into making his play. Yet the Ranger reined up, still looking northeast, and wrapped his reins around the horn, then pulled back the Greener's other hammer.

"Hold up, Browne. You, too, Injun."

Daniel tugged the hackamore, wetting his lips, watching a rider on a bay horse lope down the trail. Blake Browne nudged his big mule past Daniel, stopping beside the Ranger.

"You know him?" the Ranger asked.

"Can't make him out," the whiskey runner said, "but he's a white man."

Sunlight reflected off something on the rider's lapel, and Browne swore. "Hell, he's a lawdog."

"Maybe."

The rider slowed the bay's pace about one hundred rods away, raising a gloved right hand. As he approached, Daniel could indeed make out a six-point star pinned to his unbuttoned coat. He could also make out the lawman — a big man, tall, wearing a high-crowned hat that the weather had beaten as much as it had battered his grizzled face. The man let the bay walk the last few yards, tugging on his mustache a moment, before dropping his right hand beside a holstered revolver.

Grinning, Daniel knew he might not die this day after all.

"Howdy," the man said in a thick drawl. "Hoped I could catch up with you boys. Was headin' down to Wichita Falls myself, and it's safer than ridin' alone. You boys don't mind no comp'ny, do you? Name's Noble. Harvey P. Noble." He sprayed the ground with tobacco juice.

"Marshal, eh?" the Ranger said.

"That's right. Deputy out of Judge Parker's court in Fort Smith."

"Listen, Arkansas, we don't need . . . ," Blake Browne started.

"Name's Noble, mister." The friendliness left Noble's voice, and his eyes hardened. "That's Marshal Noble, or Deputy Noble to you."

"I'm Quantrell," the Ranger said.

"Quantrell!"

"That's right. Only it's spelled with an 'e' instead of an 'i' . . . Carl Quantrell, Comp'ny D, Texas Rangers . . . but I ain't shamed by that name no matter how you think. You ask me, Capt'n Quantrill done a lot of good during the war."

"Reckon there's plenty of folks who agree with you." Noble pushed back his hat. "And plenty who don't."

Daniel didn't know anything about any Quantrell, with an 'e' or an 'i'.

Suddenly Noble smiled underneath his

bushy mustache. "How you farin', Daniel?"

"Better," Daniel said. "Now."

"You know this buck?" Browne asked.

"I do indeed," Noble said, and the smile disappeared. "But I can't say the same of you."

Browne swallowed. "Blake Browne," he answered in a hushed voice. "Trader out of Wichita Falls."

Noble nodded. He pointed at Ranger Quantrell's Greener. "Ranger Quantrell, would you mind lowerin' the hammers on that ten-gauge?"

Slowly Quantrell did as he was asked. "Just makin' sure this Comanch' didn't try nothin'," the Ranger explained.

"That's good policy," Noble said, and he reached inside his pocket, withdrew a pencil, which he stuck in his mouth, and then, after some searching, found a note pad. He flipped until he found an open page, and began scratching something on the paper.

"You said Quantrell, right? Comp'ny D. Out of Wichita Falls?"

The Ranger barely nodded.

"Carl with a 'c' or a 'k'?"

Quantrell answered.

"And you're Blake Black?"

"Browne."

"Browne. That's right. You mind spellin' that for me?"

"What you want my name for? What you want Carl's name for?"

"Hell, let's just say I'll know what name to carve on your cross iffen we gets jumped by Comanch'."

The Ranger shot a glance at Browne. Both men wet their lips.

"You think those Injuns would jump us?" Quantrell asked.

"Daniel's right popular with his people. There was a bunch of tribal laws gatherin' at the agency when I rode up." He looked over his shoulder, scanning the empty horizon. "Hell, I wouldn't be surprised if they was hidin', watchin' us, right this minute. You're a Ranger, Quantrell, and you're a trader, Mister Browne. We got experience. And none of us is too young not to remember how the Comanches often acted before they got penned up on this agency. Now, how do you spell that name again, Mister Browne? My memory ain't what it once was."

"B-l-a-k-e . . . B-r-o-w-n-e."

"Good thing I asked, then. Else I might have spelled your last name without that 'e' on your grave marker, or some such."

Nodding, Noble finished writing, flipped

the note pad closed, and returned pad and pencil to his pocket. "Browne with an 'e' and Quantrell with an 'e' . . . ain't that a coincidence. I reckon we'd best ride, boys. Light out of this hostile country."

They camped on the Texas side of Hill's Ferry, having ridden in silence since Harvey Noble joined the party. Dark clouds threatened rain, blackening out most of the stars and moon. Chained to a post oak tree, Daniel sat away from the campfire Quantrell had started, watching the two lawmen and the whiskey runner eat and drink in silence. Finally Noble rose, let out a loud fart, and filled a cup with coffee, then spooned beans into an enamel bowl.

"I'll feed your prisoner, Ranger Quantrell," he said as he walked away.

Noble placed the food and drink in front of Daniel.

"Not really hungry," Daniel said.

"Coffee's terrible, and beans ain't cooked enough, but you best eat, son." He looked over his shoulder, then sat down, his joints popping. "You got yourself in a peck of trouble, Daniel."

"Would have been a lot worse if you hadn't come along." He decided he was hungry after all, and forked some beans into his mouth.

"Likely." He looked over his shoulder at the campfire, then leaned forward. "I'd surely like to put a pair of bracelets on Blake Browne, but never been able to catch him."

"You get the letter I asked Mister Ellenbogen to write you?" Daniel asked, mouth full, forgetting the manners they had tried to teach him back in Pennsylvania.

Noble shook his head. "Nope. Been in the Oklahoma country lookin' for a rapscallion knowed to hide out on the Canadian River. Likely your letter's waitin' for me in Fort Smith."

If Ellenbogen actually wrote and mailed it, Daniel thought. He said: "You're a long way from the Canadian."

"Can't catch 'em all. No trail. Nobody knows nothin'. Decided to ride back to Fort Smith, but wanted to drop by and see how you was. Good thing, I reckon."

After a quick smile and nod, Daniel tried some more beans. "I thought you said you were riding to Wichita Falls."

"I am," Noble said. "Now. Fort Smith can wait." He pushed back his hat. "Happened pret' much like I told them ol' boys. Rode down to the agency. Found that Ben Buffalo Bone pal of yours and another Comanche lawman. What's his name? Two Broken . . . ah . . . hell's fire. Like I told them skunks, my memory ain't so good no more."

"Twice Bent Nose?" Daniel asked.

"That'd be the one. I wasn't lyin' when I said your pards was likely followin' us. I told 'em not to, but I suspect they kept an eye on us till we crossed the Red. And I warrant they might have decided to kill them two gents over yonder if I wasn't with 'em. You got friends, Daniel. I hope you know I'm one of 'em."

Daniel had to wash down the awful food with stout coffee. "Well, I owe you."

"Nope. Just doin' my job. Can't have nobody committin' no murder in my territory."

Daniel tried another bite, then set down the plate.

"You want to tell me just what the hell's goin' on here," Noble said, "and how you got your name on a Texas arrest warrant?"

The last thing Harvey P. Noble told Daniel was that he'd try to find a lawyer. Then he followed the white-haired jailer down the dark hallway, leaving Daniel alone in the cell at Wichita Falls.

Well, not alone. He had three Negroes, two Mexicans, a Celestial, and four other Indians for company, all of whom had ignored Daniel as he found a piece of open floor and settled in for the night.

Noon had passed, and the jailer still had not brought in any grub or emptied the now overflowing slop bucket, and the stench was overpowering. Even the Apache with the yellow headband looked pale.

Across the hall, in a less crowded cell, waited six or seven white men. The prisoners might have been separated by race, but the smell sickened everyone.

Daniel's eyes watered, his head hurt, and a cramp bit into his calf, when the door opened, and a high-pitched voice yelled: "Killstraight? Daniel Killstraight!"

He pulled himself up, spotted another jailer standing in the door, and nodded.

"Step away from the bars, boy," the jailer said, rattling a Chicago nightstick on the iron bars as he walked down the hall. "All of you bastards, back up, don't move, don't talk." The smell didn't seem to bother this man. Likely he was used to it. A large key grated inside the lock, and the door pulled open with a squeak. "Outside," the jailer ordered, and Daniel limped into the hallway, felt the knob of the club push him forward as the door slammed shut. "Your lawyer wants to see you," the jailer said as he locked the cell.

As they walked toward the light, yells broke out.

"How about some chow?"

"How about emptyin' these buckets!"

"Where the hell's *my* lawyer?"

The jailer didn't answer.

"My name is Vaughan Coyne." He was a fair-skinned man, with sandy hair and long whiskers. Maybe thirty. Wearing an ill-fitting sack suit of brown and tan plaid, with a faint scar above his right eyebrow. He held out his hand, and the firm grip surprised Daniel. After a gesture from Coyne, both men sat at a table in the sheriff's office. One white lawman with a black mustache and the jailer sat across the office, neither showing any interest in the attorney and his client.

"Did Marshal Noble send you?" Daniel asked.

"I have a fondness for Indian cases," Coyne said. Daniel couldn't place the accent. Not Eastern, as he had heard in Pennsylvania, and maybe a thousand miles from the Texas and Arkansas drawls he heard so often. "I spent some time at the Standing Rock Agency. It's a travesty what my people have done to you." He shook his head, and opened a satchel, withdrawing a large note pad, and some other papers. After laying the papers on the desk, he reached inside his sack suit and withdrew a pair of spectacles, put on the glasses, and read in silence.

After two or three minutes, Coyne looked up. "The complaint says you burned a wagon owned by Blake Browne near Deep Red Run, Greer County. It says you also assaulted Browne with intent to kill. You destroyed his trade goods. That you also tried to kill his employee." Coyne slowly pulled off the glasses. "Serious charges."

"He was selling whiskey on the reservation," Daniel said.

"That would surprise no one. But you couldn't arrest him. Not on the reservation. Certainly not off it."

"But I could convince him not to come back."

"So you're pleading guilty?"

Daniel didn't answer.

"Do you know what it's like in Huntsville prison, Daniel? For an Indian?"

Daniel clasped his hands, and looked away from the lawyer.

"I want to help you, Daniel," he heard the lawyer say, "but you have to help me, too."

He thought of this. Looked back at young Coyne. At last, he sighed. "Browne had a wagon full of whiskey. I followed his trail from the Wichita Mountains. I followed him from where he had sold some of his whiskey to a Comanche man named Toyarocho. Toyarocho got drunk. He passed out on top of his daughter, and suffocated her. She was four years old. Four!"

Silence. Then: "I can understand your motive."

"There's more." Daniel's fingers tightened into fists. "At Huupi, a Comanche camp just north of the Red River, a Penateka Comanche, an old man, drank some of Blake Browne's whiskey, and died from it. Poisoned."

"Poison? Are you sure?"

"There was a kitten in his lodge. The kitten had lapped up the whiskey the old Comanche had spilled. The kitten was dead, too. They died the same way."

What interested Daniel was that the lawyer didn't take notes. Like he was remembering everything. Daniel was a lot like Harvey Noble, wanting to write everything down on paper.

"Huupi is, I think, a long way from the Wichitas," Coyne said. "How can you be certain this Comanche and cat died from drinking Blake Browne's whiskey?"

"The same kind of bottle," Daniel said.

"Cox and Coursey Bottling Works in Dallas. All the bottles Browne had were like that. And when I caught up with those two bastards, Browne said something. Something like . . . 'You ask anybody from Teepee City to Huupi and so forth that they would vouch for Blake Browne.' That made me think he had been selling whiskey in Huupi. And, like I said, it was the same kind of bottle. Every bottle in that wagon I burned was the same ceramic stoneware, stamped with the same thing."

Finally Coyne withdrew a pen from his suit coat, and wrote on one of the papers. A left-hander, Daniel noticed, who wrote really perfect, beautiful letters. Coyne set the pen aside, and stared at Daniel. "But the four-year-old girl, she wasn't poisoned. Nor was her father. Right?"

Reluctantly Daniel nodded. "I'm not saying all Browne's whiskey was poison. I don't know how whiskey works. How it's made, I mean. I don't drink it. But on the reservation, I see what it does to The People."

More silence. The lawyer scribbled some more. When he looked up, he asked: "You burned Browne's wagon. You don't deny this?"

"I burned it. I burned all the whiskey he had left."

"How much?"

Daniel had to remember. "Half of the crates had bottles. No, a little less than half. The other crates were empty."

"That's a lot of ginger beer, certainly."

Daniel waited, then said, shaking his head: "Not beer. Whiskey. Whiskey in beer bottles."

"I'm sorry," Coyne said. "Trying to make a joke. Stupid of me. So, let us surmise that he left Wichita Falls with a load of whiskey. . . ."

Daniel shook his head. "The bottles were stamped Dallas."

"Dallas is too far for whiskey runners to operate."

Daniel had to agree. The lawyer sounded pretty smart.

"He goes up through Huupi," Coyne said, "then over to the Wichitas, then cuts west. Likely headed for Teepee City, Texas."

"That's the town he mentioned," Daniel said. "Teepee City."

"A town not known for temperance," Coyne said. "You caught him at. . . ." Putting his glasses on again, he looked back at the papers. "Deep Red Run." The lawyer leaned back in his chair, chewed on the end of his pen, rocking, staring at the ceiling. "I could hire a guide. If he could find the remains of Browne's wagon, bring back evidence that proves Browne was selling whiskey. . . ." Leaning forward, he slammed the chair legs on the floor, the noise causing the jailer and sheriff to stare at the two men for a moment. "This dead Indian at Huupi. You said he had the same bottle. Did you save this bottle?"

A grimace stretched across Daniel's face. *Idiot.* "I threw the bottle at the Texas Ranger's head at the agency."

"Maybe there were other bottles in the dead man's teepee."

Daniel's head shook. "The lodge was burned. It is the way of The People."

Coyne sighed, put his elbows on the desk, and clasped his hands. "Blake Browne is a notorious character. I'd like to rid Texas and Indian Territory of his likeness. Maybe we can do it. Wichita Falls juries have little sympathy for Comanches, but I have my own motives, my own mission, and I hate Blake Browne. And I might be able to . . . should be able to . . . play Greer County against them, but you never know how a judge will act. Let me see what I can do, Daniel." He almost leaped out of his chair, and stretched a long arm across the table. "I'm your attorney, my friend. Let's fight these evil-doers together."

Hesitantly Daniel took the offered hand. Sheepishly he asked: "How much money is this going to cost?"

CHAPTER EIGHT

"You're free to go."

Daniel stared at the jailer, wondering, not moving. He recalled a half-dime novel he had read back at Carlisle. A Lakota named William had somehow managed to sneak the book into the barracks, and all the boys would laugh as Daniel read the outrageous story to them at night, when they were supposed to be asleep. *The Marshal of Magdalena; Or, Vengeance of the Colorado Kid,* by a Colonel Something-or-another. The scene that kept coming to mind now was when a mean lawman let the Colorado Kid's brother out of jail, then shot him in the back.

"You coming, or ain't you?" the jailer snapped, and Daniel moved into the stinking hallway, letting the old man slam the steel door shut, lock the bolt, and shove Daniel forward.

In the office, a deputy handed Daniel his

badge, medicine pouch, money purse, and other items they had taken from him when he arrived in Wichita Falls, made him sign a receipt. They offered no explanation, just opened the door — the bright sunlight of late afternoon almost blinding him — and sent him into the streets of Wichita Falls.

No one shot him in the back.

At first, the only person he saw was a lady in a red and white gingham dress, who quickly crossed the wide, dirty street, instead of passing near him. He didn't blame her. Even if he wasn't an Indian, she'd likely walk a mile to avoid the stench of the jail that seemed tattooed to his body. Suddenly thinking of a bath, he dug into his pocket and withdrew the money purse, surprised to find his three greenbacks, change, even the gold piece still there.

He wondered if an Indian could get a bath in Wichita Falls, or if he'd have to wash the stink off in the Wichita River. His eyes had adjusted to the daylight, and he could see now.

It was a relatively new town — maybe ten years old, if he remembered correctly — but looked ancient. Looked dirty. The sun and wind aged everything, and everyone, quickly in West Texas. He heard the scream of a locomotive's whistle, and started walking toward the boardwalk. From what Harvey P. Noble had told him, Wichita Falls had boomed since the arrival of the Fort Worth and Denver Railway Company back in '82. What once had been home to maybe a dozen families, a Methodist church, and a post office, now was the Wichita County seat, home to hundreds of families, a lumberyard, a shingle factory, and even a sorghum mill. It was the railroad that interested him, although he wasn't quite sure why.

A voice stopped him.

"Daniel!"

Turning, he saw Vaughan Coyne racing across the street from Kemp's General Mercantile, dodging a freight wagon, ignoring the bearded driver's curses, and swinging onto the boardwalk beside Daniel, hugging onto a wooden column to catch his breath. "They let you out already?" he said.

Daniel saw no need to answer.

The lawyer pointed to a bench in front of the barber shop, and Daniel sat down. "They just got the writ," Coyne said after he dropped beside him, withdrawing a handkerchief from his vest pocket and dabbing his brow.

"Got warm all of a sudden," Coyne said.

"It'll do that," Daniel said, just to say

something.

"I could use a beer . . . oh, never mind. Ignorant of me. Forgive me. How . . . how does it feel to be free?"

"Why did they let me go?"

Coyne gleamed. "I told you I could play Greer County against them, Daniel. Wasn't sure if Judge Goodman would go for it or not, but he did."

Waiting again.

Finally Vaughan Coyne caught his breath, and color began seeping back into his face. "The county solicitor and I met in the judge's chambers." Coyne adjusted his spectacles. "Greer County is disputed territory. You know that. Texas wants it. The federal government claims it. A criminal trial is the last thing the Texas government wants to see in Greer County. It would lead to appeals, of course, and, eventually, the Supreme Court would have to decide on jurisdiction, on who actually owns that country. I persuaded Judge Goodman that the last thing he'd want is a trial. Didn't take much persuasion. And Judge Goodman persuaded . . . no, he demanded . . . the county solicitor to quash the indictment right then and there. What do you say to that, Daniel?"

He didn't know how to respond. "Thank

you," he said at last.

"Thanks aren't necessary. I wish all my cases were so simple. I wish I had more cases, actually more clients."

Daniel remembered the money purse, reached for it, but the lawyer read his mind, and put his hand on Daniel's forearm. He had a surprisingly brutal grip. "I told you yesterday, Daniel, that there was no charge for this service. You're good publicity, my friend. That's payment enough."

When Coyne released his arm, Daniel found a greenback. "I could," he said hesitantly, "at the least, buy you . . . that beer."

Leaning his head back against the frame wall of the barbershop, Vaughan Coyne cackled. "As long as it's not ginger beer." And stopped immediately, shaking his head, removing his glasses, apologizing again for a bad, bad joke. "Well, anyway, I do appreciate the sentiment, but you know you couldn't have that beer with me. They won't let an Indian in the saloons here, not even a policeman."

"You have one yourself. Beer, whiskey, or wine. I must go."

He started to rise, but the vise gripped him again, and Coyne pulled him back to the bench. "Wait a minute, Daniel. What's next? As your attorney, I want to know. Do you drop this whole matter?"

His head shook.

"You must tread lightly, Daniel." He looked up and down the boardwalk, even through the windowpane to check out the barbershop. "Blake Browne is not a man to trifle with. He's been roaming these parts for forty years. And he has the Texas Rangers, at least Carl Quantrell, backing him."

Silence. Looking across the street at the mercantile. Like a Comanche.

"You're a free man. Best thing for you to do is forget Blake Browne, get back to Cache Creek, help your people, help yourself. Don't do anything foolish. Just forget everything. I warned you about Huntsville prison. The next time, the judge might decide he'd like to get his name in the papers, fight for Texas, fight against the United States. You know what happened to that Indian in Huntsville, Satanta, one of your people, don't you?"

Daniel shrugged. He remembered Satanta, though just barely, remembered his mother pointing him out when the Kwahadi were still free, when they were preparing to fight the *taibo* killers of buffalo at the place in El Llano Estacado called Adobe Walls. Only Satanta was not of The People.

110

He was a big blow-hard, who loved to hear himself talk. A Kiowa, known as Set-t'ainte, or White Bear. Twice he had been sent to the *Tejano* prison in Huntsville. When Daniel was a boy, maybe a year before the Pale Eyes had grabbed him and sent him to Pennsylvania, they had heard the news of Satanta. The big man, depressed that he would never be freed from prison a second time, had leaped from the second-story landing of the prison hospital, and fallen to his death.

But he was not Set-t'ainte, and had no plans of going to the Huntsville prison.

"You hurt Blake pretty good, and," the lawyer was saying, "trust me, he'll get his come-uppance."

"Two of my people are dead," Daniel said. "I do not forget these things."

Coyne wet his lips. "I hate Blake Browne as much as you do. I'd like to fight him. Put him behind bars."

"So would Harvey Noble."

"Noble? Oh, yes, the federal marshal. Well, let's fight him together."

A minister walked past, offering the briefest nod. The wind picked up, and the sun dropped lower.

"Have you heard of a man called Dakota?" Daniel asked.

Slowly the lawyer shook his head. "Where did you hear that name?"

Daniel shrugged. "It was something Blake Browne said. When I went to his camp, he said that I must be working for Dakota. I take it that he did not like Dakota."

"A lot of people don't like Blake Browne."

Daniel said nothing.

"So you think . . . that this Dakota . . . is . . . ? What do you think, Daniel?"

He shook his head. "I don't think anything." He was looking again at the mercantile. He was thinking, though, not about Dakota, not even about Blake Browne. He was thinking about Harvey P. Noble, remembering him opening that note pad, writing down the names of Quantrell and the whiskey runner. He was thinking of some advice the Cherokee Hugh Gunter had given him a long while back.

If you want to be a detective, a real policeman, you can't go off jumping to no conclusions. That'll get you in trouble. You got to think. Think hard. And take notes.

So, Daniel was thinking: *Could I buy an Old Glory writing tablet, a Columbus lead sharpener, and a pack of Faber's No. Two pencils at Kemp's store? Would they sell to a Comanche?*

"I'll ask around," Coyne said. "Let's work

112

together. I'll get word to you about anything I learn, about Browne, about Quantrell, about this Dakota character. Now, what are your plans? We have to stop Blake Browne. But let's do this legally. By the white man's law. I want this man to be punished as much as you do. Poisoning an old man with bad whiskey. Getting a young girl killed. That's not right."

It felt good to be back among his people. There were no repercussions from his arrest. In fact, now the Comanches, Kiowas, and Apaches treated Daniel as nothing less than a hero, a warrior who had defeated the hated *Tejanos* by their own brand of fighting.

"You are the only Nermernuh who has one of these law-yers," Rain Shower told him. "Even Quanah does not have a lawyer. A rich *taibo,* is he not, this Coyne man?"

"He did not get rich representing me," Daniel said with a shrug.

"Is he handsome?"

Daniel stopped chewing the stringy beef. He stared at the pretty girl, who giggled, but never stopped looking at him. Finally he shrugged, and reached for the pot to refill his cup with coffee.

"I missed you," Rain Shower said. "I worried for you."

He tried to think of something to say, but then Ben Buffalo Bone came charging out of his lodge, screaming Daniel's name like a mountain lion, singing out praises of Daniel's courage. With a sigh, Rain Shower returned to her place beside her mother at the cook fire. As she left, and as her brother approached, Daniel also sighed.

"Did you see Nácutsi in the jail in Texas?" Ben Buffalo Bone said.

"No," Daniel answered.

"He is there now," Ben Buffalo Bone said, taking Daniel's coffee cup as his own. "Twice Bent Nose and Mean Dog took him, and four other prisoners. They probably arrived after you left. Mean Dog likes to take his time on these matters."

Daniel considered this. The court in Wichita Falls was for serious offenders. Nácutsi had been drunk, had gotten into a fight with Daniel — although Daniel had been the one who had started it — but that was a case for Quanah's Court of Indian Offenses, not a judge in Texas.

"You were right to send me to Nácutsi's lodge, Bávi." Ben made a face, and tossed the coffee, cup and all, to his side. "There was much whiskey there. Too much for one man to drink."

"He was selling whiskey," Daniel said, as if he had known it for some time. Maybe he had.

Ben nodded.

"The bottles?"

Ben's head bobbed again. "Like the one he had. I do not know the *taibo* words, but the markings were the same. The same as the one Toyarocho held that day. The same as the one you brought from the lodge of the great Penateka who is no more, the one you threw at the head of the *taibo* man with the red hair. You know of what I speak."

"Yes," Daniel said. He knew too well.

Ceramic stoneware with blue letters.

Cox & Coursey Bottling Works
Home Brewed
GINGER BEER
Dallas, Texas

They had been speaking in Comanche. Now, Daniel muttered in English: "It doesn't make a damned bit of sense."

CHAPTER NINE

Steam floated like heavy smoke above the two coffee cups Major Becker set on his desk. Daniel watched as the doctor picked up the nearest one and drank, never flinching, while Daniel quickly pulled his hand away after burning his fingers on the handle. He decided he'd wait. Besides, it was black coffee. No sugar. No milk. The doctor didn't even offer anything, and Daniel, like most Comanches, really liked his coffee sweeter than sugar cookies.

"Sergeant," Major Becker said, "I've seen my share of whiskey poisoning in this man's army. Seen enlisted men, officers, even doctors drink themselves to death, over years, and over hours. The United States Army, apparently, has a quota to recruit drunkards by the score. What is it that you wish to know?"

Daniel nodded. "Symptoms," he said, then thought he should explain. He had told

Leviticus Ellenbogen of his suspicions, that Seven Beavers had been poisoned by bad whiskey — that if he could link Blake Browne to that man's death, then they could charge the whiskey runner with manslaughter — but the agent had suggested the old Penateka had died of alcoholism, that Daniel was letting his hatred blind him to reason. Daniel told Becker what he had found at Huupi, inside the lodge, told him as much as he could remember.

"Mister Ellenbogen has a point," Becker said softly. "I don't know that I ever met this Seven Beavers, but I have seen a lot of your people, a lot of Kiowas, too, drink too much whiskey, and die from that. I've seen a lot of my soldiers do the same."

Daniel nodded. "Symptoms," he said again.

"Yes. Of course. Well, I don't know that I ever paid that much attention to these symptoms. When I was first studying medicine, my teachers . . . including my God-fearing, liquor-hating mother . . . told me that those who were slaves to liquor had a inner weakness, lacked moral courage, and that was to blame for their drunkenness. Now I, and many other doctors, believe there is much more to it, like there is a disease. They drink, and drink more, and more. Because they cannot stop, because the disease demands this. Courage and morality have nothing to do with it. It's tougher, of course, among your people, and other Indians. They can't hold their liquor as well. Lack a tolerance for it. So alcohol has a worse effect on them."

Daniel was getting tired of nodding.

"Symptoms. Yes. Well, there is always the strong stench of alcohol. This Seven Beavers would have stunk of whiskey. He would have been unresponsive, probably unconscious. Perhaps he just passed out. That's common for a drunk, but as far as fatal poisoning, there would be more serious symptoms. His skin would be cold, clammy. Much of his color would have been gone."

Watching Daniel, Becker took another sip of coffee, and pointed the cup at him. "That's a good idea, Sergeant. Writing all this down. I should think to do this. What I'm saying sounds pretty good. Maybe I'll write an article for the *Army and Navy Journal*." Becker drank again, set the cup down, and said: "His skin might be blue."

"A blue Indian?" Daniel grinned.

"Did you see the body?" Becker asked.

Daniel shook his head. "He was on his way to The Land Beyond The Sun when I arrived at Huupi."

"Agent Ellenbogen is right, I'm afraid, Sergeant. You would have a hard time getting an indictment against Browne without any evidence. There's a difference, a big difference, between bad whiskey and too much whiskey, although some symptoms might be the same. You said you found the whiskey bottle?"

"Yes. But I threw it at the *Tejano* with the red hair."

The doctor failed to choke down his laugh. "And what of this dead kitten?"

"It had lapped up the whiskey that had spilled," Daniel said. "At least that's what I think. It had coughed up blood. So did the old Penateka."

Becker shrugged. "That could be bad whiskey. But it could also be a symptom of drinking too much whiskey. Many drunks have bleeding ulcers."

"Can a kitten drink too much whiskey?" Daniel asked. "Or get an ulcer?"

The doctor was reaching for his cup. He stopped, stroked his chin instead. "Like Mister Ellenbogen said, it's still grasping at straws. Without evidence."

"I know. You say you have seen much whiskey at this fort."

"At this fort, and many others. On battlefields. In towns. For many years."

"So you know whiskey?"

Becker laughed. "Some say I do."

"I don't know whiskey. Not well. Just from what I've seen with The People. And, yes, with your people. If the whiskey was bad, the whiskey that Blake Browne was selling, would it kill just one kitten and one Penateka?"

"I would think others would have been affected," Becker said.

"So would I," Daniel said.

"Maybe they have."

Daniel waited, wondering.

"This whiskey runner cut a wide swath, didn't he? You said your lawyer mentioned Teepee City . . . that Browne might have been selling whiskey over there, too."

Daniel nodded.

"Well, you might ask around, find out if anyone else has died. Not just Indian. A settler in Teepee City. Maybe somebody in Wichita Falls, or a farmer on the Pease River. Maybe over at Doan's Store."

"Yes," Daniel said. This doctor was smart. Smarter than he was.

"There's something else," Becker said, and Daniel waited again.

"You said you destroyed many bottles of Blake Browne's whiskey. Well, those bottles could have contained the poisoned whiskey.

Seven Beavers just had the bad luck to buy one made from the batch that was lethal. Maybe you saved a bunch of lives. We'll never know."

Daniel sighed. He didn't know how to feel. Maybe he had saved many of The People, many *taibos* who lived in Greer County, many settlers in Teepee City. Maybe he had destroyed the evidence he needed to hang or, at least, imprison Blake Browne.

"I have some bottles," Daniel said. "Outside."

"I thought you destroyed all of Browne's whiskey."

"These were found at the lodge of Nácutsi. Fifteen bottles."

"That's quite a thirst for one brave."

"He was selling the whiskey, too. I think he was selling for Blake Browne."

"There are more whiskey runners on the reservation that this omnipresent Mister Browne," Becker said.

"That is true." Daniel waited. "Maybe Nácutsi worked for Dakota."

"Dakota?"

Daniel let out a sigh. "Just a name I've heard." Then he blurted out: "Have you heard of him?"

"I'm afraid not."

Silence.

"What do you want me to do with these bottles?" asked Becker.

"See if they are poison."

Becker finished his coffee. "All right. You have more faith in me that I have in myself, but I'll help. I'm not much of a chemist, but I guess I can tell if the whiskey is just bad whiskey, regular forty-rod, or poison whiskey. Let's go."

Leading the way, Daniel left the post hospital, and showed Major Becker the two wooden cases strapped on a pack on a patient, ugly mule. Each man took a case and, bottles rattling, set the boxes on the porch. Becker grabbed one bottle by the neck and pulled it up for inspection. He stared briefly, put the bottle underneath his arm, and found another bottle. His face changed. He knelt, studying the case, wet his lips, and looked up at Daniel.

"Every bottle's the same," he said.

"Yes," said Daniel.

"I've never seen that before. Not here."

Daniel agreed. "Nácutsi had these. All of Blake Browne's bottles were these. The Penateka who is no more had this bottle. That is what was beside the dead kitten. And this is the kind of bottle we found with Toyarocho, the one who killed his daughter by accident."

Becker read the label, and sighed. Slowly he rose, and told Daniel: "You might want to talk to one of our soldiers, Sergeant, when he returns to the post. He's on patrol now. A Seventh Cavalry trooper named Fenn O'Malley."

Spring had taken root, hot, windy, with threatening dark clouds blacking out the sun. Typical.

Reining in the buckskin, Daniel dropped his right hand by the Remington in the holster, and watched the rider move between the trees to the south near the confluence of Cache Creek and the Red River. The only men he had seen were a couple of cowboys driving longhorns to the pastures they leased from The People. The man riding out of the woods, however, was not white, although it took Daniel a minute before he recognized the long graying hair and tall silk hat.

"O-si-yo," the smiling rider greeted in Cherokee.

"You're a long way from Muskogee," Daniel told Hugh Gunter.

"You ain't too close to the Comanche agency." Gunter pulled the blue roan to a stop, and offered his right hand.

They shook hands.

123

"Rode over to see you at your horse-smelling home," Gunter said. "Ben Buffalo Bone sent me down here. You're a tough guy to track down. Move like a raven."

"Looking for a cavalry patrol," Daniel said.

"Gonna ambush them?"

Daniel shook his head with amusement.

"I got the letter that Ellenbogen gent mailed," Gunter said, and Daniel's amusement faded. *Well,* he thought, *at least the agent mailed the letters.*

"Struck me as interesting," Gunter said. "Especially after what I found up 'round Stinking Creek." Gunter pointed to a stand of elms. "Let's get out of the wind. Compare notes."

"What strikes me peculiar," Gunter said, "is that you ain't seen many Creek whiskey runners in your territory. That ain't like the Creeks."

"Maybe they've seen the light." Daniel drank from an Army-issue canteen.

"Now, you're trying to be funny," Gunter said. "Creeks have been busy aplenty in the Choctaw and Cherokee nations. So when I got that letter you asked your agent to write, I started doing me some investigating. Asked around in places like the Seminole

124

Agency, Cummings, Limestone Gap, along the KATY line, and over by Fort Holmes, Johnson, and the Negro Settlement."

"Covering a lot of ground," Daniel said.

"That's right. So's I can bill the United States Indian Police for all the miles I rode. And my wife and children like it more when I ain't in sight. Seems that the Creek whiskey peddlers have been busy elsewhere, but not down here."

"Too busy to pester us," Daniel said.

"Maybe. But I ain't told you what I found 'round Stinking Creek."

"Tell me."

"Plan to. I found me a couple of dead Creeks. Wagon burned, with all the whiskey in it. Remind you of anything?"

Daniel dug out his writing tablet and pencil. Stinking Creek lay in the western edge of the Chickasaw Nation, not far from the Comanche reservation. "Maybe the Chickasaws are as tired of whiskey runners as we are."

"As *you* are," Gunter corrected.

"You think I killed those two runners?"

Gunter snorted. "That ain't your style, Daniel. And I don't think you give a tinker's dam what's going on in the Chickasaw Nation. What struck me peculiar was the way them two Creeks . . . well, one of them looked more like a half-breed . . . was laid out. Shirts stripped off, and their backs was all whipped. Whipped before they was dead or after, I don't know. But that ain't all. Then they got hauled up like they was deer carcasses thrown up a tree . . . after they had expired, I warrant . . . to bleed 'em out. Throats cut. Hanging from tree branches. Filled with arrows. Ain't what I'd call a robbery."

"No," Daniel said.

"What I'd call, maybe, a warning."

Daniel wrote in his tablet. He said: "Stay out of the Chickasaw Nation."

"Maybe so. Or maybe they was on their way to or from your country. Maybe the message was keep out of Comanche land."

"That's. . . ." Daniel shook his head.

"See, this Creek I know on Goat Creek, he gives me some stories sometimes, for a greenback or tobacco or maybe if I don't arrest him, and he says the Creeks been asked to keep out of your country."

Daniel considered this, then thought of something Ellenbogen and Becker kept telling him. "I don't think you could get an indictment with that."

"How about with this?" Gunter reached into his frock coat pocket and pulled out a long whip of braided thong, fastened to a handle made of the polished bone.

Cow bone, Daniel thought. Years ago, The People would have always used a buffalo bone, but the buffalo had all but vanished. The braided leather whip felt old, but the bone seemed rather new.

"It ain't Chickasaw," Gunter said, "and it ain't Cherokee or Creek."

"It's Comanche," Daniel said.

" 'Tain't yours, I hope."

Daniel handed the whip back to Gunter. "I never cared much for whips."

"I don't think them two Creeks cared much for this one, neither." He rolled the thong over the handle, and stuck the whip back in his coat pocket. "I buried the dead men where I found 'em, will drop off a report at Fort Arbuckle on my way back home. I didn't think two dead whiskey runners was anything to work up a sweat over. Don't think nobody in the Chickasaw Nation will give a damn, either."

He thought of the arrows. "Comanche arrows? The arrows in those Creeks? Were they Comanche?"

"Yep. Dogwood shafts, turkey feathers, metal points."

It started raining, cold, hard drops. Daniel pulled his hat tighter, and rubbed his jaw. "What was the whiskey in?" Daniel asked.

"Told you. A wagon. Piss-poor pathetic one at. . . ."

"No. The containers. Ceramic bottles?"

Gunter nodded, and Daniel felt his heartbeat increase. "Sure, ceramic bottles. Glass bottles, too. A couple of jugs, one keg, a little bottle for medicine, a gourd, two. . . ."

Daniel stopped listening. It didn't matter. He wrapped the Old Glory writing tablet in oilskin paper, and slipped the pad and pencil in his saddlebag.

"What was you looking for soldier boys for?" Gunter asked. The two men mounted, and rode north.

"We've been finding a lot of beer bottles," Daniel said. "Same bottles . . . full of whiskey." He described the bottle. Gunter showed no recognition. The rain fell harder.

"The doctor at Fort Sill says a soldier named O'Malley was busted for drunkenness on duty." As he explained, Daniel reached behind him to pull out a bottle he had stuck in his saddlebags. "He was drinking out of one of those ginger beer bottles. I wanted to ask him where he got it."

Gunter laughed. "You think he'd tell you?"

"I was hoping I might persuade him. The People can be persuasive about some things."

The Cherokee's laugh grew louder. "Daniel, I ain't never seen this side of you. I think you're growing up." He pointed to the sky, and raised his voice. "About to come a turd float, Daniel. We best find some shelter on some high ground."

CHAPTER TEN

"Never cared much for ginger beer," Hugh Gunter said. "Too hot, too spicy. Beer ought to be cool, easy to drink. Got little use for Choctaws, but they do know how to cook up a decent brew. Choc can be a fine tonic. Cures just about everything, or that's what the coal miners tell me. That's who the Choctaws sell most of their Choc to. Never cured me of nothing, though. Not enough alcohol in it to cure a cold."

Daniel wasn't interested in Choctaws or their beer. He waited for Gunter to pass the ceramic stoneware bottle back to him.

"Where'd you pick that one up?" Gunter returned the bottle.

"Ben Buffalo Bone found it at the lodge of one of The People," Daniel said. "I'm finding them everywhere."

The thunderstorm had passed quickly, pounding the ground with large, painful raindrops while bending the trees with a blistering wind in a fury, then blowing its way southeast, heralding the arrival of an early spring. In the coolness of approaching evening, the bright white orb sank behind long, purple clouds. Pushing north, Daniel and Gunter headed back to the agency near Fort Sill.

Gunter removed his tall hat, and ran his long fingers through his long graying hair. Meticulously he fastened the hat atop his head, and went on about Choctaw beer, about the tobacco and fish berries they put in it for flavor and color. Maybe more. Daniel stopped listening until the old Cherokee asked: "You know anything about this bottle works place in Dallas?"

Daniel shook his head.

"Me, neither. Seems that would be the place to start your investigation. Dallas, Texas. Hell-hole. Like most of that God-awful state full of God-awful Texicans."

"My lawyer told me Dallas is too far away for whiskey runners."

The wicked grin that immediately spread across Gunter's face told Daniel he had made another mistake. The Cherokee turned his horse closer to Daniel, gave a loud whistle, and slapped Daniel's wet back.

"You didn't told me you had yourself a lawyer, Daniel. My-oh-my, ain't you coming up in the world. A pettifogging lawyer. *Dtyhh,* we say in Cherokee. Means quarreler. How much did that quarreler charge you for that priceless piece of information and advice?"

Shaking his head, Daniel sighed, which only made Gunter laugh harder.

"He didn't quarrel too much," Daniel said when Gunter's cackling died down, and added a moment later, "I think."

"Well, your friendly *dtyhh* is absolutely right," Gunter said as they forded a small creek. "Now, mostly the whiskey runners I run across . . . them that ain't Creeks . . . light out from Van Buren or Coffeyville to the north. Down south, they come from Spanish Fort and Denison City."

"And Wichita Falls," Daniel added.

"There, too. Mostly to your people. They don't get to us civilized nations."

"How about Greer County?" Daniel asked. "Do you know of any runners operating out of Greer County?"

"I don't know a damned thing about Greer County," Gunter said. "Don't want to, neither. But you're making me lose my train of thought with all your interruptions. We was talking about these two Cox and . . . what's the other name again?"

"Coursey. Is that considered one of my

interruptions?"

"Damnation, Daniel. Not only is you getting more notional and confrontational, you are becoming a real pain-in-my-arse smart aleck."

Daniel laughed.

"All right," Gunter said, "yes, most whiskey runners don't hail from Dallas, but these bottles do. So that's what I mean, best place to start is Dallas, Texas. First, though, I'd suggest we make camp, get a fire going, dry off. Don't want to catch our death."

"Let's ride a little more," Daniel said.

"You got any food?"

"Some pemmican. Some jerky." He turned to face the Cherokee. "No Choc."

"I got some coffee. And three, four stale biscuits that won't break too many teeth. Veritable feast."

They were riding through a long path in some woods. "There's a pasture once we get out of this woods road," Daniel said. "A creek beyond that. We'll camp there."

"Suit yourself."

After slowing his horse, Daniel reached into his saddlebag, and withdrew his writing tablet and pencil. The buckskin had a smooth, easy gait, had seldom showed any notional and confrontational tendencies, so Daniel draped the reins in front of his saddle, flipped to an open page, and started writing.

"So what all do we have, other than these ginger beer bottles full of rot-gut?" Gunter asked.

"A dead Penateka," Daniel said. "Poisoned by bad whiskey."

Gunter snorted. "And two dead Creeks."

Daniel stuck the pencil behind his hear, and flipped back a page. He read: "Stay out of Comanche, Kiowa, and Apache reservation. Like that informant told you."

Gunter nodded.

"So those two dead whiskey runners you found were killed after they had come into our land?"

"It's possible. Ain't certain. But Chickasaws usually don't get angry enough over Creeks to do them that way." Gunter shook his head. "Nobody often gets angry enough to do nobody that way."

Absently Daniel chewed on the pencil until he could taste the wood, and remembered a school mother back at Carlisle jerking a pencil from his mouth, snapping at him: "Pencils are for writing, Daniel. Not eating. This horrible habit of yours must cease at once!"

He wrote again. Stopped. Turned to look at the Cherokee. "But that whip you found.

It was Comanche. Those Creeks were killed by one of The People."

First Gunter nodded, next shook his head, then spun his head in a circular movement. Daniel thought he might be drunk on memories of that Choc beer. "Yes," Gunter said, staring ahead. "They were murdered by a Comanche. The whip says so." His voice changed as he looked at Daniel. "Or maybe that whip was left behind to make a body think that the heinous crime was perpetrated by you heathen savages."

A feeling of stupidity swept across Daniel.

"How do you people pay for the whiskey you drink?" Gunter asked.

Daniel shrugged. "Barter," he said, frowning, remembering some of The People who would sell their wives, their daughters, so lost were they without that *taibo* whiskey.

"So the killer maybe picked up that whip for a bottle of ginger beer. Then shot down two Creeks infringing on his territory. Left the whip behind so all of us really intelligent peace officers would go arrest the first Comanche buck we found."

Daniel was thinking of something else. "Where's Uvalde?"

Gunter shrugged. "Don't rightly know. Texas some place, I think. South a ways. Maybe in Mexico. Why?"

"When I found the white man, Blake Browne, when I burned his wagon. . . ."

"And beat the bitter hell out of him."

"Now who's interrupting!"

With a humorous bow, Gunter apologized.

"The young man that was riding with him, Browne called him Uvalde." Daniel turned back to the first page of the Old Glory tablet. "Uvalde Ted Smith."

"Name don't ring a bell."

"He could be from Uvalde."

"That's possible. Downright likely. Mister Ted Smith's been to Uvalde, at least."

"So the whiskey runners could be operating out of Uvalde." Daniel stopped, shook his head. "No. Not if it's south. If Dallas is too far for whiskey runners. . . ."

"You'd have to ask Uvalde Ted Smith," Gunter said, "and I never heard of him."

"How about Dakota?"

"That's north of here. A good ways north."

"No, have you ever heard of a man named Dakota?"

"Can't say that I have."

"Blake Browne mentioned him, as well. I think he's a whiskey runner."

"You're starting to think everybody's running whiskey."

Silence.

"So where does your soldier boy fit in?"

He had to think for a moment, before remembering the trooper from the Fort Sill hospital.

"Fenn O'Malley." Daniel tested the name. "When he was busted, the major at Fort Sill said, he had a bottle of ginger beer. Hit a sergeant in the jaw while holding the bottle. Broke the sergeant's jaw, and broke the fingers on O'Malley's right hand."

"Right intelligent practitioner of fisticuffs, this O'Malley," Gunter said. A moment later he added: "That ginger beer sure is omniscient."

"Omnipresent," Daniel corrected.

"Watch them interruptions, Sergeant Killstraight. Else I might not give you something to ponder."

The woods road they had been following dumped into a prairie, and they startled a few longhorn cattle. Thunder rolled in the distance, but the skies ahead remained clear. Daniel had to gather the reins as they turned, and waited until they had cleared the cattle before he dropped the reins again, and wrote some more.

"What outfit is your potato-eating trooper with?" Gunter asked.

"Seventh Cavalry."

"Fairly new to your fort, ain't they?"

Daniel had to think. "I guess so."

"Custer's old outfit."

"I knew that." Back at Carlisle, the Lakota boys always bragged about how they had wiped out Yellow Hair on the Greasy Grass. What great bluecoat chief did you ever kill? they'd ask Daniel and boys from the other tribes.

"I think they was stationed," Gunter was saying, "or used to be stationed, or are still headquartered out of Fort Abraham Lincoln. That's in Dakota Territory. Don't know where Uvalde is, but I do know that for certain."

He chewed the pencil again, but when he started to write in the notebook, Gunter stopped him.

"It could be that this bluebelly is called Dakota, but that sure ain't certain. He could be from County Cork or Wisconsin. He could have just enlisted over in Missouri or Alabama. He might never been to Dakota, might not never have heard of Dakota, especially if he's just some poor, ignorant Irish farmer fresh off the boat. Hell, he could be from Uvalde, for all that we know. All that be is a theory."

"I understand that," Daniel said.

"Well, here's something I understand, Daniel. Granted, it's just theory, too, but I've been studying hard on it since that thunderstorm, and been thinking about it since I found those dead Creeks. The Creeks have been warned to keep their whiskey off your reservation. Two Creeks are dead. Maybe they was killed as a warning, too. That tells me that somebody is claiming the Kiowa, Comanche, and Apache Reservation as their territory. They want it for themselves."

"Why?"

Gunter shrugged. "Money."

"Why not spread into the Chickasaw Nation?" Daniel said.

"Fair question. But they might be like locusts. Start at one place, eat everything that's green, then move with the wind. Could be they want to start small, and your reservation's fairly small, fairly new, pretty wild, and wildly lawless. Good place to get your whiskey business started, and you people . . . no offense . . . tend to have a thirst for whiskey. Judge Parker's deputies don't ride over here that often. The government'll likely divide up this court before long, if that Senator Dawes and his crew ain't butchered up Indian country before then. Anyway, we keep Harvey P. Noble and his pals right busy in the Chickasaw, Choctaw, Creek, and Cherokee Nations. I got no authority here. I ain't slighting you, Daniel, or your tribal police, but, if I wanted to get me a toehold in Indian Territory, was I of mind to peddle whiskey, I might start my business in this country."

"The Army patrols for whiskey runners, too."

"Piss on them bluecoats," Gunter said. "Texas Rangers and Texas sheriffs likely keep an eye out for them south of the Red River."

The face of Carl Quantrell appeared before Daniel.

"That ain't ginger beer, and it certainly ain't Choc, they's filling them bottles with," Gunter said. "These whiskey runners are big."

"And organized."

"More so than the Creeks." Gunter shook his head and spit. "Hell, I never arrested no Creek that'd ever fill that bill. Organized. Now, don't get me wrong, Daniel. I'm not fretting that two whiskey runners got cut up and strung up and shot up over in the Chickasaw Nation, not when I got murderers and robbers and rapists to hunt down, but that's my territory, and I don't like that."

"I don't like a dead girl and a dead old man killed because of these whiskey runners," Daniel said.

"And Harv Noble, he don't like nothing. So the way I see it, the three of us are like them Three Musketeers."

Daniel liked that. Even if he had never read that book.

"So we should work together?" Daniel asked.

"I'd like that, my young Comanche friend. Like your letter said. I'll work my territory, you work yours, and I'll make sure Marshal Noble knows he has volunteered to join our war party."

"I think he already has."

"But one of us should get to Dallas, Texas." For some reason, Gunter was staring hard at Daniel.

"I couldn't do that. I'm Comanche. They don't allow us to go riding into Texas. That should be Marshal Noble."

"I'm in Muskogee. Harv's in Fort Smith. You're closest."

"But I'm Indian."

"Get a pass."

"You get a pass!"

"I don't need no damned pass. I'm an officer of the United States Indian Police. I go where I damned well please, and I surely don't please to go to Dallas."

"We should just write or wire the town marshal in Dallas," Daniel said.

"There's only us Three Musketeers," Gunter said. "You trust any white man down in Texas? You think a peace officer in Dallas gives a fig what's going on in Indian Territory? You think the Dallas city marshal is crying that two Creeks and two Comanches got buried?"

"My lawyer in Wichita Falls said he would ask around, too. Maybe. . . ."

"Piss on that *dtyhh,* too."

"Well, I can't go."

"Then don't. Maybe Harv knows somebody."

"Good." He had ended that subject. "Here's a good place to camp."

"It'll do," Gunter said dryly.

They unsaddled and grained the horses. Once they had a fire going, and coffee brewing, they squatted near the flames, holding out their hands to pull the warmth closer.

"Well," Daniel said a moment later. "We have something to go on. For our investigation, I mean."

Gunter was shaking his head before Daniel had finished. "Nope. What you got in your Old Glory tablet is a few pages of some words. What I've got is a few ideas. What it all adds up to be is a bunch of nothing. We got nothing, Daniel. Nothing that'll get anybody arrested, let alone hung. But we

142

got us a place to start."

Dallas, Texas. Daniel sighed.

CHAPTER ELEVEN

As they rode into the agency grounds, a crowd had gathered, and more kept coming, some of them running, talking with excitement. Only it was too early for ration day, and soldiers rarely came to the agency. Unless there had been trouble. Gunter snorted something in Cherokee, but Daniel ignored him, focusing on the multitude. Indian policemen. Including Ben Buffalo Bone and Twice Bent Nose. Seven haggard troopers from Fort Sill, with a young, mustached, cherry-faced lieutenant. Major Becker squatted in the bed of an old buckboard, peering down at something, then shaking his head, pulling up a woolen blanket, and talking to Agent Leviticus Ellenbogen, who stood sweating, wringing his large hands. Teepee That Stands Alone was there, too, with maybe a dozen other Comanches and Kiowas — and several more hurrying that way. Leaning against the wall of the agency headquarters, head bowed, stood a man Daniel never expected to see in Indian Territory.

Becker stopped talking, Teepee That Stands Alone turned around, arms folded, his face a mask, and the black bluecoats shuffled about uncomfortably as Gunter and Daniel entered the compound. The young officer barked an order, Ben Buffalo Bone started to shout something, but the Indian agent commanded him to be silent, and Vaughan Coyne lifted his head.

Daniel and Gunter reined in their horses.

The Wichita Falls attorney stepped forward, speaking urgently: "Daniel, don't say anything until you and I have had a chance to talk."

He looked at the wagon, saw the worn brogans sticking out of the blanket.

"Bávi!" Ben Buffalo Bone started.

"Shut up!" the agent yelled at him.

"Run," Ben Buffalo Bone said. "It is the bad white man."

"They think you killed him," Twice Bent Nose added in Comanche.

A murmur followed. A Comanche woman began singing. The afternoon sun broke through gray clouds.

Daniel shot a quick glance to Hugh Gunter, who slowly swung down from his horse, and said — "Well, let's take a look-see." — and strode to the wagon. Silently Daniel followed, aware of the stares, the pressing silence that was quickly broken when the young lieutenant told them to stay away. Major Becker, however, countermanded the order, saying: "They can't hurt this man any more, Mister Newly." Carefully Becker stepped around the covered corpse, and helped Gunter, then Daniel, up onto the wagon bed. The Army surgeon then knelt, and pulled back the blanket.

Daniel turned his head in disgust, panic.

Gunter whistled, and squatted.

After swallowing down the bile quickly climbing up his throat, Daniel faced the dead man again.

Blake Browne's body had swollen like an overripe plum, like it was about to burst open. His eyes were gone. So was his topknot. Two small but ugly wounds looked black against the pale flesh of his bare chest and stomach. Two arrows lay between his side and broken arm, the point missing from one, the other, shaft broken, stained with dark, dried blood.

Gunter picked up the arrows, and held them out toward Daniel.

"Comanche?" the Cherokee asked.

Daniel sank beside him, thankful his knees

didn't buckle. He looked at the broken arrow. "Maybe," Daniel said. "It's dogwood." He examined the feathers, shaking his head. "Hawk feathers." He pursed his lips.

The white lieutenant started yelling again. "Everybody on the reservation knows that the hawk is Killstraight's medicine. That alone should be enough to hang that son-of-a-bitch!"

"You got plenty of friends," Gunter whispered to Daniel, and took the arrow away.

The crowd was talking again, Ben Buffalo Bone translating what had been said, Vaughan Coyne telling Daniel again to remain silent. Then Teepee That Stands Alone's voice thundered in the guttural language of The People.

"Listen to the words of Teepee That Stands Alone," Ben Buffalo said, smiling after the old Kwahadi *puhakat* fell silent. "The People would never use hawk feathers on an arrow."

"It is true," another voice drawled. Daniel saw Frank Striker, the agency interpreter, sitting on an overturned bucket, whittling.

Twice Bent Nose's head bobbed in agreement.

"Well, he was killed by an Injun," a black-bearded trooper said. "That's certain."

"Killed and scalped," another voice

chimed in.

"Shut up!" Major Becker demanded.

Daniel looked at the arrow again, then lifted his head toward the surgeon. "Did you break the arrow pulling it out?"

"It was like that when Mister Coyne discovered the body."

Daniel looked above the wagon at the pale attorney. "Where did you find him?"

The young lawyer swallowed. "Between Middle Cache Creek and West Cache Creek. I saw the buzzards." He lowered his head again. "Thought it was probably just a Texas steer. . . ."

"Busted arrow's no good," Major Becker said, "but why leave the other arrow in Browne's chest?"

"The People will not use an arrow that has taken the life of a human, even a *taibo*," Daniel said.

Gunter whispered: "You sure no Comanche did this?"

"I'm not sure of anything," Daniel said. "Except I didn't do it."

"I know that. You ain't got the look, no matter how mean you want to be, no matter how much you hated this rank sumbitch. What about that big, mean-looking fellow yonder?"

"Teepee That Stands Alone?"

"He don't look happy."

"It was his granddaughter that was killed. Remember? Her father passed out on top of her."

"With one of them Coursey and Cox ginger beer bottles," Gunter said. "He's got a motive."

Daniel shook his head. "Teepee That Stands Alone follows the old traditions of The People." He pointed at the arrowhead. "That's metal. He'd never use that. Would only use a stone head. Nor would he use hawk feathers."

"What are those two bucks whispering about?" the lieutenant of the Long Knives demanded.

Hugh Gunter slowly rose, stretching out his tall form, and staring hard with black, bitter eyes at the young officer. "I'm not buck, soldier boy," he said. "I am Hugh Gunter of the Long Hair Clan. I am an officer with the United States Indian Police, and you will speak to me . . . and Sergeant Killstraight . . . with respect, else I climb down off this wagon and whup you to a frazzle."

Lieutenant Newly looked away. Frank Striker laughed and went back to his whittling.

"I was going to take him back to the

hospital," Becker said, "perform a postmortem examination there. But I want you to see this." He pulled back the rest of the blanket, revealing Blake Browne's naked corpse.

His thigh was slashed, deeply, to the bone, long, ugly.

"These two are likely the death wounds," Becker said, pointing at Browne's chest.

"What about his eyes?" Daniel asked.

Becker shook his head. "Ravens, I warrant. Turkey buzzards. Some sort of carrion."

Mein Gott, Ellenbogen muttered, the first words he had spoken since their arrival.

"As I was pointing out," Becker continued. "Two death wounds. The scalping, and this." He pointed at the slashed thigh. "Mean anything?"

"It means Indian butchery." Young Newly had regained his voice, and courage. "Comanche arrow or not, Major, Blake Browne is dead."

"Glory to heaven," one of the troopers said.

Newly whirled, face flushed, started for the soldier, then spun around, focusing his wrath on Daniel. "We have enough evidence. We should arrest this Indian, hold him in the guardhouse, transport him for trial and execution to Fort Smith. Or Wichita Falls. Killstraight had motive. He had means."

"No opportunity, though," Gunter said. He waved a hand over his nose. "This boy's mighty ripe." Looking now at Major Becker. "How long you reckon he's been dead?"

With a shrug, Becker answered: "Three days, perhaps four. Hard to tell."

"Well, Daniel couldn't have done it. He's been riding with me for the past five days. Down south. We've been investigating two other dead whiskey runners we found. A couple of Creeks, and they was butchered a hell of a lot more than this old boy. That's three dead whiskey runners. Now this boy, being white . . ." — pointing at the corpse — "he's a federal matter, but those Creeks, that's my matter. Daniel's been helping me. I expect a passel of Judge Parker's deputies will be helping, too. We got three murders. Somebody's killing the whiskey runners on your reservation. That's my report."

As he helped Daniel down off the wagon, Gunter whispered: "Don't be tormenting over my lying soul, Daniel. Let's go talk to your *dtyhh.*"

"That's great news, Daniel," Vaughan Coyne said, inside the stifling agency. "You have an alibi. You couldn't have killed Blake Browne."

Daniel started to speak, to admit that the Cherokee policeman had lied about being with Daniel all that time, but Gunter grunted. Agent Ellenbogen cleared his throat, decided he had nothing to say, and Daniel said: "Why are you in Indian Territory?"

"Coming to see you, Daniel," the lawyer said. "I told you I would investigate Browne, Quantrell, and this Dakota you mentioned."

"And?" Daniel asked.

The lawyer went pale. He sat down. Probably the heat. Fanned himself, shook his head, looked up, speaking slowly, barely audible. "I thought it was just a steer. Those buzzards."

Ellenbogen fetched a glass of water, and the lawyer drank. Slowly his face regained its color. He finished the water.

"Quantrell is no friend of law and order," Coyne said. "I think he's involved with this whiskey operation. I think he and Blake Browne are. . . ." The paleness returned. "Were," Coyne corrected, bowing his head. He looked up, his face pleading. "I just can't get the sight of that man . . . just can't . . . forget him. It was . . . horrible."

They waited.

152

"Browne and Carl were partners. I think Carl Quantrell is Dakota."

Daniel cursed himself silently. He ought to be writing all this down, but he had stupidly left his Old Glory tablet in the saddlebags.

"How you come to that?" Gunter asked.

Coyne said: "He's from Company D. Out of Wichita Falls. But before that he was assigned for eleven months in Dallas. Dallas is where you said those ginger beer bottles hail from."

"Excuse me," Daniel said, standing. "Mister Ellenbogen, do you have pencil and paper? I'd like to write this down." He'd never remember all that.

When he had settled back in his chair, Coyne continued.

"He and Browne were known associates. They could be spotted together at one of Wichita Falls's grog shops, and lately Quantrell has been patrolling the Red River area." He paused. No questions. "Instead of patrolling the river, I think he was guarding it, letting Blake Browne slip across into Indian Territory with whiskey."

"Something to consider," Gunter said without commitment.

"I think so." Coyne pushed back his bangs with his left hand, revealing the thin line of a wicked cut, probably from a knife, just below the hairline on the right side of his face. "Quantrell found out I had been asking about him. He gave me this, told me it was a warning, told me I could easily wind up dead."

"Why did you not prefer charges against that scoundrel?" Agent Ellenbogen demanded.

"Swear out a complaint against a Texas Ranger? In Texas? I've been practicing law long enough, sir, to know when I have a case and when I have nothing, Mister Ellenbogen. And Quantrell . . . well, sir, he scares the hell out of me. He's a dangerous and treacherous man. If you come across him, I would not give him a chance. He'll kill you."

That, Daniel believed, was true enough.

"Is he from Dakota? Is he called Dakota?" Daniel asked.

"I'm not sure where he comes from, but I was thinking Company D. D for Dakota. Just a code."

Daniel started to say something, stopped, wrote.

"I feel sick," Coyne said.

"Better than Blake Browne feels," said Hugh Gunter.

CHAPTER TWELVE

The arrow entered the abdomen, slicing deep, downward, and to the left. Having nicked the splenic artery and pierced the stomach chamber, the arrow would have killed Blake Browne, but it would have been a long, agonizing death. Therefore, the other arrow, higher, glancing off a rib and into a lung, likely proved to be a blessing. It followed the same down, left trajectory, a mortal injury that would have brought death a little more quickly that the gut wound.

Of course, Major Becker couldn't tell which arrow struck first. The lung shot might have been the first wound. The shot to the stomach, in fact, might have happened after Blake Browne was dead.

"They could have even hit him at the same time," Becker told Daniel. "If there had been two killers."

Daniel shook his head. "Both arrows had hawk feathers. I'd say they came from the

155

same quiver." Again he studied one arrow, the one not broken, crudely made, no Comanche markings, and a wild thought ran through his mind: *If it came from any quiver.*

"Well." Becker sipped his Scotch. "You'd know better than me. I'm not much of a detective."

"Nor am I," Daniel said.

"Some say I'm not much of a physician."

They sat in Becker's office at Fort Sill, the post hospital surprisingly quiet, the windows open to let in the cooling breeze and let out the smell of sickness and medicine. Outside, came the commands of officers and non-commissioned officers, even the popping of the American flag, the jingle of traces, and curses of saddlers over at the corrals.

"But I missed one thing when I examined the corpse in the wagon," Major Becker told Daniel after he finished his whiskey. "His skull was crushed. From behind. That would have killed Browne, too, and faster than either of the two arrow shots."

"Which killed him?" Daniel asked.

"Does it matter?"

"I guess not."

"My guess is that the head injury came from falling off the wagon. That killed him."

Daniel wrote that down, thinking. The

first arrow struck him, then the second, and he fell off the wagon, striking his head. He sketched the scene, crudely, in his notebook.

"The killer would have been higher."

"Absolutely."

"Like on a boulder."

"A good guess."

"Browne was ambushed. From a high place."

"Naturally."

Daniel closed the writing tablet. Frowning, he tried to picture the country between Middle and West Cache Creeks. Vaughan Coyne had returned to Wichita Falls. Too bad. Daniel would have liked to see exactly where the lawyer had found the dead whiskey runner.

"But there's another possibility," Becker said. "He was knocked off the wagon, and the killer stood over him . . . Browne was likely already dead . . . and shot him twice, scalped him, slashed his thigh."

He opened the Old Glory, wrote that down, closed it again.

More voices, closer, sang out along the parade grounds.

"You might want to get out of here, Sergeant Killstraight," Major Becker said. "Lieutenant Newly is officer of the day."

■ ■ ■ ■

"You are distracted."

Daniel quickly looked at Rain Shower, who smiled her shy smile, holding a gourd of water, offering him something to drink, as he sat outside the cabin where he and the horses lived.

"I am sorry," he said, took the gourd, and drank.

She sat across from him. "Your mood has soured since you went to see the Pale Eyes agent yesterday," she said.

He set the gourd beside him. The way he saw it, Daniel's mood had been soured for weeks. For at least an hour, he had been sitting outside on this Sunday, his day off, reading and rereading the notes he had scribbled in his Old Glory tablet.

"I wanted to get a pass," Daniel decided to explain to her. "To go to Dallas."

"The *Tejano* city?"

"Haa," he answered.

She turned up her nose in disgust. "I have never been to this place called Dallas, but there are many lodges in those cities," she said. "Many places like that." Pointing at the cabin behind him.

"Not as many as some cities that I have

seen," he said, first in English, out of habit, then in Comanche.

"The Pale Eyes agent," she said, "he would not give you this pass?"

"No. Agent Ellenbogen was skeptical." Which was a mild description. Downright defiant.

"I once rode to a *Tejano* town," she said. "Wichita Falls. I did not like it. But I gladly would go to this place in Texas, if you wish. I did not have a pass when I rode to Wichita Falls. It was to help you."

"It was a big help," he said.

Hugh Gunter had sent her galloping those hard miles — more than fifty — to Wichita Falls to fetch Deputy Marshal Harvey P. Noble. Daniel had worried about her, but Rain Shower was Nermernuh. She could ride better than many warriors of The People, certainly better than Daniel.

"Then I will go again." She started to rise, but Daniel reached, took her arm, gently pulled her back. Smiling, he stared at her, slowly shaking his head.

"It is too far. I will keep asking Agent Ellenbogen. I will attempt to be . . . ahem . . . more persuasive."

"And he will keep telling you no. He can be as stubborn as you are. My brother tells me so."

He joked with her. "Your brother tells you that I am stubborn or that Agent Ellenbogen is stubborn?"

She didn't laugh, not even smile. "The agent. He needs not tell me about you."

With a laugh, Daniel shook his head, but Rain Shower cut off his humor with a defiant statement. "No, I will go."

"It is too dangerous for you to go alone," he argued. "And you do not know the way."

"I will not go alone. I will go with Quanah."

For the longest moment, he just stared at Rain Shower, trying to understand what she had just told him. Tried to find the words, but the only thing he could say was: "Quanah?"

Enthusiastically she nodded. "*Haa.* In two suns, he is going to Texas. He and Coyote Chaser and Teepee That Stands Alone, and A'do-eete and Tséeyñ of our friends the Kiowa. They go to another *Tejano* town to talk to the *taibos* who wish to use the grass of The People and the Kiowa to feed their cows. Fort Worth. It is not far from Dallas, or so Quanah tells me. He tells me the people of Fort Worth hate the people of Dallas. Like The People hate the Pawnees." The look on Daniel's face must have stopped her. She looked at him, curious, then suspicious, and said: "Perhaps you could come with Quanah and me."

Leaning over, he kissed her, then stood, heading inside to fetch his buckskin, calling back over his shoulder: "Rain Shower, you are not only lovely, you are brilliant!"

Reluctantly Leviticus Ellenbogen handed Daniel a signed pass permitting him, as a sergeant of the tribal police, to accompany Quanah Parker and a delegation of Comanche and Kiowa Indians to Texas, where the Indians would discuss grazing rights for the big Texas cattlemen. Daniel had no illusions. Ellenbogen would have turned Daniel down again had it not been for Quanah.

Since the death of Yellow Bear roughly two years ago, Quanah had been named — by the Pale Eyes, not The People — as chief of the Comanche Nation. The People were not like the Pale Eyes. Never had they let one man, such as the Great White Father, govern them. Yet if any one warrior could lead The People back to their glory, Quanah Parker was that man.

He was a man in his thirties or forties — no one, neither white nor red, knew for sure, except Quanah, and he wouldn't say. His mother had been a *Tejano* girl The People had captured on a raid. As a warrior, Quanah — which meant Fragrance — had fought against the Long Knives, Texas Rangers, and other enemies with the Destanyuka band, then joined the Kwahadis to continue the fight until he realized the inevitable, that The People must learn to live with the Pale Eyes, must surrender, or starve and die.

Haa, Daniel thought, *he is our chief.* Daniel might need Quanah's help on the reservation, might need him to help wipe away Rain Shower's anger. When Ellenbogen gave Daniel the pass to travel to Texas, he told Rain Shower that she could not go. Her pouting did not last long, replaced in seconds by wild anger, and she had cursed the agent, Daniel, and Quanah, before storming out of the agency and heading for her camp.

Quanah lived as a *taibo,* lived in the Star House, a two-story, wooden mansion near Cache Creek that the Pale Eyes had built for him, with four giant white stars painted on the red shingles. Often he dressed in the finest clothes he could buy from the post sutler. He even wore a bowler from Washington City and a diamond stickpin in his black, silk cravat — gifts from rich Pale Eyes. Yet, also, always, Quanah lived as a Kwahadi. His hair hung in long braids, wrapped in otter skins. He kept as many wives as he needed. He could write his name in English, but he usually spoke in the language of The People. He still fought for The People. He would always fight for The People. He would always be Kwahadi.

"Daniel," Frank Striker had told Ellenbogen back at the agency, interpreting for Quanah, "will be our voice. Like Aaron was to speak for Moses."

That surprised Daniel almost as much as it had stunned Leviticus Ellenbogen. The agent had no argument, so now Daniel found himself sitting, cross-legged, on the lush grass in front of Quanah's Star House, waiting with the other Comanche and Kiowa (but no Apache) diplomats for the wagons that would take them to Texas, wondering if Rain Shower remained furious at him.

Waiting for the Long Knives who would escort them as far as the railroad depot in Wichita Falls.

For three hours, they wondered if the Pale Eyes had forgotten, then A'do-eete heard the hoofs, and a few minutes later six Long Knives, mounted on dun horses, rode down the road to the Star House. White men, like those under Lieutenant Newly. Not the black buffalo soldiers Daniel was used to seeing at Fort Sill.

His eyes locked hard on one rider, a black-headed lanky man with hard green eyes, and his right hand in a dirty cast. Daniel remembered him from the post hospital.

So, Daniel thought, *I've found Fenn O'Malley at last.*

They camped that night on the Texas side of the Red River, just beyond Hill's Ferry.

Daniel had spent much of the day studying the Irish trooper, the one Major Becker had said had been busted for drunkenness on duty, had smashed another bluecoat while holding a ginger beer bottle. His blue blouse was faded, but a darkness on the sleeves told Daniel that O'Malley had once worn the chevrons of a sergeant, the same as Daniel wore on his scratchy, ill-fitting uniform.

At camp, the Long Knives picketed the horses and mules between the Indians, closest to the river, and the soldiers, one bluecoat guarding the livestock. Separate fires. Separate food. Separate. Yet there was also a separation among The People. Quanah lay near Daniel, but Coyote Chaser was off in the opposite corner, and Teepee That Stands Alone even farther away.

The soldiers complained loudly; the Kiowas and The People were silent. Reading a tattered three-year-old issue of the *Police Gazette,* Daniel waited until his supper had settled in his stomach, then walked toward the horses, nodding politely at the yellow-mustached sentry, and moving into the soldier camp.

The bluecoats fell silent, staring hard as Daniel approached, removing his hat, running his fingers nervously on the inside of the crown. One man unfastened the cover of his holster. Another spit a stream of tobacco juice. Daniel stopped in front of the slouched Fenn O'Malley, and, remembering a technique he had read about in the *Police Gazette,* he said: "I've been looking for you, Dakota."

"The hell are you talking about, buck?"

Well, the author of the *Gazette* piece had said his trick worked when he questioned a suspected arsonist.

An informant from the southern side of Chicago told me that Lucifer Salzburger had been using a bogus name, Hans Fritz, so when two bad eggs walked out of the bar room and one called the other "Fritz", I decided to take a chance, stepping off the step and calling out in a friendly voice: "Hey, Salzburger, your mother's been look-

165

ing for you."

Both men stopped, and J.C. "Lucifer" Salzburger, alias Hans Fritz, the notorious fire fiend, whirled, eyes wide, saying: "My mother?"

Grinning, I drew and cocked my Bulldog revolver, and said to this notorious arsonist: "Hello, Lucifer."

"I was told you were called Dakota."

"No red nigger calls me nothing. Get out of here, buck."

O'Malley looked away. Daniel kept staring. *Read the fellow's face,* Hugh Gunter once told him. *Watch his eyes. You can tell if a man's lying, most times, once you get the knack. Not always, but more often than not. Listen to his voice. That's another way of telling.*

Daniel decided the soldier wasn't lying. The man wasn't called Dakota. He decided not to read the *Police Gazette* to learn how to be a detective. The editors loved more of those crazy, violent stories, anyway. The magazine wasn't really known as a training manual for Comanche policemen.

He waited, kept staring at Fenn O'Malley. Finally the Irishman looked up. "What the hell do you want? You don't get back to your side of camp, I'll carve your damned eyes out."

"Where did you get the whiskey bottle?"

"What whiskey bottle? The hell you talking about?"

"Ginger beer. Coursey and Cox Bottling Works."

"Beer?" one of the other Pale Eyes soldiers said, and the others snorted. "Sergeant O'Malley has never touched a drop of beer in his life, Sergeant Comanche."

"Yeah," said another, "that's why he's no sergeant no more."

Fenn O'Malley glared. "You watch your mouth, Dutchie. I can carve your eyes out as quick as I can blind this buck."

"Not with no busted hand, mick."

"My fingers'll mend, Dutchie."

Daniel spoke again. "Where did you get the bottle?"

"I answer no questions from no savage."

"The bottle?"

"I don't know nothing about no beer bottle."

"Sure you do, mick," the one called Dutchie said. "That's how you busted Sergeant Gasquet's jaw."

"He was asking for it," O'Malley said. "Same as you."

Dutchie laughed. " 'Course, that was

Lieutenant Newly's mistake, dumb green-horn of an officer. Send the Irish on a scout to catch whiskey runners, and they'll find whiskey, sure as hell."

"Fenn found it, all right," another soldier said.

"The hell with all of you," O'Malley said.

Daniel decided to give the *Police Gazette* one more chance. "Carl Quantrell told me they called you Dakota."

This time O'Malley stood. He towered over Daniel, and his good left hand clenched into a hard, hard fist. "I told you. My name ain't Dakota. And I never heard of Carl Quantrell, neither."

"Company D," Daniel said. "Texas Rangers."

Nothing. No expression on O'Malley's face, other than contempt and hatred for Daniel.

"Get the hell out of my sight. Else I'll give you what you savages gave Custer."

"How would you know?" Daniel said. "You weren't there." He turned, walked away, half expecting Fenn O'Malley to come after him, but the Irishman had turned his frustrations against the one called Dutchie. The two cursed each other for the next five minutes, before the sergeant, who had been silent while Daniel had been trying to interview O'Malley, threatened them with the stockade. By the time Daniel had settled on his bedroll, Dutchie's voice sang out, surprisingly pleasant, serenading the camp, Indians and soldiers alike, with "Is That Mister Reilly?"

Daniel picked up the *Gazette,* sighed, and tossed it into the fire, then reached for his Old Glory tablet.

CHAPTER THIRTEEN

Dallas made him nervous.

He arrived late, after leaving Quanah Parker and the Indian delegation at the Hotel Texas, and riding an almost empty T&P smoking car — even though he didn't smoke — some twenty or thirty miles across rolling prairie and scrub trees to the Dallas depot. It was a growing city, a big city, but didn't seem as lively as Fort Worth. Men and women crowded the streets and dance halls in Fort Worth, but Dallas looked practically deserted. *Maybe,* Daniel thought, *that is because Fort Worth caters to the cattle industry, and Dallas cottons to farmers.*

The three men in sack suits who got off at Dallas with Daniel quickly disappeared into the night. Daniel found a grouchy, balding clerk in a dirty collarless shirt at the ticket window, and asked for directions to the Coursey & Cox Bottling Works.

The grouch removed an unlit, soggy cigar

clamped between his dentures. "Never heard of it."

"Would you have a city directory?"

Spitting out an oath, the ticket agent ducked out of view, knocked over a bottle, cursed again, scattered some papers, and popped back into sight, sliding an old book, pages yellowed, swollen after getting wet years ago, toward Daniel.

He looked at the date. The directory was four years old.

"Best I can do," the grouch said. "This isn't City Hall."

Daniel turned the pages, reading the small type, sighing upon discovering that several pages had been torn out, a few stained with something that blotted out the words and numbers, but at last he found what he wanted.

Coursey & Cox Bottling Works, Mfct., Brewery, 1992 Houston Street, at River Road. No telephone. Prop., S.W. Zeske.

He turned to the back of the directory, found an address and telephone number for Mr. S.W. Zeske, no wife, no children, occupation not listed.

After scribbling the information into his tablet, he slid the weathered book back to the grouch.

"Where's Houston Street?" Daniel asked.

"Right out that door."

"And River Road?"

"Where'd you expect it to be. Over toward the Trinity River."

He glanced at his notes. "And the Mother Bagwell's House on Commerce?"

"Do I look like a city map? It's that way." He pointed. "Houston runs into Commerce, but it's opposite of River Road."

"Thanks," Daniel said.

"Good night," the ticket agent snapped.

A Regulator clock on the wall chimed. It was 1:15 A.M.

Too late to call on S.W. Zeske. Too late to visit the bottling plant and brewery, for that matter, but Daniel had to be back at the Hotel Texas before breakfast to interpret for The People and the Kiowas, and the Texas cattlemen. He hoped he could find a night watchman at Coursey & Cox, get some information from him, then, if needed, use the Hotel Texas telephone to call Mr. S.W. Zeske. The prospect of using a telephone excited him. He wondered what it would be like, what S.W. Zeske's voice would sound like, what his voice would sound like. Yet when he stepped outside, his excitement waned.

Outside, the night air remained heavy with the smell of coal smoke and oil. The flames

172

in the gas lamps shown eerily, and, above him, telegraph and telephone wires resembled long black lines, forming nets at some places. A piano banged out a tune somewhere, and a Houston and Texas Central locomotive coughed and belched on one of the side tracks. He heard a voice, quickly turned, startled, but found only a couple of black men dragging crates onto the depot platform. Moments later, bells sang out, hoofs thundered, and a hook-and-ladder tore down the street toward some fire that no one could see from the depot. Daniel and the two black men watched the darkness swallow the firemen, then they looked at each other. One of the workers shrugged.

"Beg your pardon, but where's Houston Street?" Daniel asked.

"Why, you're standing on it," the bigger man said.

"Which way's the river?"

The other one pointed.

Daniel thanked them. He slid a Faber's No. 2 pencil over his right ear, stuck the writing tablet under his arm, and pulled a folded piece of paper from his coat pocket, rereading the note that had been delivered to him when he was about to board the Fort Worth and Denver Railway car in

Wichita Falls.

My Dear Friend Daniel:

*Sorry I must miss you, but I have con-
tracted a driver to take me to Teepee City.
Hope to learn more about the whiskey
operation there. I have uncovered nothing
more about the Coursey & Cox Bottling
Works or the late Blake Browne. His assistant, the man known as Uvalde Ted
Smith, departed our fair city. At present,
his whereabouts are unknown.*

*Daniel, please be careful if you go to
Dallas. Yesterday, I learned that Carl
Quantrell has returned to that city for
reasons unknown. Be on guard, and good
luck.*

*Let me know what you learn. I shall do
the same.*

Your obt. servant,
Vaughan Coyne
Attorney-at-law

This far down Houston Street, there were
no gas lamps. There was hardly a city any
more, and the cobblestone road had deterio-
rated into a muddy bog. Daniel walked on
the grass, stopping at one intersection and
looking hopelessly for a street sign. There
was none. He decided that this was not

River Road, and pressed on. Bullfrogs croaked, and bats whipped their wings. He no longer heard the sounds of the city. A cloudless night provided him with some light, but not enough, so he kept walking onward, sweating, panting, uneasy. He was about to turn back, return to the other road, take a chance that it was River Road, when he spotted a giant black cross.

No, not a cross. Two beams forming a leaning cross, next to a ghostly palisade of timber. Daniel walked through the thick grass. He touched one piece of wood, felt something on his hand, wiped it off on his trousers. Soot. But not recent. He stepped over a rock, heard the crunching of glass beneath his moccasins, used the quarter moon and stars to study his surroundings. He had stepped inside the shell of a burned building.

Somehow, he knew he had found Coursey & Cox Bottling Works.

The lights appeared suddenly, and Daniel stumbled back, wishing he had brought his Remington revolver with him, but Agent Ellenbogen had refused to allow a ward of the government to cross into Texas with a firearm. Flames flickered from the shadows, and he counted. One. Two. Three. Four.

Torches.

Voices. A drunken laugh.

Suddenly Daniel was surrounded, bathed in light. Stupid, he thought, and he cursed Hugh Gunter and his insistence that Daniel go to Dallas. Only he couldn't blame the Cherokee for everything. Coming here this late. Alone. That was stupid. This was his own fault.

He counted seven men. One, a raw-boned, broad-shouldered man, much taller than Daniel, stepped out of the circle the men had formed around Daniel.

"Welcome to Coursey and Cox, buck-o. What do you think?"

He saw the knife, thin blade and bone handle, in the man's left hand.

Ducking, leaping back he avoided the slicing blade, but strong arms grabbed him from behind. A fist rocked his head. He saw the orange flames of the torches. No. His eyes were closed. The light came from elsewhere.

"They tell me you's Comanche," a voice whispered. "Comanches killed my uncle on the Salt Fork thirteen years ago."

"Don't kill him, Trent!" someone cried.

"I ain't," Trent said. "But he's gonna wish he was dead."

Someone rammed an anvil into his stomach. He felt sick. His long hair was jerked back. Another punch rocked his jaw, loosened three teeth. He tasted blood in his mouth.

"Maybe I'll scalp the bloody savage," Trent said.

Daniel threw up.

"Damnation!" another man roared. "He puked all over my Oxfords!"

He felt his nose give way. Then vomited again. Realized he was on his knees. Someone kicked him in the back, and he fell into the ash. Bits of glass scratched his face. He was jerked back by the hair, thrown onto the grass.

Then came a gunshot.

"Jesus!"

Another shot. Daniel heard the whine of a ricochet.

Trent's voice, suddenly high pitched: "Let's get the hell out of here!"

Running feet. A third shot prodded them on their way.

Slowly Daniel rolled over, opened his eyes, saw another orange light coming for him, flickering, weaving, then lowering, revealing red hair that flowed beneath a large hat, touching the collar of a black broadcloth suit, a mustache, under-lip beard, and three days of stubble across the rest of his pockmarked face, and those cold deadly almost pale blue eyes of the *Tejano* Ranger named Carl Quantrell.

"Well," he heard the Ranger's drawl, "if it ain't the Comanche detective. You're off the federal reserve, *amigo*. Hope you learnt your lesson."

Daniel closed his eyes, heard sounds. Flipping of pages. The Ranger was looking at his Old Glory tablet. Daniel didn't know what happened to his pencil. Those things didn't come cheap. The Wichita Falls merchant had charged him 37¢ for a dozen. Then rough fingers dived into his pockets, removing his pouch, his medicine bag, and papers.

The voice started moving far, far away, like it was inside a cave.

"Well, hell, boy, you got yourself a pass. Don't you rate, eh? A pass giving you permission to come to the great state of Texas with a party of other red devils."

Paper crumpling.

A heavy sigh. A curse. "Vaughan Coyne. That contemptible shyster." The ripping of paper. "That son-of-a-bitch."

A new voice cried out: "What is going on out there? Speak to me! Who are you?"

"Shit." Daniel wasn't sure if he had cursed, or if it was Carl Quantrell.

"I warn you," the voice came louder. "I

178

have a three-dollar Smoker in my hand, and I sha'n't miss."

"You're lucky, Sergeant Killstraight," Carl Quantrell's voice whispered, and the Ranger was gone.

So was Daniel. He dived into that opening, as black as midnight, and fell forever.

The woman with the Irish brogue and .38 Smoker also had a beautiful smile. The city policeman, likewise, had an Irish accent, a much larger, much more expensive revolver, and a permanent scowl.

"Seven men," the policeman said. "One of them called Trent. Another wearing Oxford shoes. I do not have much bloody evidence to go on, Patty."

"What about the Texas Ranger, Carl Quantrell?" she asked.

"What about him? He didn't do a thing, except, maybe, if the boy's story is right, save the Indian's life. This Indian might should thank Ranger Quantrell."

"Thank him?" Patty Mullen sprayed the side of a brass spittoon with her saliva. "Some gentleman, some Ranger. He ran into the darkness. Didn't even offer to help me with Sergeant Killstraight. Likely would have killed him had I not happened along."

"Now, Patty."

"Now Patty nothing."

"He's a Texas Ranger, Patty. A Texas Ranger."

"Who's likely enslaved by demon rum, who thinks his badge makes him a god, who runs away in the dead of night like a craven coward."

Daniel's brain remained in a slowly dissipating fog. He knew he was inside a newspaper office, lying on a sofa, knew that his head hurt, that his stomach ached, that it hurt to breathe through his nose, knew that he had been talking to the city peace officer and Patty Mullen. He looked outside.

He knew that it was daylight.

He knew that he was in trouble.

"I need to get to Fort Worth," he said. His voice had an odd, nasal tone. "Hotel Texas. Quanah Parker."

"You rest, Sergeant," Patty Mullen ordered. "I'll take you to the Panther City myself. I'll explain everything to Chief Quanah Parker, and the Northern Texas Stock Growers' Association officers. It'll be a great story for my newspaper. But not as great as the scathing editorial I shall write about our city police."

The policeman sighed. "I'll see what I can do, Patty. Just don't expect much with what I have to go on."

"You do that, Timothy." Her voice and eyes softened. "Do it for me, please."

"Talk to you tonight."

A bell rang over the door. Somewhere, a train whistle blew. Daniel tried to sit up. He slid back down, mumbling: "Shit."

"I don't know where Doctor O'Brien is," Patty Mullen said. "Well, I do, most likely. In his cups. Or sleeping off another drunk. I should have known better than try to get him here on a Friday night, Saturday morning, rather. Can I make you hot tea, Sergeant?"

He seemed to shake his head. "I'll be all right."

"In a pig's eye."

He felt a warm, wet towel on his face. He felt Patty Mullen take his right hand in hers. He felt better.

"Tell me again, Daniel." Testing his first name. "What were you doing at that old building? At nigh two in the morning, mind you."

"Coursey and Cox Bottling Works," Daniel said vaguely. "Ginger beer."

"You wanted beer? Ginger beer?"

"No. I don't drink."

"Good for you, Daniel. But. . . ."

"There have been some murders on the reservation."

"Really?" With much interest.

"The only clue I have is a bunch of ginger beer bottles from Coursey and Cox."

"Aye. But that burned down a month ago."

He used his left hand, let Patty keep running her soft fingers over his right hand, and removed the wet towel. He seemed to see her for the first time.

A tall, slim woman, hair the color of corn silk tucked up in a bun. She wore a fancy gown — long sleeves of black, yellow, blue, and white checks, with gold cuffs, a gold-trimmed collar, the rest of the dress a rich gold satin, fastened in the back with hooks and eyes. Her eyes were bright blue, her soft fingers stained with ink. She even smelled of ink. He saw the door, a name spelled backwards on the glass, couldn't quite read it. Finally it came to him.

The Dallas Temperance Leader
Patricia Anne Mullen
Editor & Publisher

"When did it burn down?"

"The Ides of March," she answered rather quickly.

"March Fifteen," he said, and she stared, intrigued, sizing him up.

"That's correct," she said. "I remember because it was my lead story. I publish on Tuesdays. The fire was late the Fifteenth. It was my March Twentieth edition." Her smile was warm. "I remember everything. I'll give you a copy of that paper if you like."

"How did it burn?"

"Arson," she answered.

He sighed, and slowly sat up. The room no longer spun around like a *taibo* children's top.

"Lucifer Salzburger," he said in disgust.

"Huh?"

"Nothing," he said. "A joke."

"Ahh."

"What did S.W. Zeske have to say about his business burning to the ground?"

"Zeske?" Patty Mullen laughed. "Zeske. He sold the business two years ago. Left Dallas for Denison. After I ran the whiskey-rotted fool out of Dallas."

He looked for his Old Glory tablet, couldn't find it, asked her about it, hoped she hadn't left it in the grass or mud along Houston Street and River Road.

"It's on my desk. Your penmanship leaves something to be desired. It's almost as bad as mine."

"May I have it?"

She returned with two more notebooks,

along with a pack of pencils. The tablets weren't Old Glory, and the pencils weren't Faber's, but Daniel didn't complain.

"Yours is practically filled up," she said. "You'll need some more."

"Thanks." A creature of superstition, he looked at the notebooks and pencils in his lap. Uncomfortable. Didn't think he really trusted the Echo pencil tablet or American Eclectic pencils, but maybe he could use them until he found a mercantile that sold Old Glory tablets and Faber's.

"Now." She had a tablet and pencil in her own hands. "You mind telling me about those murders, about everything?"

"I have to get back to Fort Worth," he said.

"Fine. I'm coming with you."

CHAPTER FOURTEEN

Coursey and Cox Bottling Works was founded by M.W. Coursey and his grandmother, Bessie Cox, shortly after the Houston and Texas Central Railway arrived in the summer of 1872. The following year, the Texas & Pacific reached Dallas, and the city, and the brewery and bottle manufacturing company boomed. The business moved from a wooden frame building on Pacific Avenue to a larger lot on the outskirts of town near the Trinity River bottoms, to be closer to a water source. Mr. Coursey and Mrs. Cox were lucky. They sold out to S.W. Zeske shortly before the Panic struck in 1873. Zeske managed to hang on — "probably just so he could drink free ginger beer," Patty Mullen said — until he sold out to a gambler known in Dallas, Denton, and Tarrant counties as Show Low Beeber, who kept it for about eighteen months.

"Two years ago," Daniel said.

Patty Mullen started to reply but had to take a quick lick of ice cream before it dripped onto her lap. "Yes. Two months after I started my newspaper in Dallas."

Daniel carved the cold cream with his spoon, and ate, liking the softness, the coolness, the sweetness. Having not eaten ice cream since one 4th of July in Carlisle, Pennsylvania, he had forgotten how good this Pale Eyes concoction tasted.

They sat at a corner table in the Queen City Ice Cream Parlor in Fort Worth, guests of the Northern Texas Stock Growers' Association. Outside, women, children, and even one or two cowboys crowded the boardwalk along Belknap Street to watch Kiowa and Comanche Indians eat ice cream and talk to newspaper reporters and cattle barons. Quanah and Coyote Chaser seemed to relish their peach ice cream. A'do-eete wolfed down chocolate, and Tséeyñ took incredibly small bites of vanilla. Daniel and Patty Mullen had followed Quanah's example, choosing peach ice cream. Teepee That Stands Alone sat alone, arms folded, refusing to try the Pale Eyes dessert.

Daniel had arrived in Fort Worth shortly before noon, having to apologize for his tardiness, then sitting through four hours of meetings, translating, asking questions, answering questions, explaining, discussing Senator Henry Dawes and what the passage of his act that would divide the reservation meant, talking, talking, listening, arguing. Negotiating. His heart wasn't in it, though. He kept thinking about the Coursey & Cox Bottling Works, about Patty Mullen, about Carl Quantrell, and seven Dallas ruffians.

Of course, he had reason to thank those Dallas toughs. In Fort Worth, he had been treated as someone just short of hero status. He wore bandages on his cheeks and broken nose. Quanah had asked him if he had counted first coup. Even the Texas cattlemen had slapped his back, congratulated him on his round of fisticuffs, even if he had lost the fight. Once the newspaper reporters learned what had happened, they had hurriedly scribbled stories for the next editions that would illustrate just how rotten a city Dallas had become. Fort Worth, much closer to the Indian frontier, proved to be a city where Comanches and Kiowas could walk the streets safely, could enjoy wonderful treats such as prairie oysters, thick steaks, biscuits flavored with pecans, and ice cream for dessert. But step into Dallas, and an Indian walked right into harm's way.

Now in the ice cream parlor, he was thankful that the attention had turned to the real Comanche and Kiowa leaders, so that he could talk to Patty Mullen. And eat ice cream.

"You wouldn't happen to know what Show Low Beeber's real name was, would you?" Daniel asked the Irish newspaper editor, publisher, and temperance leader.

"Not hardly."

"I'd like to find him."

"That's easy, Daniel. He's buried in the Odd Fellows Cemetery." She swallowed more ice cream. "It happens to a lot of gamblers. Dallas isn't some tame farm town. Doc Holliday lived here for a while. So did Sam Bass. Ever hear of them?"

He shook his head.

"Bad men. We get our share of bad men."

"Like a man named Trent and some fellow with Oxford shoes and a sledge-hammer for a fist."

She giggled. The first time he had heard her laugh, but it didn't last long.

"And many wicked peddlers of spirituous liquors. I'm for temperance. I founded my newspaper on that very principle."

"I guess I'm the same. Temperance I mean."

"Good for you. We're allies."

"So, what happened to Show Low Bee-ber?"

"Shot and killed. There wasn't much interest in ginger beer any more, or there was too much competition. He lost the Coursey and Cox Bottling Works in a dice game. The story I hear, though, is that he lost on purpose. The dumb oaf that won it thought he had a gold mine when, in fact, he had a bankrupt company, a ton of debt, hardly any ginger beer, and crates and crates of worthless, empty bottles."

He stopped eating, started writing. By the time he had finished, most of his ice cream was nothing but a thick soup. He ate it anyway. It still tasted mighty fine.

"How do you remember all this?" He tapped his writing tablet. "I'm nothing without my notes in front of me."

"It was my story, Daniel. I covered it. Wrote about it. Any scandal that I can blame on drunkenness. I don't need writing tablets." She tapped her temple. "I keep it all up here. The Ides of March. Coursey and Cox Bottling Works. Show Low Beeber. Important news for my cause. Important stories that can turn public opinion, that can help us wipe out this blight, make the United States and her territories free of evil liquor forever. I covered these stories, so I remember them well. Covered them all. Up until Show Low's death, it was big news in Dallas. Maybe bigger news in the *Temperance Leader* than the *Times Herald.* Exciting stories to write about. Then it got all bogged down with lawyers trying to sort everything out, argue everything. Lawyers. That's too boring for my paper, listening to overpaid barristers say this and that. I want action. I write with action, about action, and demand action."

He interrupted her before she started another sermon.

"What do you know about the fire that burned down the place? You said it was arson."

"It was arson. It's still under investigation. Maybe it was the new owner that burned it down. Some say it was the creditors. Some say it was friends of Show Low Beeber. Some say it was just some drunken tramps." She winked. "Some say it was me."

He smiled. "Was it you?"

"No. Not my style. I burn with ink and paper, not matches and coal oil. And I had no need to burn it down. I had done my job by shutting it down."

"Who won it from the late Mister Beeber?"

"A drunken Irishman," she said. "Gives

my people a bad name. A soldier. Claimed self-defense, and, maybe it was, so the grand jury did not indict him."

Daniel felt a chill race up his spine. His spoon rattled in the empty bowl. He knew the name before Patty Mullen said it.

"Fenn O'Malley."

A bowl crashed and shattered on the floor, and the din of conversation immediately stopped. Daniel turned, saw Teepee That Stands Alone looming over a freckle-faced clerk who must have brought the *puhakat* a bowl of vanilla ice cream.

"You try to destroy my *puha!*" the old man roared in Comanche. "I do not wish to be here."

"What's the matter with him?" Patty whispered.

"He's what you would call a medicine man. What the soldiers and agents call. . . ."

"I am Nermernuh," the tall Comanche said, striding across the parlor to tower over Quanah and Coyote Chaser. He certainly looked as a leader of The People, his feathered headdress, and elk-skin war shirt, dyed black and decorated with images of hailstones, partially covered by a breastplate of coyote rib bones. That contrasted sharply with Quanah's suit of black broadcloth and Coyote Chaser's mix of trade goods and buckskin. He raised a ceremonial lance over his head.

"I am Teepee That Stands Alone. I fight for The People. Who do you fight for? Who calls you the chief of The People? You dress as a *taibo*. You smell like a *taibo*. You eat this stupid food of the *taibo*. You sell the grass of The People to these fool Pale Eyes so that they can feed us their cows. Food for the weak. I want to eat buffalo. I want to see the buffalo return."

"So do I," Quanah said softly. "But this will not happen."

"No. For you will not let it happen. And you. . . ." His face hardened as he stared at Coyote Chaser. "What of you?" Teepee That Stands Alone said.

Coyote Chaser stared at his bowl of peach ice cream.

"You are no leader. Your power is bad. You are no better than Maman-ti of the Kiowas. You are lower than Maman-ti. You curse all of The People yet you brag of how the Yam-parika are the only true people. So I curse you, for all that you have done. Hear me. I am Kwahadi. I am the last true Kwahadi. I am all that is left of The People."

Facing Quanah again. "I did not want to come here. You made me come."

"I asked you to come," Quanah said. "I

seek your foresight. Always I have heard your counsel."

"But you never listen. You bring us away from the buffalo, from the great plains where once we roamed at our will. You bring us to die slowly among the Long Knives and other Pale Eyes. You bring us to a place of sickness. You brought a curse onto my son. The curse of whiskey. You sent my granddaughter to The Land Beyond The Sun. You will sell our homes to the *taibo*. Turn us all into *taibo*. I do not wish to be here."

Quanah nodded. "Then go." He found Daniel, speaking with his eyes.

"Come on," Daniel told Patty Mullen. "I need to escort Teepee That Stands Alone back to the hotel."

"What was he saying? Why is he so angry?"

"I'll tell you on the way. You might want to interview Teepee That Stands Alone for your paper. I'm not sure he'll talk to a Pale Eyes woman, but his story is right for the *Temperance Leader.*"

He donned his hat, crossed the room, surprised to find the face of Teepee That Stands Alone streaked with tears. Coyote Chaser was also crying.

"You will take care of him," Quanah told Daniel.

"It will be done," Daniel said in Comanche. He held out his right hand, but the tall *puhakat* stepped back.

"You are more *taibo,* too," Teepee That Stands Alone said. "But you were stolen from us. And you honored The People by fighting the *taibo.* Your face, your nose carry the wounds you earned, even if the wounds are covered with *taibo* medicine. Your heart is sometimes good." He lowered the lance, and cast a look of disgust at Quanah and Coyote Chaser. "Unlike these."

"I will take you back to the hotel," Daniel said.

"I do not wish to go to that place. I want to go home."

Daniel nodded. "You will. But first we must return to the Pale Eyes' place."

He stared at Patty Mullen. "Who is this ugly woman?"

"She is called Patty Mullen. She wishes to talk to you. She fights with words, but her words are read by many. She wishes to punish the *taibo* who bring whiskey to our land. She wishes to avenge your granddaughter who is no more."

Teepee That Stands Alone spit. "I will not talk of such things to a *taibo* woman."

"You do not have to. But she is a friend. She wants to help us. And we should leave this place."

"I leave this place." He shifted the lance, leaning the carved wooden point at Patty Mullen, grinning. "Tell this *taibo* woman this . . . in the old days, I would have taken this woman. I would have used her as I wanted to, then passed her around to the warriors who rode with me. Then I would have cut her throat, pulled out her heart and liver, eaten them raw. I would have left her to the coyotes and wolves. I would have taken her scalp, but would have no use for such an ugly, pale thing. I would have stuck it in her mouth. That is the way of The People. The way things would be. The way things should be. You will tell her this."

"I will not tell her this," Daniel said, "because I know you, Teepee That Stands Alone, and I know you would never have done such things."

"No?" He straightened, turned his rage on Daniel. "What would you know, a boy raised by Pale Eyes, a boy whose mother was not even one of The People?"

Daniel fought down his anger, found wisdom from Quanah Parker. Quanah had let the *puhakat* rage on, had controlled his temper, would never let cattlemen, store clerks, and gawkers on the street see The People fight among themselves.

"I know that the *puha* of the great Teepee

That Stands Alone cannot wear, cannot touch anything that is not made by The People. Teepee That Stands Alone would not disgrace himself on a *taibo* woman. Or his *puha* would be destroyed. The *puha* of Teepee That Stands Alone was always great. Rarely would he fight, for his power was in his wisdom, his medicine, not a war lance, and, when he fought, he fought men. Not women. That much I know, Teepee That Stands Alone."

The old man's shoulders slouched. His voice softened. "I do not wish to be in this place any more," he said, his voice breaking.

"Let us go," Daniel said, and took the *puhakat*'s arm.

"Do I have to talk to this woman?"

"Only if your heart tells you to do so."

"We shall see. After I smoke my pipe. Will you smoke with me, my son?"

"It would honor me to do so."

Exhaustion would soon overtake him. Softly he pulled the door closed, and walked down the carpeted hallway with Patty Mullen.

"What a sad, sad man," she said. "What a terrible story."

"Yes." It was all Daniel could think to say.

"Whiskey kills." She sounded as tired as

Daniel felt.

"Yes."

"It kills everything it touches. It killed my father. Did I tell you that?"

He shook his head.

"We lived in Omaha. Omaha, Nebraska. My father was an alki-stiff. Ever heard of that?"

"No."

"They wouldn't let him in the saloons any more, so he drank druggists' alcohol. Till it killed him."

"I am sorry."

She stopped, leaned against the paneled wall near a gas lamp. "Do you believe in visions, Daniel?"

He studied her without answering.

"I've been fighting for the wrong people. Fighting for my people. White men, women, and children. I had no idea how bad whiskey was on the reservation. I had no idea. I'm changing the name of my newspaper, Daniel. *The Dallas Temperance Leader* is too small, too narrow. It has to be the *National Temperance Leader.* And the story of you, of the Comanches, of Teepee That Stands Alone will be the center . . . no, the entire . . . focus of the new edition."

She came close to him then, closer than he liked, but he did not move. Couldn't move. She no longer smelled of newspaper ink, and he tried to swallow. Her smile was lovely, but footsteps sounded softly on the stairs, and, by the time a sweating man with a big mustache appeared on the second floor, Patty Mullen was leaning against the wall again.

"Sergeant Killstraight?" the man gasped.

"Yes?"

"Telegram for you."

Daniel took the envelope, tried to find his money purse, but the man insisted there was no charge, no tip necessary, and then he hurried down the stairs. Daniel opened the envelope, pulled out a slip of yellow paper.

WHITE WHISKEY RUNNER MURDERED STOP BODY FOUND IN HILLS FERRY STOP WAGON BURNED THROAT CUT THIGH SLASHED SCALPED STOP NO WITNESS STOP MEET YOU IN WICHITA FALLS STOP HP NOBLE DEP US MARSHAL

CHAPTER FIFTEEN

He stepped off the Fort Worth and Denver Railway car and onto a crowded platform, wanting to use his luggage to push through the *taibos* in their broadcloth suits and big hats, wanting to find Deputy Marshal Harvey P. Noble, but he stopped, turned, held out his free hand, and helped Teepee That Stands Alone climb down from the passenger car. Quanah Parker, Coyote Chaser, and the other Indians followed.

"I want to go home," Teepee That Stands Alone said in the language of The People.

"Haa," Daniel said. *"Kemarukwisu."* But thinking: *Not soon enough, though.* He looked at Quanah, saying: "We should find the Long Knives."

Quanah nodded, and Daniel led the Comanches and Kiowas off the platform, down the street, and to the wagon yard on the north end of town. The bluecoats were pretty much where they had left them, stretched out on the hay, in the shade, playing cards with about a half-dozen bottles sitting in a bucket of water. Beer bottles. Two of them empty. Daniel watched one trooper pull one out, open it, and take a long pull. Dark glass, though, not ceramic stoneware. Not ginger beer.

The sergeant looked up, grunted something, and tossed his cards onto the ground. "How was your trip?"

"Good," Daniel said.

The sergeant squinted. "What the Sam Hill happened to your face?"

"It's a tough town," Daniel said, and the soldiers laughed.

"Tougher than this town," one of the bluecoats added. "Not a damned thing to do here but play cards, watch the dust blow, and drink beer."

"Beats being back at Sill," another said.

"Damned right."

The sergeant sighed. "Reckon we should get ready to move out."

Daniel pressed his lips together. *Not yet,* he thought. "If you don't mind, Sergeant," he said, "it's late. Teepee That Stands Alone is depressed. Something's bothering Coyote Chaser. Probably sick from the rocking train. Perhaps we should wait till first light."

"Suits me," one soldier said. "I'm in no

hurry to get back to Sill and that idiot Lieutenant Newly."

"It would suit you, Dutchie," the sergeant said, keeping his eyes on Daniel. "You're winning." He stared at Daniel for a while, then at the Comanches and Kiowas finding cool spots in the stable. "But I reckon we could wait till morn. Give me a chance to get some of my money back."

"Have you seen a deputy marshal?" Daniel asked. "Name of Harvey P. Noble?"

"No." The sergeant had turned, gathered his cards, and the deck, while the man named Dutchie clawed at the coins and greenbacks left in the center. As the bluecoat dealt another hand, Daniel looked at the soldiers. He cleared his throat.

"Where's O'Malley?" Daniel asked.

"Gone," the sergeant said.

"Gone? Gone where? I need to talk to him."

The soldiers were more interested in their cards than anything Daniel had to say.

"Where is he?" Daniel put more urgency in his voice. "I need to find him."

"So does Lieutenant Newly. So does the provost marshal. He run off."

"Run off? Where?"

The sergeant tossed his cards onto the ground with a curse. "Hell, I can't even deal myself a decent hand."

"It's pretty important," Daniel said.

"So's desertion." The sergeant turned back to Daniel. "I don't know where that loud-mouthed mick run off to. Deserters generally don't tell me things like that."

"He deserted." Daniel tested the fact, not liking it.

"Don't reckon he run back to Fort Sill," Dutchie said, and bet $5.

"Shouldn't you . . . ?" Daniel stopped himself. No need to irritate the sergeant more. The bluecoats knew their business, and, if they'd rather play cards than go chasing a deserter, that was their business.

"I'm going to look for Marshal Noble," Daniel announced. "Be back as soon as I can."

"Make sure that you do." The sergeant turned back to reach for a beer. "Newly will want to nail my hide because of O'Malley. I don't need your agent gunning for me, too."

As he turned to go, another man entered the wagon yard, and Daniel stopped, not believing. His grin widening, Nácutsi walked until he stood right in front of Daniel.

"Why aren't you in jail?" Daniel asked in Comanche. His temper flared, but he controlled his voice.

"You want to arrest me again, Metal Shirt? You want me to split your head open again? Even though somebody else has done it."

The soldier known as Dutchie suddenly called out to the Kwahadi. "Hey, Gunpowder. Welcome back. Come over here and sit in this white man's game!"

Daniel barely heard the words. Clenching his fists, facing that damned dog of a Kwahadi who wanted to court Rain Shower, he said: "Ben Buffalo Bone and Twice Bent Nose brought you to jail. You were running whiskey."

The warrior laughed. "I run nothing. Your Pale Eyes laws are nothing against my *puha*. I am free. My case dismissed. I am too important to rot away in some *taibo* jail like Toyarocho. I am a wolf for these bluecoats. I am free. But if you want to arrest me again, Metal Shirt, please." The smile vanished. "Try it."

Daniel fought down the anger, pushed Nácutsi aside, left the wagon yard as quickly as possible, the Comanche brave's cackles following him like smoke from a campfire.

"Nácutsi should be in jail."

"I can't help you, Daniel," Vaughan Coyne said. "Judge Goodman dismissed the charges."

"He was running whiskey," Daniel argued. "Ben Buffalo Bone said he found whiskey in his lodge . . . 'Too much for one man to drink.' The same ginger beer bottles that Blake Browne had, that Seven Beavers had." He broke a taboo of The People, speaking the name of a dead man, but Daniel did not care. "That is what Ben Buffalo Bone told me. They brought him to jail. And now he is free."

The young attorney sighed. "There was no proof, Daniel, that he was running whiskey. There was no proof, or little proof, that it was his whiskey. From what I've heard, Judge Goodman had to let Gunpowder go."

"He hit me," Daniel said, knowing he sounded like a child, but he couldn't help it. "Used one of those damned bottles."

"That's a matter for your Court of Indian Offenses, Daniel. You know that better than I do. It's not for a white man's court. I'm sorry."

With a defeated sigh, Daniel reached for the cup of coffee. The lawyer was right. It was over. Nácutsi was free. He'd return to the reservation with the others tomorrow. There was nothing Daniel could do. File a complaint? Let Quanah don his robe and act like a judge? No, Quanah was smarter than that. He'd know what truly maddened Daniel, and it wasn't the fact that Nácutsi had laid Daniel out with a whiskey bottle, wasn't even the fact that Daniel knew that Nácutsi — how could that man be Kwahadi? — was part of that gang of whiskey runners. It was all about Rain Shower.

What could a bright, beautiful Kotsoteka girl see in an arrogant dog with a violent temper? A whiskey drinker? A son-of-a-bitch?

"What did you learn in Dallas?" Coyne asked.

Daniel shrugged. "The place that made those beer bottles burned to the ground."

"That's great news, Daniel. That means there will be no more whiskey bottles. No more bottles. No more whiskey. Right?"

He drank coffee instead of answering. Vaughan Coyne was damned naïve. There would always be whiskey bottles. There would always be whiskey.

"What else?" Coyne asked. "And, forgive me if I'm intruding, but . . . well . . . what in God's name happened to you? You look like you got run over by a locomotive."

He told him. About the thugs near the Trinity River. About Carl Quantrell, at least, the parts he could remember. About Patty Mullen, the temperance newspaper editor.

"Good thing she happened along," Coyne said. "Quantrell would have killed you." He pointed to the healing cut above his right eye. "Like he almost killed me."

"Lucky," Daniel said. "Both of us."

The lawyer dropped his head. "I don't feel lucky."

"I don't, either."

"Feel like . . . I don't know . . . lost."

"I thought I had something," Daniel said. "Well, I learned something." He told his lawyer about Fenn O'Malley, how the soldier had won Coursey & Cox gambling in Dallas.

"We need to talk to this soldier." Vaughan Coyne sounded like a different man, a fighter, ready to attack, but Daniel shook his head.

"He's gone. Deserted."

"Damnation!" Coyne's right fist knocked a book off his desk. "Every time we get something, we lose it."

"I still have nothing," he said. "Nothing to go on. Nothing to stop these bad men." He slid the empty cup onto the attorney's desk. "What did you find in Teepee City?"

Coyne sighed. "Probably less than you discovered in Dallas. There's nothing in Teepee City. Well, there's no Uvalde Ted Smith, and nobody I talked to knew . . . at

least, they wouldn't admit to knowing . . .
Blake Browne."

"Another whiskey runner was killed in the
territory," Daniel said.

"What?"

Daniel fished out the telegram. "North of
Hill's Ferry," he said. "Same as Blake
Browne. White man, scalped, his thigh
slashed. I've been looking for Marshal Noble. I need to find him. We return to the
reservation tomorrow." He stopped, ran
what he had just said through his mind, and
repeated three words, almost in a whisper.
"His thigh slashed."

"Yes?" Coyne said. "Like the other one.
Indian mutilation." He tried to cut off the
word, but couldn't, dropped his head again,
and looked up sheepishly, apologizing. But
Daniel was headed for the door. Vaughan
Coyne called his name. "I didn't mean
anything, Daniel. I. . . ."

"Huh? I didn't even hear what you said."
Daniel opened the door, headed into the
fading light, hearing his lawyer's words: "We
will win this battle. Justice isn't always swift,
but it's usually just. Trust me."

He was worried. Harvey P. Noble said he'd
be in Wichita Falls, but Daniel hadn't found
him. The sheriff, the town marshal, his at-

torney, a clerk at the courthouse — nobody had seen Noble, at least not recently. Daniel couldn't wait. He had to leave with the soldiers and Indians in the morning. His trip to Texas would end in failure. He couldn't find Harvey Noble. Nácutsi was free. He couldn't even interrogate Fenn O'Malley.

"Boys, I've said it before and I'll say it again . . . I surely hate to leave Wichita Falls," one of the soldiers said in the wagon yard, and laughed.

"Shut up, Dutchie!" the sergeant barked. "I'll get my money back when we're back at Sill. I'll get it back through your hide."

"Oh, Sergeant, watch your temper. You're worse than that drunken mick. I'll loan you some money, Sergeant. But, first, I need to piss."

Footsteps sounded. Nácutsi snored. The wind blew. Daniel closed his eyes, then opened them, tossed off his blanket, and stood, moving for the privy, stopping underneath a lantern at the gate to the yard, waiting for the bluecoat named Dutchie to finish Nature's call.

The door to the outhouse flew open, and the soldier stumbled from too much beer, wiping his hands on his trousers and whistling as he weaved his way back toward the

wagon yard. The whistling stopped, and
Dutchie straightened, his face cautious,
maybe frightened, at the sight of Daniel
waiting for him.

"I'd like to talk to you," Daniel said.

A long moment. Then: "About what?"

"Fenn O'Malley."

Dutchie laughed drunkenly. "Injun, I can't
help you there. That bastard didn't tell me
where he was skedaddling to?"

The wind blew. Dutchie shuffled his feet.
"Listen, no offense, but you Injuns make
me nervous. I've been in this man's army
too long, seen what the Sioux can do to a
white man."

"I'm not Lakota."

"I've heard about what you Comanches
used to do."

"I spent seven years back East." His smile
was a façade. "Learning to be a white man."

The wind blew.

"Did O'Malley tell you he won a brewery
in Dallas?" Daniel said. He wasn't about to
let Dutchie get away from him, not until he
was finished. "In a card game." *No,* Daniel
thought, *it had been a dice game,* but he
didn't correct himself.

"Me and Fenn wasn't exactly on speaking
terms."

Daniel frowned.

"But," Dutchie said, "that would explain it."

He brightened. "Explain what?"

"Oh, that blow-hard talked all the time. Said he'd be rich soon enough, too rich to be a horse soldier, said he'd be lighting a shuck to San Francisco, that we could all kiss his arse. Won himself a brewery, eh? Hell, he wouldn't buy me a round."

"He say anything else?"

Dutchie shook his head. "Like I said, we wasn't bunkies or friends. You know that, Sergeant . . . Killstraight, ain't it?"

Sergeant Killstraight. Well, that was better than Injun. Daniel was making progress.

"He busted another sergeant's jaw with a whiskey bottle," Daniel said. "That's what Major Becker told me at Fort Sill."

"That's right. But it wasn't a whiskey bottle. It was a ginger beer bottle. Hard as a rock."

"I know." Daniel smiled.

The bluecoat grinned back.

Definite progress.

"But it didn't have beer in it. It was full of whiskey," Daniel said.

"Could be. Sergeant Andrews yonder, he's a beer drinker, like me, but O'Malley, he was pure Irish. Pure drunkard. He'd want whiskey."

"They've been selling it on the reservation. Some of it poison."

"Yeah, I've heard. We haven't been down here long, Sergeant. Us Seventh Cavalry boys. You think O'Malley was peddling whiskey to your braves, right?"

"That's right." He tested the name. "Dutchie."

"The name's Brink, Sergeant. Actually, it's Dirk Brinkerhoff, but my friends call me Brink. I just ain't got many friends." He smiled again. "Least, not when I'm on a winning streak playing draw poker."

"Call me Daniel."

"All right, Daniel. O'Malley sold whiskey when he could to Indians when we were at Fort Robinson and Fort Lincoln. Well, not just Indians. He'd sell to anybody. Got arrested once in Bismarck, but he beat the charges. Civilian charges. You know how them things go, I expect, and Army courts-martial ain't never really stopped him, neither. Been busted twice, but he's always gotten his stripes back. Expect this time'll be no different. So this is an old story with him. Whiskey running and whiskey drinking."

"He ever mention a Texas Ranger named Quantrell?"

With a shrug, the trooper replied: "I can't

say. Don't recall. Like I said. . . ." He smiled weakly.

"Have you heard of him? Quantrell? Carl Quantrell?"

The head shook. "Just you mentioning the name. But the latest orders we got was what Lieutenant Newly calls a joint action. Looking for whiskey runners to protect you Indians. We work the Indian Territory side with the federal marshals, while the Rangers patrol south of the Red."

"Cut any sign?" Daniel asked.

"Not really. Nothing much anyway. That's why the lieutenant signed on that Comanche. Gunpowder."

Gunpowder? Daniel frowned. Yet that would help explain how Nácutsi got his charges dismissed. Too valuable for the Army. The soldiers needed a scout — wolves, The People called them. Wolves for the Long Knives. Traitors. Of course, some of The People said the same about the Metal Shirts like Daniel.

"You know him? He's Comanche like you. Kwahadi, I think."

"I know him."

"You might ask Gunpowder, Sergeant . . . I mean, Daniel. Gunpowder was O'Malley's pet. Before he got into that row with Sergeant Gasquet, O'Malley was always volunteering, pleading with Lieutenant Newly to let him lead a patrol to go get them whiskey runners. 'Course, any soldier at Sill could tell you Fenn O'Malley, the drunken, lying, thieving bastard, would find whiskey, but never report it. Any soldier, that is, but some damned West Pointer like that greenhorn Newly."

Silence. "I'd best turn in," Dutchie said. "Before the sergeant thinks I've deserted like O'Malley."

"Thanks, Brink."

The bluecoat grinned. "If I was you, Daniel, I'd ask that other Comanch', Gunpowder, what he knows. He and O'Malley was tighter than thieves. He could likely tell you more. A hell of a lot more than I could."

With a wry grin, Daniel let the soldier pass. "The problem there, Brink, is that me and Nácutsi . . . Gunpowder, you call him . . . aren't exactly on speaking terms."

CHAPTER SIXTEEN

Whoever had named this stuff hardtack, Daniel thought, should have won a prize. He dipped the cracker in his coffee to soften it up, and wondered why the United States Army tortured its soldiers with this food. It lasts forever, he had heard a soldier say once, and Daniel had to agree. This tooth-duller likely had been baked back when George Washington commanded the U.S. Army, but that's all these 7th Cavalry boys and the Indian delegation had for breakfast.

Staring at his tin cup, he suddenly wished he hadn't tried to soften the cracker, for now weevil larvae floated to the top. When he looked up, he saw Trooper Dutchie Brinkerhoff and Sergeant Andrews skimming off the insects with their fingers before eating the hardtack and drinking their coffee. Among the Indians, Teepee That Stands Alone apparently had no problems drinking the coffee or eating the tooth-breaking biscuits. Nor did Coyote Chaser. They didn't even try to soften up the hardtack. A'do-eete, the tall Kiowa, just stared into his coffee cup, mesmerized by the magic that had produced these bugs. Daniel poured his coffee onto the ground, insects, hardtack, and all.

Then he heard the racket. The din grew louder. Angry voices. Too angry for this early in the morning. Slowly he stood, looked at Quanah, turned as Sergeant Andrews barked an order.

"Look sharp, men!"

"What the hell's going on, Sergeant?"

"The Texans!" cried the other Kiowa, Tséeyñ, in guttural English. "Come kill us. Like kill Set-t'ainte." He began singing the death song of the Kiowa's Ko-eet-senko Society.

"Killstraight!" the sergeant barked. "Shut that buck up. Look alive men. Sharp."

"What's going on, Sergeant?" a young trooper cried.

"How the hell would I know! But that buck might be right. Damned Texas sons-of-bitches."

"I ain't getting killed protecting no red nigger!"

"You do like I say, Johnston, or I'll shoot you myself."

Tséeyñ still sang his death song.

"Killstraight. Shut him the hell up!"

Daniel knew better. He couldn't stop Tséeyñ's death song. Nor could A'do-eete. Instead, he motioned Quanah to lead Teepee That Stands Alone and Coyote Chaser back into the corner, nodded at A'do-eete to follow. As Daniel walked to the line of Long Knives, he spotted about a dozen or more angry *taibos* heading for the wagon yard.

"Halt!" Sergeant Andrews yelled.

They didn't listen. Men in muslin, and broadcloth suits. Farmers, drovers, and merchants. One or two carrying repeating rifles in their sweating hands. Another with a rope.

"Cock arms!" Sergeant Andrews ordered.

That stopped them. At least for a moment. The leader stepped forward, a farmer in duck trousers and a homespun shirt, a wide straw hat, and bronzed face. "You won't shoot us, bluebelly."

"One more step, mister, and I give the command to fire at will."

"He's bluffin'!" yelled another.

"Try me. I'm sick of your damned town. I'm sick of eating Texas dust."

The farmer wet his lips. "We come for that one. That's all we want, Sergeant. You can have the others."

Daniel blinked. The farmer was pointing at him.

"What did I do?" Daniel asked.

"You know what you done. You butchered Horace Benson."

"I don't know anyone by that name."

"Scalped him. Left him for the buzzards and crows. Ripped him to pieces. Cut his manhood off, and stuck it in his mouth."

"Red bastard!" another man yelled.

"Aim!" Sergeant Andrews ordered.

The Kiowa sang.

"You can't kill us all, bluebelly." The farmer grinned.

"We can kill our fair share," Sergeant Andrews said. "Killed my share at Chattanooga and Spotsylvania. Reckon I can kill a few more at Wichita Falls."

Daniel walked around the soldiers, stepped a little to the right. He didn't want these bluecoats to die for him, and he certainly didn't want Quanah and the other Indians to die because of him. Nor did he want to die.

"Where," he began, his voice shaking, "was this Horace Benson killed?"

"Killstraight," Sergeant Andrews whispered. "Just keep quiet and get back behind us."

Daniel ignored him.

"You know where he was killed. Same as you know you killed him. Don't matter how good you speak English."

"Where?" Daniel tried again. "And when?"

"Three, four days back, likely," someone in the crowd said. "Three miles above Hill's Ferry."

Daniel understood. "The whiskey runner." Regretting those words. Like he had just admitted to the crime. Quickly he added: "I got a telegram from U.S. Marshal Noble." Adding with more urgency. "Three or four days ago, I was. . . ." Where was he? "Here. Or on my way here. I couldn't have killed this man."

"Don't try that, you murdering Comanche buck. We know all about you. Damned Injun lawdog. You killed him. We know it. Everybody knows it. Because we know all about you and those damned papers you're always jotting on."

"Papers?"

"Killstraight," Sergeant Andrews demanded.

The Kiowa sang.

"Fine, fancy paper, with that damned Stars and Stripes on the cover." The farmer spit, looked away from Daniel, stared hard at Sergeant Andrews. "I hate that damned flag. And I killed me a fair amount of Yankees in that damned war. Wouldn't bother me to kill a few more here in Wichita Falls."

Another Texian said: "They found one of 'em books full of white paper under Horace's body. Just like one we hear that buck writes on."

The Old Glory tablet. He was sweating now, but he thought of something. "Hold on, just a minute," he said, and he was running back, finding his grip, bringing it forward, setting it on the ground, opening it, shoving his full Old Glory deep underneath his dirty clothes, pulling out the tablets Patty Mullen had given him.

"These are what I use," he said. Standing, holding an Echo pencil tablet in each hand. "Not Old Glory. No flags, and this paper is gold. Not white. Not fancy." He was gambling. "Who told you I used Old Glory?"

Shit! he thought. He had bought an Old Glory tablet at the mercantile when he first came to town. If that merchant was in this crowd, if somebody had seen him. . . .

"That don't mean nothing!" a man with a black hat and Spencer rifle yelled. "Nothing!"

"Means something to me," said a new voice, surprisingly steady, and the farmers, merchants, cowboys, soldiers, Indians, and

Daniel watched two men ride easily along the road. One aimed a big Winchester at the farmer, reins draped over the withers of his horse. The other tapped the six-point badge pinned to his vest with the barrel of his revolver, which he then aimed at the cowboy with the Spencer, and slowly, ominously thumbed back the hammer.

"Best clear out, boys," Harvey P. Noble said. *"Pronto."*

"But . . ." The farmer swallowed, eyes fixed on Hugh Gunter's cannon of a rifle. Suddenly he lost his voice, and his face paled.

"He killed Horace!" the man with the Winchester shouted.

"He did no such thing," Noble snapped. "I found that whiskey runner's body myself."

"He cut his pecker off. . . ."

"Bullshit! Now clear out, or let's start the ball."

The Kiowa sang.

The wind blew, refreshingly cool, and Daniel watched the mob stumble away, back to the saloons, swallowing their pride. Noble turned around as Hugh Gunter lowered the hammer on the big repeater. "Make sure they don't stop, Hugh," he whispered, and the tall Cherokee nudged his horse into a walk.

Someone ran around the corner, slowing, sweating, pulling a suspender over his undershirt. Vaughan Coyne walked past Hugh Gunter, eyes wide, confused, worried, mouth hanging open, trying to figure out what question he should ask first.

Harvey P. Noble swung down from his horse, shaking his head as he looked at Daniel. Smiling, he said softly: "You're about the luckiest fellow I've ever knowed."

They didn't stop until they had crossed the Red River and deposited Coyote Chaser and camped near the Comanche village of Huupi. They didn't talk until that night. No one had wanted to talk, not even when Vaughan Coyne had caught up with them later that day. After Sergeant Andrews hurried the Indians out of town, and out of Texas, the lawyer had dressed, and rented a horse from the livery, but he still didn't know what to say, and the soldiers didn't want to talk, too scared — Daniel knew that feeling — after such a close brush with death.

Yet now, in what felt safe in Indian Territory, Harvey Noble, Hugh Gunter, Vaughan Coyne, and Daniel found a spot away from the soldiers and Indians.

"I could use a snort," Hugh Gunter said.

Daniel opened his Echo tablet to a new page, started to write, but his hand kept shaking. He set the pencil aside, and let Marshal Noble examine the pencil tablet.

"Where'd you find this?" the lawman asked.

"Dallas. Newspaper woman gave it to me."

"You off Old Glory?"

Daniel wet his lip. "There's one . . . a full one . . . in my grip."

Gunter shook his head. "Now I could really use a snort. Them Texas cads found that thing, the lead would have started flying thick."

"So." Daniel swallowed. "There was . . . a tablet . . . when you found that dead runner?"

Noble nodded. "Old Glory. Me and Hugh know it pretty good."

"Jesus!" Coyne stared hard at Daniel.

"But. . . ." Daniel didn't know where to begin.

"Where were you," Noble said, "say, eight, nine days ago?"

"That man at Wichita Falls." Daniel tried to swallow, but couldn't. His throat was dry. "He said it was three or four days ago."

"When me and Hugh found the

corpse . . . wired you from Henrietta . . .
he'd been dead a spell."

"Oh, God, Daniel," Coyne said.

Now he felt a little angry. At his lawyer,
Gunter, and Harvey P. Noble. "You think I
did it?" he snapped.

"I don't. . . . I don't know what to think,"
Coyne said.

"You gonna answer Harv's question?"
Gunter asked.

"I don't know," Daniel sang out. "Somewhere. On the reservation. But I didn't kill
that whiskey runner."

"Hell," Noble said easily. "Me and Hugh
know that."

Gunter chuckled. "You're green, Danny
boy. But you're not a fool. You wouldn't
leave one of your notebooks underneath no
dead man."

"It was left behind on purpose." Coyne
looked up, snapping his fingers. "Someone
tried to make it look like Daniel killed that
man."

"Plain enough," Noble said. "To me and
Hugh." He frowned. "Maybe not to that
hardheaded, ill-tempered prosecutor in Fort
Smith. Maybe not to Judge Parker. Certainly not to the judge's hangman. Probably
not to a jury of white gents."

"Glad you got to Wichita Falls when you

did," Daniel said.

Noble grinned. "Well, I'm right sorry to have delayed our arrival. Sent you that wire, thought we'd just catch a train to Wichita Falls, but then me and Harv decided to go back to Hill's Ferry, nose around some."

Daniel took his tablet, found the pencil, turned back to that new page. "You said in your telegram that this man was scalped."

"That's correct."

"Those men said he had been . . . well . . . his. . . ."

"No. That's just a mob talking. Scalped, yes. And, like I said, his thigh was cut deep and cruel. But that's all."

"God," Coyne said. "That's all? That's enough."

Gunter laughed. "You're greener than Daniel."

Noble pushed back his hat. "This Horace fellow, from what me and Hugh could tell, he was sitting alone at his camp. Gents just rode up, all friendly like, and killed him."

"Like he knew them," Gunter said. "Didn't appear to put up a fight, and he was shot at close range."

"Shot." Daniel wrote this down. "Two men?"

"Two horses," Gunter said. "Shod horses.

That's another reason me and Harv ain't ready to arrest you yet for murder. You Comanch' still favor unshod ponies."

"But he was hacked up a mite," Noble said. "Now, I've seen a bunch of butchery in the Nations, but this cutting a gash in a dead man's thigh, that's new to me."

"It's Indian . . . ," Coyne said. "Mutilation." He dropped his head. "I learned that. They . . . well. . . ."

Daniel smiled. "Indians mutilate their enemies," he said. "Make it hard for them in the next life." He blinked, curious. Certainly Noble knew that about what the Pale Eyes would call "Indian depredations" but what The People, and other Indians, considered natural.

After biting off a mouthful of tobacco and working the quid into his right cheek, Harvey P. Noble found his own pencil and notebook. "Let's compare what we've all learnt," he said. "See what we got."

Coyne started, explaining that he had gone to Teepee City, but had learned nothing about a man named Dakota, Blake Browne, or Carl Quantrell.

"Quantrell, eh?" Noble said.

"Yes. The way Daniel and I think, Quantrell is this Dakota. He damned near tried to scalp me." He pointed at the cut above his eye. "And he almost killed Daniel in Dallas."

Noble spit, looked at Daniel. "That right?"

Daniel explained all that had happened in Dallas, and about Fenn O'Malley winning Coursey & Cox Bottling Works in a dice game. Remembering, he spun and faced the lawyer. "You better watch yourself, Mister Coyne. Quantrell found that note you left for me. It just came back to me. After those ruffians had beaten me up. He found the note. Cursed your name. He'll probably come after you."

Coyne pulled back his coat to reveal a small revolver in a shoulder harness. "I'm new here, but I'm learning," he said with a greenhorn's grin. "I'm ready for Carl Quantrell."

"Quantrell's tough," Noble warned.

A short silence followed.

"So," Gunter said, "you think that Ranger and O'Malley are in this together?"

"I do," Daniel said. "It makes sense. Rangers and the soldiers are looking for whiskey runners, but, the truth is, Quantrell and O'Malley are running the whiskey. Nácutsi's helping them."

Noble nodded, considering, let out a long breath, and shook his head. "Still need more evidence before I can get an arrest warrant naming 'em."

"What was O'Malley doing in Dallas," Gunter asked, "when he won that ginger beer place?"

Daniel frowned. He felt stupid again. "I . . . didn't ask. Didn't think of it."

Noble spit. "Might not matter. The building burned down. Dallas ain't no jumping-off spot for whiskey runners in the Nations. Hell, he was whoring or visiting his ma or gambling. He was there."

"And now he's gone," Coyne said. "Deserted."

"Good riddance," Noble said. "All right." He flipped back a few pages in his notebook. "Here's what I learned. Ain't none of them ginger beer bottles been seen lately in Wichita Falls. So that ain't the place they're operating out of. But I did telegraph me a lawman in Dallas, and he done some detective work, found out that six dozen crates of bottles from Coursey and Cox was shipped by the Fort Worth and Denver Railway to Wichita Falls."

Daniel blinked. His mouth fell open.

"But. . . ." Coyne sounded equally as stunned. "You said there were no bottles like those in town."

"That's right. Freighted off somewhere after they reached Wichita Falls. Couldn't find where, though. The man that picked up them crates at the depot signed his name as Theodore Smith."

"I'll look into it when I get back to town," Coyne said.

"You do that," Noble said.

"I don't know that name, though," the lawyer added.

Daniel stared at the name he had written on the paper. "Ted Smith." It hit him like a mule's kick. "Uvalde Ted Smith."

Coyne's fingers snapped. "But of course. Blake Browne's partner. Smart thinking, Daniel."

Daniel's shoulders sagged. He wasn't much of a detective. Muttering a curse, he thumbed back two pages in his Echo tablet.

"What is it?" Gunter asked.

"It's something Nácutsi said yesterday. He said he wouldn't rot in a jail like Toyarocho. Said he was too important."

"Who the hell's Toyarocho?" Noble asked.

"He's the one who killed his daughter. He's the first one I found with that ceramic stoneware bottle." He cursed again, kicking at the dirt in front of him. "He was in the Wichita Falls jail. I should have thought to question him."

"Well, you sure ain't going back to Wichita Falls till we get this mess cleared up," Noble said.

"I'll question him," Coyne said. "What should I ask?"

"He speaks almost no English," Daniel said.

"I'll find an interpreter. What else? I'll keep looking for Uvalde Ted Smith, too, but it's not likely we'll find him. Apparently you scared him out of the country, Daniel."

Gunter and Noble laughed.

"We need to move fast," Noble said. "Before our killer strikes again and murders another whiskey runner. He's already killed four men."

Suddenly Daniel closed his notebook. "No," he said softly. "He hasn't."

CHAPTER SEVENTEEN

"What do you mean?" Gunter asked.

To Daniel, it was clear. Well, clearer. He took a drink from his canteen.

"Blake Browne and that other fellow," Daniel began. He couldn't remember the name of the second dead Pale Eyes whiskey runner, not without looking at his notes. "They were killed, scalped, their thighs slashed."

"Yeah," Gunter said.

"But those two Creeks you found . . . ," Daniel began, looking at the Cherokee, who, grinning, tipped back his tall hat.

"Strung up," Gunter said. "Shot full of arrows. Whipped. Left to rot."

"I don't get it," Coyne said.

Harvey Noble spit again. "I do. That's smart detecting, Daniel. Should have seen it myself. We got two killers out there. One killed them Creeks, strung them up, left 'em as a warning, but didn't do nothing to their legs. The other killer bushwhacked and cut up Browne and Benson, and slashed their thighs. Nothing similar about them two deals," Noble went on, shifting the tobacco to his other cheek. "Yep, it's two different people. Might have two different reasons."

"But there is one thing similar," Gunter said. "The gent who sent those Creeks to hell, he left behind a Comanche whip. Ain't that right, Daniel? And the one who killed those two ol' white boys. One was filled with arrows with hawk feathers. The other had an Old Glory pencil tablet soaking up his blood. Whoever is killing them runners, Daniel, they surely don't like you. They seem to want you to hang."

Every time he saw a turkey buzzard, his stomach practically turned over, fearing he'd find another dead whiskey runner, but the next few days proved relatively quiet after he returned to the agency.

On this afternoon, Twice Bent Nose had tracked Daniel down at the teepee of Nácutsi, where he was searching for some clue, something that would shackle him to those whiskey runners. He knew Nácutsi was scouting for a 7th Cavalry patrol. Daniel had hoped he'd find something here, but, no, Nácutsi was too smart for that.

"What is it?" Daniel asked Twice Bent Nose.

"Agent Elbow," the old warrior said. "Say come."

With a sigh, Daniel kicked over a rack of drying meat, mounted the buckskin, and rode for the agency.

Arms tucked behind his back, Leviticus Ellenbogen paced in front of the agency headquarters, hair matted on his sweaty forehead, brooding, not even noticing that Daniel and Twice Bent Nose had arrived. Sensing the agent's temperament, Twice Bent Nose stayed just long enough to water his horse. By the time Daniel had unsaddled the buckskin, Twice Bent Nose was trotting toward the trees lining Cache Creek's banks.

"You wanted to see me?" Daniel said, and Agent Ellenbogen stopped, looked up, tried to find the right words. He found nothing, so pulled his hands from behind his back. One held a rolled-up newspaper, which he shoved in front of Daniel.

"This came," Ellenbogen said at last. "For you. Read it."

Carefully Daniel unrolled the paper.

"Read it!" Ellenbogen bellowed.

He pushed back his hat, walked to a lean-to, the angry agent just a few steps behind him, sat down, and studied *The National Temperance Leader,* trying to find the article the agent wanted him to read. That was easy enough. The headline screamed a war cry next to the advertising rates, a column titled "National Reports of Demon Rum", a poem, some quotes from Shakespeare, and a list of Dallas County places to worship.

WHISKEY KILLS!
Sorrowful account
of a Comanche warrior.
His sad story.
A daughter dead.
A race dying.
Killed by Liquor Most Foul.
One Indian's Fight
To Rid His Land
OF DEMON RUM!
Daniel Killstraight,
a true soldier of the Lord,
a great peace officer.
Our New Voice For Temperance!
Whiskey runners found dead.
GOD'S JUSTICE

COMANCHE
JUSTICE
A Most Moving Testament.

"Shit," Daniel said where he sat underneath the lean-to. Slowly he raised his eyes, found Agent Ellenbogen looming above him.

"Read the whole thing, Sergeant Kill-straight. It continues on Page Three. The publisher's editorial is on the second page. You might want to read that one, too, but first, the story about you and Teepee That Stands Alone."

Daniel felt his stomach turning over again, and there were no buzzards in sight.

He is not the typical guest you'll find at The Hotel Texas in Fort Worth. Slowly, uncertainly this impressive, silent, red-skinned man — more than six feet in height, by my estimate — settles into a rattan rocker in a room that looks as if it has not been occupied for days, even though this is where the Comanche medicine man who is called Teepee That Stands Alone has been staying while negotiating with Texas cattle barons about grazing rights on their reservation in the Indian Territory.

He has removed a magnificent war bonnet of dozens of eagle feathers, revealing his shiny, silver hair that has been trimmed short for an Indian man. The braids should be long, but instead are ragged, roughly cut, although slowly growing back in uneven strands. He smells of grease, of wood smoke, and wears only the traditional clothing of the Comanche. Yes, dear reader, he is an Indian. Noble red man to some. Brutal savage to others. He is dressed in britches of some animal skin and a fine leather shirt painted black and white. His moccasins are unadorned. A breastplate, white bones and dark leather, complements his attire.

I am told by an interpreter that he is of the Kwahadi, the last band of the wild, free-roving, hard-fighting Indians that only surrendered to the white supremacy a short decade ago. Ten, twelve, or thirteen years is not a long time, but in that short period the Comanches have been victimized and brutalized.

Yes, I hear those bellicose protests of the hardy frontiersmen and women who settled in Indian Country across Texas, across Kansas, through Colorado, and the eastern ranges of New Mexico Territory. They can remember when they were victimized and brutalized by these Comanche savages. But the Comanches are at peace with the white men now. Comanches no longer commit depredations. No, they are now victims of evil depredations — perpetrated by white men.

These peaceful Indians are being victimized by the white race's intoxicating, soul-destroying liquors. John Barleycorn. Demon rum. Whiskey, foul, terrible, ardent and IL-LEGAL! spirits.

Teepee That Stands Alone knows this too well, and, thanks to our mutual friend, a young Comanche policeman named Daniel Killstraight, this grand medicine man — a healer, a leader, an advisor — is willing to share his hardships and terrible, heartbreaking story with our national audience.

Toward the close of last winter, Teepee That Stands Alone laughed as all proud grandfathers laugh. Joy and pride filled his heart, and he sang the songs of his people, told the stories grandfathers tell, enjoyed the company of his granddaughter. Her name was Sehebi among the Comanches. It is translated, Sergeant Killstraight tells me, as Willow. A beautiful name. A beautiful girl.

She was four years old. She had all her life in front of her. Yet this innocent life was taken, taken savagely, without mercy, for whiskey has no mercy.

Her father, the son of Teepee That Stands Alone, returned to his lodge, drunk on whiskey that he had bought from some mysterious drummer with no soul, no mercy, no innocence, just savageness. Intoxicated, her father passed out, and fell on top of his young, sleeping daughter. Brace yourself, dear reader. Hold on to your loved one's arm for *support. Close your eyes. Blink away tears, but, please, you must read on. You must read past this. You must fight the pain that Teepee That Stands Alone has fought.*

Poor Willow's life was snuffed out. She suffocated underneath the weight of her drunken father, an Indian recently convicted of manslaughter, who, rather than face a lengthy prison sentence in Huntsville, only yesterday was found hanging by the neck in a dungeon at Wichita Falls.

Daniel stopped, stunned. "Toyarocho," he said. "Is he dead?"

"Took the coward's way," Agent Ellenbogen said. "I'm not crying over his soul. I'm waiting, Sergeant Killstraight. Read it. All of it."

He shook his head. Vaughan Coyne said he'd try to question him, find out where Toyarocho had gotten the liquor. Vaughan Coyne. Daniel mouthed the name. He said it aloud, testing it, wondering.

"Read it, Sergeant. Now!"

He picked up the paper, picturing Toyarocho hanging by the neck, wondering what he had used for a rope. He remembered watching his childhood friend, Jimmy Comes Last, hang at Fort Smith for two murders he had committed in the Nations, remembered thinking: *How does one travel to The Land Beyond The Sun with a neck so crooked?*

"I'm waiting," the agent said.

Daniel found his place, and read on.

So be it.

Yet the father of sweet Willow is not alone to blame for her terrible, terrible death.

Sergeant Daniel Killstraight knows this. They are opposites, Killstraight and Teepee That Stands Alone. The sergeant is young, more boy than man, dressed partly in the manner of our white race, dressed partly as a Comanche brave. He speaks English, but speaks Comanche, too, despite our race's best efforts to remove his given language from his mouth. He is unassuming, handsome in an Indian sort of way, with a barrel chest and long hair, shorter and more rotund than the Comanche medicine man. Teepee That Stands Alone is an old man. He is entirely Indian, utterly impressive, a man that commands respect no matter the race. He refuses to wear or touch anything that the white race has created. If he does such a thing, I am told, his power will turn into dust and blow away.

"It does not matter," Teepee That Stands Alone says. "I am dead already. My heart is dead. I will soon travel to The Land Beyond

The Sun."

Others in Indian Territory, on the Comanche, Kiowa, and Apache Reservation, have also gone to The Land Beyond The Sun. One is an old Comanche man, a leader named Seven Beavers who was killed by drinking poisoned whiskey. He died a horrible death, coughing up blood. The whiskey was so wretched, it also murdered a kitten that had lapped up the liquid death that claimed its master.

Whiskey has no mercy. It kills a four-year-old Comanche girl. It kills an ancient warrior and chief more than seventy years old. Killed by a bottle made by a brewery and bottling factory on the banks of the Trinity River in Dallas. Coursey & Cox Bottling Works, once known for its foul ginger beer, is no more. The business went bankrupt, the building burned to the ground, but the bottles still transport death. Instead of ginger beer, these bottles now contain whiskey — and some of that whiskey is poison.

Of course, all whiskey is poison. But some is more lethal than others. Whiskey kills, but now the Comanches are striking back.

A notorious whiskey runner named Blake Browne was found murdered on the reservation. The evidence points to some unknown Comanche as his killer. Two foul, evil ped-

dlers from the Creek Nation were also killed after trying to sell their illegal concoction to the Comanches. And yet another, it has been recently reported, was found dead, his cargo of illegal, deadly liquor burned beside his body. Killed, they were — murder, some might claim — as a warning to all those who attempt to transport death to these poor people.

This avenger remains at large. Some might think the killer is Teepee That Stands Alone, for he certainly has a reason, a reason that any white jury would find it impossible to convict. Some have blamed Sergeant Daniel Killstraight. Yet he is a protector of his people, and, if this is his handiwork, many would call it just.

The crimes — if you call these crimes — remain under investigation, but the real crime is what the white man's whiskey is doing to these Indians. They have no stamina against our liquor. They have no buffalo, and little pride. They are wards of our federal government, yet our wise leaders in Washington ignore their pleas, ignore our pleas.

Sergeant Killstraight believes that the man responsible for this latest assault on these now peaceful Indians is a whiskey runner known only as Dakota. He has vowed to find this man, and bring him to justice. And what help has he gotten from our civilized laws?

In Dallas, this noble, lionhearted, and UN-ARMED! peace officer was beaten ruthlessly by a gang of white thugs. One of these men is a notorious, cowardly member of the Texas Rangers, a blight on that grand organization's record, a hardened, callous man named Carl Quantrell who rides for Company D, a frequenter of saloons. Quantrell remains at large, as does this phantom called Dakota, unless they are one and the same.

Whiskey kills, and it will keep on killing unless we outlaw this demon liquid killer across the continent, unless we remove the blinders that keep us from seeing, unless we forget the sadness in the face of a broken-hearted grandfather named Teepee That Stands Alone.

How much longer will we let whiskey kill? Someone in the Indian Territory is striking back. These "Whiskey kills" are righteous, some people say. Maybe these "Whiskey kills" will make the leaders in Washington City take notice. Maybe The Great White Father will see the light.

Maybe these attacks against whiskey runners is the beginning of a new Indian War. Do our leaders in Washington, in Austin, in Topeka and Denver, want another war? Can they blame peaceful Indians fighting to protect their granddaughters and grandfathers against men who kill with poison whiskey? Would you do anything less than these Comanches are doing?

His Will Be Done. Comanche will is being done.

If I were a whiskey runner in the Indian Territory, I would fear for my life. Especially were my name Dakota.

Daniel lowered the paper. Leviticus Ellenbogen, face flushed, fists clenched, snarled. "Read the editorial, Killstraight."

"I think I just did," Daniel said.

A hand struck at him. Daniel closed his eyes, expecting a blow, but the agent ripped the paper from his hands. "I despise a smart aleck, Killstraight. Almost as much as I hate being made a fool of." He turned the page. "Here, let me just find a section. Yes, here. 'We do not know the temperament or philosophy of the newest agent in charge of the Comanches, Kiowas, and Apaches, but we do know that the last such agent is now serving a prison sentence for collaboration with whiskey runners!' She implies that I am as corrupt as my predecessor. I shall sue the wench for libel."

He wadded the first edition of *The National Temperance Leader* into a ball and threw it at Daniel. "Frank Striker, my interpreter, brought this from Dallas this afternoon. He was down there at my request, trying to raise funds from Texas churches of all faiths to help you people! Needless to say, once they read that paper, the priests, the preachers, and the rabbis were all hesitant to donate any funds to help you! To help me! And this . . . this . . . Patty Mullen, curse her soul, she was not content to print this inflammatory prose in Dallas County. She wired her story to various papers in Philadelphia, New York, Baltimore, San Francisco, Detroit, and Washington. Even before Mister Striker galloped back here, I was being delivered telegrams by the score."

Ellenbogen stopped only to catch his breath.

"The Secretary of the Interior wonders what I am doing here. President Cleveland is questioning the judgment of putting me in charge. Reporters from Washington and New York want to know the same. On the other hand, a Dallas editor wired to ask why I have a renegade Indian policeman running around killing white men!"

"I haven't killed anybody." Daniel rose, his own anger building.

"No? I'm starting to wonder. I've tried to help you, Killstraight. I've tried with all my might, within all my means. But this has gone too far."

"It had gone too far when Sehebi's life was snuffed out," Daniel said. "It had gone too far when Seven Beavers was poisoned. I did not ask this woman to write such an article."

"She's a firebrand." Ellenbogen's shoulders sagged. "Like you. We don't need firebrands."

He would get nowhere fighting with Agent Ellenbogen. So Daniel walked away.

CHAPTER EIGHTEEN

Some of what Patty Mullen had written disturbed him. For one, she had suggested that Daniel might be the one running around avenging Comanche deaths by murdering and mutilating whiskey runners. More importantly, Daniel feared that Carl Quantrell would not let her attacks on him go without retaliation. On the other hand, Daniel had never seen his name in a newspaper before, and that made him feel, well, important, although some of her phrases irked his pride.

More boy than man. . . .

Shorter and more rotund. . . .

Handsome, she had described him, but then had to add *in an Indian sort of way.*

What had she meant by that?

He took the newspaper with him when he left Ellenbogen, and rode home, read the *Leader* again, including the editorial this time. After that, he tried to translate what he could for Rain Shower, Ben Buffalo Bone, and their uncle. Cuhtz Bávi, however, listened only a few minutes before yawning and saying that such Pale Eyes stories bored him, and he retired to his teepee for an afternoon nap. At least Ben Buffalo Bone and his sister listened until Daniel had finished, and let him read without interruption.

Once he had finished, he folded the crumpled paper, and looked at his friends for a reaction.

Ben Buffalo Bone's yawn matched that of his uncle's. "I am hungry," he told his sister.

"That's all you have to say?" Daniel said. "What do you think of this woman's words?"

He shrugged. "Pale Eyes words. They mean nothing to The People. My uncle is right. This story, it is good, I think, and I am glad you like it, that you enjoy how she is writing about you, but The People tell better stories. Stories with buffalo and ravens and bears and wolves. Stories about counting coup and stealing horses and killing Mexicans. I do not think many people will pay Pale Eyes money for such a thing as that. It is not hard like a Pale Eyes book. It will not last long. It will not last as long as the stories The People tell." He pointed at the paper, then shrugged again. "Have you told this story to Teepee That Stands Alone?"

"Not yet."

"It is hard to believe that he would talk to a Pale Eyes woman. There is his power to think of."

"He just talked to her," Daniel said, "through me. He did not touch this woman, did not use anything made by any *taibo.* His *puha* remains strong."

"I am still hungry." Ben Buffalo nudged his sister.

"Why don't you find a wife?" Rain Shower snapped. "I tire of making food for you."

"Why don't you take a husband?" He grinned at Daniel.

She rose rapidly.

"What do you think of this story?" Daniel blurted out.

"She finds you handsome." Rain Shower glared at him. Daniel swallowed. In his translation, he had edited out in an Indian sort of way. "Why does she say this?"

"Haa!" Ben Buffalo Bone laughed. "Pale Eyes woman does not speak the truth. My brother is not so handsome. Not as handsome as Teepee That Stands Alone, at least, not according to this teller of stories. Don't be angry at my brother, Rain Shower. The

Pale Eyes woman who tells this story likes that old *puhakat* more than she admires this Metal Shirt. Is that not right, Bávi?"

Big mistake, Daniel thought. I never should have read this article to them. He felt a little hurt, maybe angry, at their response, Ben Buffalo Bone's indifference, Rain Shower's anger. What would they know, anyway?

"News-pa-per," Rain Shower said in English, then returned to her own language. "My brother is right. What good are such words? What good is such paper? It makes your hands dirty with black dye. It is good to help start a fire, but not as good as wood. Such pa-per is good only to stuff in a *chimal* to protect a warrior from the arrow of an enemy. I do not think much of this story. It does not tell you anything that you did not already know."

Daniel stared. *Except for the death of Toya-rocho,* he thought. He'd have to send a wire to Vaughan Coyne about that suicide, find out what his lawyer knew, or would say, about the death. In fact, he had plenty of questions for Vaughan Coyne. His lawyer claimed to be his friend, a protector, but Daniel was starting to think otherwise. Maybe he should write Hugh Gunter or Harvey Noble, instead. Maybe he should write all of them.

After they had arrived at the reservation, Gunter said he had to return to Muskogee. Noble had decided that he wanted to nose around some more. The federal deputy hadn't exactly said where he intended to do this nosing, but he had ridden west. Toward Greer County, Daniel expected. Still, Daniel could send word to Noble at Fort Smith. Maybe it would be there when he returned. He could definitely write Gunter. And Coyne. But what should he say to Coyne? What . . . ?

"You like this Pale Eyes woman?" Rain Shower's voice brought him out of his deep thoughts.

"She saved my life," Daniel explained. "Stopped Quantrell from killing me."

Rain Shower snorted. "Did you ask this Pale Eyes woman if she was called Da-ko-ta?"

Daniel laughed. "Why would I do that?"

"Maybe you should!" she barked, and ran for the teepee.

Ben Buffalo Bone laughed. Daniel didn't find anything amusing. Shaking his head, he balled up the newspaper and pitched it into the fire.

"My sister is right. It burns good," Ben Buffalo said. "But not long."

"I need to write the lawyer in Wichita Falls," Daniel said, staring at the blackened ball slowly crumbling in the flames.

"More Pale Eyes words." Ben Buffalo Bone yawned again. His stomach growled.

"Toyarocho is dead," Daniel said.

His friend straightened, suddenly somber. "You should not speak the name of he who is traveling to The Land Beyond The Sun."

"I know." Daniel sighed, eyes fixed on the remnants of the newspaper in the fire. "What do you know about the slash of an enemy's thigh?"

"Ah. Yes, I have never done such a thing. But I have never taken coup. I am too young. I was too young, I mean, when we rode free as the wind. That is a question for someone older, wiser. Quanah or Teepee That Stands Alone. I asked my uncle, but he says it is not the way of The People."

Impressed, Daniel looked away from the fire and into the eyes of his best friend. "You asked this?"

"Haa." Tapping his badge. "I am a Metal Shirt. We are to ask questions. Is that not so?"

"It is so."

"I told Agent Elbow. Did he not tell you what my uncle said?"

Daniel's eyes narrowed. "No. He did not."

Shaking his head, Ben Buffalo Bone leaned forward. "I do not know what to think of this agent. He should have told you. I told him while you were visiting the *Tejanos*. He should have told you. I thought it might be important."

"It is important. You tell me."

"I will. It is a sign. That is what Cuhtz Bávi tells me. It is the mark of a *Papitsinima*."

"Papitsinima," Daniel repeated. Lakota. Sioux.

Nodding, Ben Buffalo Bone said: "There are no *Papitsinima* here. *Papitsinima* dare not come to the land of The People."

Daniel agreed. "They are penned on their own reservation," he said sadly in English, then, head bobbing, spoke to Ben Buffalo Bone in Comanche. "These marks were not made by *Papitsinima*. No, but there are people who would have seen that sign. In Dakota Territory." He rose. "Dakota," he said again, and went to his cabin to read his pencil tablets.

"Do you believe in visions?"

The voice, Patty Mullen's voice, wakes him. He rises, uncertain, lost in the gloaming. Above him, he hears the cry of a hawk. The wind blows, pushing toward a garden on some small hill. Long Knives have planted trees, but they are young, and he does not think they will survive. The wind bends them like the blades of grass.

He hears the death song of a Kiowa.

He walks through a field of yellow flowers, up the rise, to a stone house. The Kiowa, Tséeyñ, stands in front of the house. His chant stops. The wind blows harder.

"Why do you sing your death song?" Daniel asks.

"I don't."

Daniel steps back. It is no longer Tséeyñ, but Coyote Chaser, the ancient Yamparika.

"Why are you here?" Daniel asks.

"I am old. It is the way of The People. I die alone."

"It is true," Daniel says, bowing his head. The People would abandon the old. Men or women; it did not matter. When a Comanche became too old to help, too big of a burden, The People cast them out. Harsh. Too harsh for some taibo to understand, but The People lived in a harsh land.

"You are no better than Maman-ti of the Kiowa!" a voice cries out. The voice is that of Teepee That Stands Alone, but it is a marsh hawk, sitting on the stone building, that is talking. "You are lower than Maman-ti."

"What happened to Coyote Chaser?" Daniel

asks the hawk.

Laughing, the hawk flies away.

"Look inside," the bird calls.

Daniel looks. The yellow flowers are now wooden crosses, and marble stones. A grave-yard. Yet the house of stone remains, only the building is small. White and gray stones set in dark mortar, a smooth roof of stone, and a door of iron, but the door is secured with a padlock.

"Come out," Daniel says, and steps away.

The wind blows the padlock away, and the door swings open. Seven Beavers, the dead Penateka, crawls out of the house. No, not a house, but a tomb. Worms have eaten his flesh. His eyes are gone.

"Why am I here?" the dead warrior asks.

A kitten, lying on Seven Beavers's shoulder, mews. It spits out blood.

Daniel steps back. "You are dead," he says. Eyes locked on Seven Beavers, and the baby cat. "You are both dead."

Seven Beavers lifts his right hand. He's holding a ceramic stone- ware bottle. He drinks. Crimson pours from both corners of his mouth. He is drinking blood.

The dead kitten mews.

The bottle falls, but the wind blows it away.

"Remember," the hawk cries from above the wind, "Maman-ti."

■ ■ ■ ■

His eyes opened wide, and he unclenched his clammy hands. It had been a nightmare. No. He realized he was sitting up, an Echo pencil tablet in his lap. He hadn't been dreaming. He had been wide awake.

The People had never been what Daniel would call deeply religious, certainly not as devout as the school fathers and school mothers back at the Carlisle Industrial School, not even as religious as Agent Leviticus Ellenbogen. Yet all of The People held magical dreams and visions as sacred.

Not that what he had just experienced was a vision, but it sure felt like it. Sweating, he shook his head, gripped his pencil, and began writing what he could remember, what the people had said, everything, before his recollections of the nightmare or vision quickly vanished.

He was still writing when hoofs sounded, and someone shouted his name. Daniel closed the tablet, stuck the pencil on his ear, and scrambled outside.

Twice Bent Nose dropped from his saddle as Ben Buffalo Bone darted out of his tee-pee.

"It is Coyote Chaser!" Twice Bent Nose

yelled at Daniel. "The medicine man at the soldier fort says for you to come quick. Coyote Chaser is dying."

CHAPTER NINETEEN

Guilt rocked his stomach like waves in a gale. He stood at the cot in the post hospital, staring down at the pale features of the old Yamparika. Coyote Chaser's breath rumbled, his eyelids lay heavy, Roman nose prominent on a slackened face, silver hair wet from sweat, plastered on a dingy pillow. No longer did the cocky chief look arrogant. Instead, he seemed feeble, ancient. . . .

A dying old man.

Dying alone.

Just a few weeks ago, Daniel had ridden to Huupi in the southern edge of the reservation trying to gather evidence that would prove Coyote Chaser had poisoned the Penateka named Seven Beavers, but Daniel knew better now. He wondered why he had even suspected Coyote Chaser of such a crime.

"I am told he has no family," Major Becker said behind him.

Nodding, Daniel sighed. "No one." Thinking: *Not any more. His wife, his family, they will not help him now. It is not The People's way.*

He recalled the words of Twice Bent Nose: *Do not grow old.*

"Patrol found him at the confluence of West Cache Creek and the Red. Sergeant Andrews probably would have left the old man there, but they found this with him."

Daniel turned to the doctor, saw the bottle in his hand. "That's why I sent for you, Sergeant."

He took the bottle, shaking it, finding it empty, turning the cold piece of stoneware in his hand, looking at the letters chiseled into his brain.

Cox & Coursey Bottling Works
Home Brewed
GINGER BEER
Dallas, Texas

"Bad whiskey?" Daniel asked. "Poisoned?"

Becker shook his head. "I don't think so. He won't eat. Won't respond to any treatment. He just lies there, wasting away. Like he's willing himself to death. His lungs are in wretched condition, and I can only guess his age, but he could be near or even past eighty. He has just worn himself out."

"Yes." Daniel handed the bottle back to the surgeon. He remembered the trip to Fort Worth. "He should not have come with us to Texas. He was too old for such a trip."

Yet he suddenly smiled, picturing Coyote Chaser sitting in the Queen City Ice Cream Parlor beside Quanah Parker, licking the peach ice cream with the relish of a young boy. He had looked fine then, hadn't turned sick until later. The smile disappeared. He remembered how Teepee That Stands Alone had lost his temper in the parlor. Daniel saw the marsh hawk from his dream, and his dark eyes narrowed.

Major Becker was talking. "Sergeant Andrews brought him to the agency, but Mister Ellenbogen wasn't there, and Frank Striker didn't know when he would return. So he came here."

"I'm glad," Daniel said.

"Well." Becker tossed the bottle onto a nearby cot.

The hospital was crowded again, windows open but failing to cool off the building. Soldiers complained, sweating, cursing their ill luck and their maladies, a few of them staring silently at the doctor, Indian policeman, and dying man.

"I can't keep him here, Sergeant," Becker

said apologetically. "There's nothing I can do for him. He'd be better off among his own kind. And I'll need every bed I can get. We're seeing a rash of malaria and dysentery, which comes like clockwork this time of year."

"I understand." Although he didn't.

"Sergeant Andrews's patrol found a case of those bottles," Becker said. "Most of them were empty. Trooper Brinkerhoff asked me to tell you that, when you came in. They rode off back south after they got fresh mounts and more rations. Brinkerhoff said he needed to tell you something, too, something about a man named Dakota."

Daniel straightened. "Dakota?"

"That's what he said. He said you'd understand. That's another reason I sent for you."

"He didn't happen to leave a note, did he?"

"I'm afraid not."

"When will they be back?"

"They requisitioned rations for six days. Ordinarily I'd say they'd return earlier, but not with the malaria and dysentery."

"Where were they going?"

"I assume they'll patrol the Red between Huupi and Hill's Ferry. But you'd have to ask Lieutenant Newly. Well . . . no. I'll ask him, and get word to you."

"Thanks." He looked back at the weakening Yamparika, then turned suddenly toward Major Becker. "You said a case of bottles?"

"Yes. They were cached in some rocks, not far from where they found that old man."

"Just one case?"

"According to Sergeant Andrews and Trooper Brinkerhoff, yes."

A black soldier lying near a window cried out for the doctor.

"I have to go, Sergeant. Is there anything else?"

Probably, Daniel thought, but he shook his head, and the doctor began crossing the room, only to stop after a few steps, and turn around. He took a deep breath, choosing his words, glanced at Coyote Chaser, then, exhaling, stared at Daniel. "Can you . . . take care of . . . him?"

"I'll see to him," Daniel said.

Ration day. A chorus of excited cries, of Comanche songs and English curses rose above the wind and rain that pelted the agency. Leviticus Ellenbogen grunted as he eased the dirty feet of Coyote Chaser onto a bunk in the far corner of the cabin.

"I'm not sure how I got appointed this

man's nurse." Ellenbogen straightened, and mopped sweat and rain water from his brow.

Daniel pulled a sheet over the old man's chest, placed a hand on his cheek, warm to his touch, and shook his head.

"Reckon the Army threw him away same as the Comanch'," Frank Striker said from the doorway.

"A miserable life of barbarity," Ellenbogen said. "Both Army and savage." He looked cruelly at Daniel. "You people just toss an old man out." He shook his head. "Your tribe's customs make things hard for me to understand, Sergeant."

"It is hard sometimes for me to understand," he whispered in Comanche.

"What's that?"

"A Comanche prayer," Daniel lied.

Striker guffawed. "Comanches don't pray."

"Well," Ellenbogen said, "I shall attend him as best I can. The Army might not take care of him, but they will have to bury him."

"I'm sure them bluecoats will agree to that," Striker said. "Rain's startin' to slack a mite. I'll play nursemaid to this ol' boy while y'all police the fandango outside."

Pulling his hat down, Daniel left Coyote Chaser's cot and stepped outside. Ration day. The People refused to let the thunderstorm drown their joy, although Daniel saw little reason for their songs and laughter. *Tejano* cowhands had driven a herd to the agency corrals, and now old, young, and middle-aged men ran around shooting cattle while the cowboys and a few soldiers watched, some in awe, several in horror, many simply bewildered.

At least the rain kept away the flies.

Daniel sighed. Rain Shower was already at work, butchering a brindle steer beside her mother. Away from the corrals, Indians lined up to gather the rest of their supplies: flour, sugar, coffee, corn — much of it unfit to eat — soap, bolts of calico or linsey-woolsey, and, for some reason, boxes of jew's harps. Oajuicauojué, Rain Shower's younger sister, tested the cheap instrument, but quickly gave up.

Jew's harps. Daniel shook his head. Last month, or maybe the month before, the federal government had sent iron hoops for barrels. No barrels, just the iron hoops, good for nothing except scrap metal. As worthless as some of the food.

As a member of the tribal police, Daniel received no rations. Maybe, he often thought, that was a blessing, although Ben Buffalo Bone's family always shared what they got with their son and his loyal friend.

"Keep that line in some semblance of order, Sergeant," Agent Ellenbogen said as he walked quickly to the assistant agent to oversee the checking off of names in the ledger.

Daniel walked down the line, nodding at the men he knew, smiling hopefully at the women, watching horses lope across the rolling plains, bringing in more Indians, many of them shouting, full of joy because of this day. Near the end of the line, he spotted a hardened face, which caused him to stop.

"I did not expect to find Teepee That Stands Alone here," Daniel said.

The Kwahadi *puhakat* slowly turned and stared. He said nothing.

"I wish to speak to you," Daniel said. "It was my plan to ride to the Wichita Mountains to visit you."

"You would be welcome," he said without enthusiasm.

Daniel fought for the words. "First, I have news that will sadden your heart." He pointed at the row of trees the soldiers had planted years ago to block the wind. "Come with me." The old man did not budge. "I will save your place in this line." He tapped the tin shield. "This gives me the power to do so."

Straightening, Teepee That Stands Alone protested. "I do not come for the gifts of the *taibo*. I take no gifts from such a wretched animal. I come to watch my people shame themselves."

A younger man, standing in front of the *puhakat,* turned. "Old man, you shut your mouth. You have no power. You have no pride."

"Watch your tongue!" Teepee That Stands Alone snapped.

"You pretend to be some powerful holy man, but you are nothing. You watch what you say, old man, or you will feel my bow across your back."

Daniel moved between the two. "There will be no fighting in this line," he said, directing the words at the younger man he did not know. "You fight, and I will arrest you. You will get no rations this month or next."

The Comanche spit between Daniel's moccasins. "Metal Shirt," he said in disgust.

"Come," Teepee That Stands Alone barked. "I have seen enough here." He headed for the trees, and Daniel glared at the young man before following the *puhakat*.

"What is it you wish from me?" Teepee That Stands Alone said when they reached the trees. The wind picked up again, driving a harder rain at an angry angle. Daniel was grateful for these small trees and their leaf-heavy branches.

"First, I must tell you something that will sadden your heart. It is news I learned. It is news of your son."

"I have no son." The words slammed like a door.

Daniel searched the old man's hate-filled eyes, but saw nothing beyond that hate.

"Toyarocho is dead," he said, and still saw nothing in the eyes.

"I have no son. The name means nothing to me."

"Should I tell your wife? Should I tell his widow?"

"Tell anyone," Teepee That Stands Alone said. "Perhaps they will mourn. I mourn no more."

"He died in the jail in Wichita Falls."

Teepee That Stands Alone shook his head in anger. "Is this all that you have to tell me? I have no time for this. I go now." He was going, too, until Daniel called for him to wait.

The old man walked back under the trees.

"I need the help of you, Teepee That Stands Alone. I need help explaining a special dream. A . . . a . . . vision."

The dark eyes brightened. "You?" He almost laughed. "You had a vision?"

"Will you help me learn what this dream means?"

"That is what a *puhakat* does. Tell me about this dream."

Daniel looked at the ration line. Looked to be going smoothly. Beyond that, Ben Buffalo Bone and Twice Bent Nose had everything under control in the corral. Agent Ellenbogen's head was buried in his ledger.

"I am following a hawk," Daniel began, trying to remember.

"What kind of hawk?" the *puhakat* interrupted.

"A marsh hawk."

Teepee That Stands Alone nodded. "That is good. The marsh hawk is your *puha.* Your father gave you his power when he took the name of the marsh hawk. He got his power from the marsh hawk. This, I remember."

"Yes," Daniel said.

"Go on."

"Before that," Daniel said, recalling something else from the dream, wishing he had that Echo notebook with him. "There was a voice. The voice of the woman from Texas, the woman you talked to. The writer of stories."

"I remember her."

266

"She asks me in the dream if I believe in visions."

"Do you?"

That stopped Daniel. "Maybe. That is why I come to you. Tséeyñ is there."

"The Kiowa?"

"Yes. He is singing his death song."

"The song of the Ko-eet-senko." The holy man nodded.

"Yes. I ask him why he sings this song, but he becomes Coyote Chaser."

Teepee That Stands Alone suddenly frowned.

"I ask him why he is there," Daniel continued, "and he says it is the way. He says he must die alone." Daniel tried to shake off the chill brought on by the wind and rain, or, at least, he blamed it on the weather. "And now, Coyote Chaser has been thrown away."

"It is the way of The People. It has always been the way."

"Yes. Coyote Chaser is in the agent's office. He is dying."

"Perhaps that is your vision. Perhaps the marsh hawk was showing you the future. You should trust the marsh hawk. You should believe what your *puha* tells you."

"There is more."

"Tell me."

"I hear your voice. You are saying . . . 'You are no better than Maman-ti.' You are saying . . . 'You are lower than Maman-ti.' "

The eyes of Teepee That Stands Alone turned darker, a bottomless pit.

"Words. They mean nothing."

"It is your voice," Daniel explained, "but the words are spoken by the marsh hawk." He threw the holy man's words at him. "I should believe what my *puha* tells me, is it not so?" And then said, for his own heart: "I should believe what my father tells me."

"Words," was all Teepee That Stands Alone said.

"You said those words before," Daniel said. "I remembered them after my vision. You said them in Fort Worth. You spoke them to Coyote Chaser. Who is Maman-ti?"

"Perhaps you should ask Coyote Chaser," Teepee That Stands Alone said.

"His *puha* is not as strong as yours."

"That is so." Softer, sadder he added: "Once so."

The dam broke, and the raindrops fell in hard, painful blasts, driven by a furious wind.

"I do not talk in the rain," Teepee That Stands Alone said, the potency returning to his voice. "You come to my lodge in the holy mountains. You come and we shall smoke

the pipe. We shall find the meaning of your
vision. In three suns, you come."

CHAPTER TWENTY

"Who is Maman-ti?" Daniel asked. "I know he's Kiowa."

"Was Kiowa," Frank Striker replied before biting off a mouthful from a twist of tobacco. "He's dead."

"Dead." Daniel let out the word in a sigh. Chasing a ghost. Chasing a dream. He shook his head, disappointed in the answer, but mainly in himself. He should be out chasing evidence, not a vision — if it had been a vision — catching up with Brink Brinkerhoff to find out what his message about Dakota meant, or doing something that might get results.

Instead, he found himself sitting in the shade outside the agency headquarters, talking to the interpreter, every now and then glancing through the open doorway to check on Coyote Chaser. Leviticus Ellenbogen had ridden to the fort with his assistant, leaving Daniel and Frank Striker in charge of the agency until they returned after dinner. The sun was hot, the sky a pale blue, cloudless. Daniel flipped to a new page in the Echo tablet and wrote.

"When did he die?" he asked.

"Oh, hell, I don't know for certain. Better than a decade ago. Why don't you ask some Kiowa?"

"You married one."

After a chuckle, Striker drenched a scorpion with tobacco juice, wiped his mouth with a dirty shirt sleeve, and said: "Yeah, that I did. Well, let me cogitate on it." He chewed and thought, thought and spit, finally nodded. "It was Eighteen and Seventy-Five. That's the year. You were here then, but just a kid. Likely don't remember much of what was going on then, probably scared to death like most Comanch' kids and women was. Like a bunch of Comanch' and Kiowa men was. Couldn't blame 'em. Yep, it was after Quanah give up the fight, come limpin' in to give up to Mackenzie. Before they shipped you off down the white man's road. Summer of Eighteen Seventy-Five. Yes, Dan'l, that was the year, but, if you need month and date, I can't help you there. What you interested in a Kiowa *dohate* for?"

Daniel shrugged. He wasn't about to

271

explain a vision to the agency interpreter, but the word *dohate* interested him. He knew only a few Kiowa words — the language might be the hardest of all the Plains tribes to grasp, even for a Comanche — but *dohate* was one word he knew. *Puhakat,* The People would say. Holy man.

"Maman-ti," Striker went on. "It means Walks In The Sky, or that's how I say it. Sky Walker, Man On A Cloud, you know the Kiowa tongue can be a holy handful. Anyway, he was a lot like your old Teepee That Stands Alone. Mean as a rattler that just got stepped on. Ornery sumbitch. Didn't want no peace with us white men. They say he was one of the leaders of the raid in Jack County, Texas, back in 'Seventy, 'Seventy-One thereabouts. The raid that got Satanta sent to prison the first time. They say Maman-ti led or preached in a lot of raids. Mean, he was."

He spit again, shifted the tobacco, and continued. "But Kickin' Bird was a big peace chief, and more and more Kiowas started seein' things his way, and not Maman-ti's. That riled him some. So when the Kiowas surrendered in 'Seventy-Five, a few months before you Kwahadis give up, Mackenzie makes Kickin' Bird pick the boys they're gonna lock up in Florida. You know how that was."

Daniel felt like spitting. Yes, he knew. The People had been forced to send many of their own brave warriors to Florida. Daniel's father had been one of those, and he had never returned.

"Kickin' Bird chose Maman-ti." The interpreter chuckled. "No surprise there. Not no differenter than some white politician would do. Yes, sir, you ask Grover Cleveland to pick who he's sendin' to prison, I bet he'd name some Republican. Might be your Agent Ellenbogen right about now after that ruction you and that Dallas newspaper lady stirred up." Another spit. "Where the hell was I, Dan'l?"

"Kicking Bird sent Maman-ti to Fort Marion."

"Right. Well, Maman-ti's off to prison, so he puts a hex on Kickin' Bird. That's the story, anyhow. Big Kiowa *dohate* casts a spell on Kiowa peace chief. And Kickin' Bird up and dies. That's one story, anyway. Or somebody . . . and maybe Maman-ti was behind it . . . poisoned Kicking Bird. That's a likely possibility, too. Or maybe, as my wife sees it, Kicking Bird just worried hisself to death."

"And Maman-ti?" Daniel asked.

"Well, a Kiowa can't go around killin' no

other Kiowa. Bad medicine. Maman-ti knowed that, and he said that hex he put on Kickin' Bird would kill him, too. Justice, I guess. If you believe that story. So when the Kiowas arrive at Saint Augustine, Maman-ti gets sicker than a dog. The doctors wrote it up as dysentery. Maman-ti says he's done for, shakes hands with some other prisoners, and sometime that summer he's deader'n dirt." He punctuated his story with another stream of tobacco juice.

Daniel considered this, shook his head, and asked: "Where's Maman-ti buried?"

"Fort Marion, I warrant."

Daniel looked at what he had just written, and asked: "What does he have to do with all this?"

"Huh?"

Daniel looked up. "I'm just thinking. Sorry." He scratched his head, looked inside the agency. The thin sheets covering Coyote Chaser's chest rose and fell unevenly, but the old man was still alive. Another thought came to him. "How about Kicking Bird?" Daniel asked. "Where's he buried? Do you know?"

"Sure. Chief's Knoll. You can't miss his grave. I guaran-damn-tee you Maman-ti didn't get no tomb as fancy as Kickin' Bird got."

■ ■ ■ ■

It was the stone building from his vision.

The Army had buried a number of Indian leaders — those that fought for peace, as well as those that died for their freedom — at the post cemetery at Fort Sill. Chief's Knoll. Satank, the great Kiowa leader of the Ko-eet-senko Society, was here. So was Ten Bears, the humble peace chief of The People. Below the small rise rose wildflowers from his dream, weathered wooden crosses and marble monuments marking the burial places of many soldiers. Frank Striker had been right. Kicking Bird's tomb was fancier than any grave at Fort Sill, even the graves of white officers and buffalo soldiers.

Yet the dream, the vision, meant nothing to Daniel. He flipped back in this pencil tablet, rereading his notes. He stared at the iron door, bracing himself, fearing that the dead Seven Beavers would somehow come out as he had in the dream, that the wind would blow the door open and he would see that terrible, worm-eaten face. Yet the air was still, heavy, and the door remained locked.

Nothing.

He could not find the meaning of his

dream, not without help from Teepee That Stands Alone. Shaking his head, he turned, and walked down the crooked rows of graves, stopping, thinking he had heard someone. He looked back at Kicking Bird's tomb, eyes locked on the iron door, and he recalled the words of the marsh hawk.

Remember Maman-ti.

The surrey in front of the agency cabin was like nothing he had seen in Indian Territory, nothing he had seen since Pennsylvania, wide-tracked with leather seats that shone brilliantly, covered with a sparkling canopy from which hung golden tassels.

Daniel swung down from the saddle, and was leading the buckskin to the corral when Patty Mullen's voice stopped him. As he turned, he saw her come from the agency, her smile radiant, followed by a thin, gray-bearded man in a fancy striped suit, and Leviticus Ellenbogen. Daniel ground-reined his horse, and moved toward them, stopping when a third man exited the headquarters.

"Hello, Daniel," Vaughan Coyne said.

Patty was saying something, but Daniel's eyes bore into his lawyer, who smiled, moving easily, until Daniel asked sharply: "What happened to Toyarocho?"

The lawyer frowned. "He's dead. Hanged himself. I'm sorry."

"I'm sorry you had to learn about it through my newspaper, Daniel," Patty said. "I never thought. . . ."

"Did he kill himself before you talked to him?" Daniel's voice remained sharp, edgy. He felt his anger boiling at the lawyer, had barely even heard Patty Mullen's apology. "Or after?" He took a step, made himself stop, but it proved hard. "Or did you talk to him at all?"

"Daniel," Patty began.

Vaughan Coyne let out a long breath. "Miss Mullen, gentlemen, would you excuse Daniel and me?" He turned back toward the cabin. "Come on, Daniel. Let's talk. Get what you have off your chest." He looked back, forcing a smile. "Come on, Daniel. This is what lawyers do. You're not the first client of mine to explode on me, but let's do this as gentlemen, as civilized men. Inside."

Coyne's smile vanished as soon as Daniel stepped into the agency, and the door slammed behind him. Coyne raised his left hand, wagging a finger under Daniel's nose.

"I tolerate a lot, Daniel, but you watch your attitude. You watch your tone."

"You never answered my question."

"Toyarocho hanged himself. You think I killed him?"

"The thought struck me." He clenched his teeth, looked beyond his lawyer, saw Coyote Chaser lying on his cot, barely alive.

"Why would I kill him? You tell me that. He was dead by the time I returned to Wichita Falls. After our talk with Marshal Noble and that Cherokee. You don't believe me? Ask the jailer in Wichita Falls. You ask the town marshal. He hanged himself in his cell with his leggings. Choked to death. Whip Windsor, the jailer, told me it was a miracle that Comanche lived as long as he did. They expected one of his cellmates to kill him. Wouldn't have bothered anybody there. Everyone considered him a child killer. That's what Windsor said. And you tell me this, Daniel. What would you do, what would your conscience tell you to do, if you had been Toyarocho? If you had killed your four-year-old daughter?"

Daniel felt the tension pour out of him, replaced by a weariness. He shut his eyelids tight.

"I didn't kill him," Coyne said, his voice a hurt whisper. "As God is my witness, I didn't kill him. Don't try my patience, Daniel. I put up with a lot, but you can push me only so far."

He bowed his head, remembered something Hugh Gunter and Harvey Noble had been trying to teach him. Don't go off accusing anybody until you had proof, until you were satisfied, until you could get an arrest warrant or an indictment. He hadn't done that with Vaughan Coyne, had let his temper beat him.

When he opened his eyes, Daniel asked: "What are you doing here?"

Coyne smiled, put a gentle hand on Daniel's right shoulder. "That's another reason I wanted to speak to you alone. There's trouble in Texas, Daniel. Carl Quantrell hasn't been spotted since you saw him in Dallas."

Daniel considered this. "How about Fenn O'Malley?"

"Nobody's seen him, either. I asked the officer of the day at Fort Sill when we arrived."

"Could they be together?"

"I don't know. Maybe. But that's not the problem. The problem is people in Texas are starting to say Quantrell's dead. They expect to find him scalped, with his thigh slashed." He removed his hand, looked deep into Daniel's eyes. "They're starting to say you killed him."

"Me?" He took a step back. "I haven't

seen him. . . ."

"There's no evidence, Daniel. It's just talk. That's why I was coming here before I met Miss Mullen and Mister Caldwell."

"Caldwell," Daniel tried. He pictured the gray-haired man with the silk hat outside. "Who's Caldwell?"

"Jonathan Caldwell. He's an Indian commissioner. You should be introduced to him. He's here to help. Thanks to Miss Mullen."

Deputy Commissioner Jonathan W. Caldwell III removed his cigar, blew a plume of smoke toward the moon, and smiled. "Do you understand what Congress passage of Henry Dawes's proposal means to you, Daniel?"

He shrugged. Congress had passed the act back in February, meaning that the reservations would be ended at some point in time, but truthfully Daniel hadn't paid much attention to any ramifications. Whiskey runners, and more recently whiskey murders, had consumed him.

"It's private property, Daniel," Caldwell said. "Private property is the essence of civilization. Henry says that to be civilized means you wear civilized clothes, you cultivate the land, you live in houses, ride in Studebakers, you send your children to school, and you drink whiskey." He laughed.

Vaughan Coyne cleared his throat, but Caldwell seemed drunk on his own voice. Patty Mullen's mouth fell open, but the deputy commissioner didn't notice. "Most importantly, you own land. You, Daniel, as a single man over eighteen years of age, will receive, when the President directs the allotment, one-eighth of a section. You have no idea how much land that is, do you, Daniel?"

Daniel frowned. "Eighty acres."

The tall man stared at his cigar with sudden distaste, flicked the ash, spit, and put the long thing back in his mouth, dragging on the foul-smelling stick until the tip glowed red. He sent another plume of blue smoke into the sky. "Eighty acres is correct. I forgot you were educated at Captain Pratt's fine school. Eighty acres is a lot of land."

It is nothing, Daniel wanted to say. The People had never owned land. Who could own the earth? The land belonged to all of The People, to the Kiowas, even to the *taibos*. No one person could own land, and eighty acres . . . . Nothing. Even Pale Eyes farmers knew you could not make a living in Indian Territory on eighty acres. He did not like Jonathan Caldwell.

"I have been in Tahlequah since early March," Caldwell said. "Working with the Cherokees, explaining to them what this change will bring. Then the charming Miss Mullen wired her articles to Washington City, and so I was directed first to Dallas, and now to here. We happened upon Attorney Coyne in Wichita Falls, and, as he has been a fine representative for you, he asked to come with us as he had business here, too, and so we are here." He placed the cigar aside. "I have never seen such stars. The sky here is big. The Western skies are magnificent, Daniel." Caldwell looked across the fire. "How do you like it, Leviticus?"

"It's big."

"Big. Grand. At night, I forget how wretched this territory is. Look at that."

"Esiavit," Daniel said.

The deputy commissioner stared across the fire at him. He tried the word, couldn't make the muscles in his mouth work, and sighed. "What's that?"

"Esiavit," Daniel repeated. "The Milky Way."

"Yes. You should forget that heathen word, Daniel. Remember, you're civilized now. Milky Way."

"Why are you here?" Daniel asked.

282

The commissioner laughed. "Why, to see that old medicine man of yours, Daniel. What else? What's his name, dear?"

"Teepee That Stands Alone," Patty said.

"Per President Cleveland's directive, Commissioner Caldwell has asked for a meeting with Teepee That Stands Alone," Leviticus Ellenbogen explained. "To smooth things over, get this controversy ended. We will go to his lodge the first thing tomorrow morning."

Daniel nodded. "Good. I was going to see him anyway."

CHAPTER
TWENTY-ONE

The surrey shifted when Leviticus Ellenbogen climbed into the back, squeezing between Vaughan Coyne and the deputy commissioner. Daniel helped Patty Mullen into the front, moved around the wagon, and climbed into the driver's seat.

Frank Striker put his hand on the brake as Daniel gathered the reins. "Know how to handle a rig like this, Dan'l?"

"I'll figure it out," Daniel said with a grin.

Striker spit, fought down a grin, and looked at Patty Mullen. "You need anything, Dallas?"

"No," she said. "Just another newspaper article."

"You'll likely get that, madam," the commissioner began, but Daniel cut off the rest of his words, snapping his head back to Frank Striker, and demanding: "What did you call her?"

Bewildered, Striker shook his head.

284

"Nothin'. I didn't call her nothin'."

"Dallas," Daniel said.

"Yeah." Striker still didn't understand. Daniel wasn't sure he understood it all, either. "Dallas," Striker said. "It don't mean nothin'."

" 'It don't mean nothing,' " Daniel repeated. "Excuse me. I'll be right back."

Ellenbogen was shouting his name when he leaped from the surrey, and ran to the corral. Frank Striker patted the back of the bay horse, and furiously worked on his tobacco, still perplexed, while Daniel found his notebooks, all of them, and hurried back to the wagon.

"That's good thinking," the commissioner said. "You can be our stenographer when we interview this medicine man of yours. I'd trust a heathen like you before I'd trust this alleged journalist or a damned attorney to take accurate notes. And I was once an attorney."

Jonathan W. Caldwell III didn't know how to shut up. For three hours, his jaws had been working, producing nothing important. "Tahlequah wasn't the end of the earth, but you could see it from there," he was saying, stopping only to light another cigar. "But this . . . Jesus . . . this is perdition itself."

He wondered if Hugh Gunter had met this insufferable son-of-a-bitch.

"Last night, you admired the stars," Patty Mullen said.

"How much farther?" Caldwell asked, ignoring Patty's statement.

"Good bit." Daniel jutted his jaw toward the rising blue-gray hills to the west.

"God," the deputy commissioner said in disgust, then laughed. "Teepee That Stands Alone. I guess his name says it all."

"I find this country beautiful," Patty Mullen said.

"The People do, also," Daniel said. "And the Wichitas are even more breathtaking."

"Perhaps the scenery will improve after the allotment of this unholy reservation," Caldwell said. "When this desolation is turned into civilization, with farms and fences, acres and acres of ripening wheat, pastures of Jersey cows, church steeples, and telegraph poles." He started to light another cigar. "I don't know why President Cleveland insisted on me meeting this holy man."

"Politics," Leviticus Ellenbogen said.

Daniel yawned.

"How long have you been practicing law?" the commissioner asked, changing the subject, trying to pull Coyne into his worthless conversation.

No response. Caldwell tried again.

"Pardon?" Coyne coughed slightly. "I'm sorry, sir. You were saying?"

"How long have you been practicing law?"

"Oh. Eight years. No, nine."

"I had a practice myself for twenty-three years. I found being a lawyer is much like being a Thespian."

"I think you are right, sir," Coyne said.

"Good training for politics."

"That I wouldn't know." Coyne sounded bored.

"In Pittsfield, that's where I practiced," Caldwell continued. "Tried one murder case."

"That's plenty," Coyne said.

"A grand case. I was defense counsel." The commissioner laughed. "I proved that the man slain had been killed by a left-handed individual. The wounds on the deceased showed no alternative, then I used testimony after testimony to show that my defendant was right-handed."

"I'm a left-hander myself," Coyne said, just to say something.

"Perhaps you were the killer." Leviticus Ellenbogen displayed a rare moment of levity.

Coyne laughed. "Not me. Never been to

Pittsfield."

"You're safe there, sir," Caldwell said. "The man I defended was the culprit."

That pulled Patty Mullen into the conversation. Turning around, she said: "But you said you proved. . . ."

The deputy commissioner laughed. "He was ambidextrous, madam. Used his left hand as well as his right. Luckily we didn't prove that to the jury."

"More proof of my innocence," Coyne said, smiling. "I can barely hold a fork in my right hand."

Caldwell had no interest in Coyne's words. He was enjoying the expression on Patty Mullen's face. "Oh, don't look so shocked, so repulsed, Miss Mullen," Caldwell said. "I didn't know of my client's guilt at the time. Only afterward, after the jury found him innocent, did he confide in me. Got away scotfree, but here's justice for you. Two weeks later, he stepped out of a dram shop and was run over by a hack. Broke his neck. There's God's justice for you."

Daniel sighed. The Wichita Mountains didn't seem to be getting any closer.

Grace Morning Star offered the guests dried meat and bread that looked more rigid than Army hardtack. She busied herself around the lodge, bringing water to drink, humming a song as she worked, talking to Daniel, apologizing that her husband was not here.

"Ask her when Teepee That Stands Alone will return," Leviticus Ellenbogen said again.

"She does not know," Daniel said for the third time, and thanked the silver-haired woman again for the water.

"Ask her where the hell she learned to make biscuits?" Jonathan Caldwell said, and flung his biscuit into the bushes.

When the old Comanche woman's head dropped, Daniel turned angrily. "She speaks English well enough."

"It doesn't make her a cook." Caldwell cackled.

"Mister Caldwell!" Patty Mullen demanded. "Your rudeness knows no bounds."

"You're one to talk, lady. Your diatribe in that newspaper showed no Christian charity." He snorted. "No offense, Ellenbogen." Underneath his breath: "Damned Jews." Then the commissioner tasted the dried meat.

"I sorry," Grace Morning Star said in English, then spoke in Comanche. "There is not much I can do with the flour I am given at ration day."

Daniel patted her hand. "Do not let his words sting, Grandmother. He is a fool. Even the Pale Eyes dislike him."

Caldwell blurted out. "Killstraight . . . tell her the meat's not bad. Not prime, but an interesting taste."

"My husband should be here," the woman told Daniel.

"I thought you said that squaw spoke English," Caldwell called out. "She should use it. Become civilized. . . ."

Daniel ignored him. "When did he leave?"

"You should speak English, too, Killstraight," Caldwell tried again, but, getting no response, he focused on eating the dried meat.

Grace Morning Star answered Daniel's question. "This morning, he left. He knew you would come this day. Perhaps he went to seek his own vision. To help you."

"Perhaps."

She shook her head. "Maybe he will not come. While these Pale Eyes are here."

"I would not blame him."

Daniel pushed back his hat, and tasted the biscuit. He made little progress, and placed it on a stone, his face changing, curious. "I did not see you at ration day."

"I did not go."

He tried something. "Your husband went."

"It is true. You spoke to him there."

"Yes."

"I am fortunate to have a good man," she said with pride. "Especially. . . ." Her eyes filled with tears, and she dropped her head. Daniel stared at the shorn locks, then at her hand. He remembered the day of Sehebi's death, and he looked at the stub of her pinky, still red, ugly, filled with puss. He remembered her chopping off the fingertip with a knife, an act of mourning by a grieving Comanche woman who had lost her granddaughter.

"He goes for you," Daniel said. "To ration day?"

"Yes. It is far."

"He is a good man." The words sounded forced, but Grace Morning Star did not notice.

"You need more meat," she said, rising. "Your ribs stick out like the dog I killed three suns ago."

He smiled. Patty Mullen had written that he was rotund, but the wife of Teepee That Stands Alone found him skinny. He chewed on the meat, and laughed, wondering what Mr. Caldwell would think when he found out he was eating dog. Daniel stopped chewing. When was the last time he had eaten dog? He made sure Grace Morning

Star wasn't looking, then spit out the partially chewed food between his legs, and covered it with dirt.

Teepee That Stands Alone did not return that night, or the next morning, frustrating Ellenbogen, but mostly Caldwell, and causing Grace Morning Star to apologize more.

Patty Mullen wandered around the camp, Vaughan Coyne stared at the mountains, Leviticus Ellenbogen took a nap, and Caldwell complained. Daniel busied himself reading his notebooks, making new notes in the margins, scratching through some words, underlining others, sorting things in his mind.

"Shit!"

He looked up, saw Patty Mullen clutching her bare foot near the brush arbor, saw the blood, and he slammed the tablet shut, went to her, but Grace Morning Star reached her first, apologizing in broken English.

"Such language," Caldwell said with a snort, "from a lady!"

Sitting on a boulder, Patty Mullen bit back something stronger than her first epitaph. "I'm all right," Patty protested as Grace Morning Star lifted her leg. "Cut my foot on a rock."

"What were you doing in your bare feet?"

Daniel asked.

"Shut up!" Patty displayed her rare Irish temper.

"Sorry," Grace Morning Star said in English. She looked at Daniel. "I fix." And to Patty: "You wait. Cut bad not. Here." She thrust the leg into Daniel's hand. "Keep this like."

"Will you be all right, Miss Mullen?" A groggy Ellenbogen, at least, had the courtesy to walk over to see her, whereas Caldwell remained near the lodge, savoring his last cigar.

"Yes." She sighed. "My shoes were pinching my feet." She wriggled her toes. "My socks are filthy."

Daniel felt like he was blushing. He wasn't comfortable holding a woman's leg, her foot bare, bleeding. It was a nice foot, and the cut wasn't deep, but bled profusely. He wished Grace Morning Star would hurry back with her medicine and wrappings. He stopped staring at her foot and calf, focused on the dirt around the brush arbor, found an old bone near a rock, a worn bone, with a drilled hole in one end, smooth from age and use. The bone from a buffalo's leg. He studied it for what seemed an eternity.

"Perhaps we should give up this fool's errand and get Miss Mullen back to Fort Sill,"

Ellenbogen said. "Major Becker should attend her."

"I'm all right," Patty protested. "It was just a rock."

"Not a rock, ma'am." With a grunt, Ellenbogen squatted and found a piece of metal in the sand. He held it with his finger. "Rusty iron. It can be dangerous."

"Lockjaw would definitely silence *The National Temperance Leader.*" Caldwell, who had just walked over, laughed hard. The last to arrive, Vaughan Coyne, sighed, shaking his head at the commissioner's attempt at a joke.

Grace Morning Star returned, and took Patty's foot from Daniel, who stared at the iron in Leviticus Ellenbogen's fingers. His heart sank, and he whispered an oath.

"What is it?" Ellenbogen asked, but looked away when Patty cried out in pain and told Grace Morning Star: "That hurts."

Daniel wet his lips, walked away, not answering Ellenbogen's questions, knowing that Teepee That Stands Alone would not come. Not this day. Not tomorrow. Not with the *taibos* here. Maybe not even if Daniel had come here alone.

"Agent Ellenbogen's right. Let's quit chasing this ghost of a Comanche heathen," Caldwell said. "Let's get Miss Mullen back

to Fort Sill to see the Army's idiot sawbones. More importantly, let's get back to
see if the post sutler in this abysmal place
has any decent cigars for sale."

CHAPTER
TWENTY-TWO

"Tell your husband that we are sorry we have missed him, but we cannot wait." Daniel looked into Grace Morning Star's old eyes. "Tell him that I have found what I sought from my vision."

She smiled. "He will be pleased. He will be proud of you."

He couldn't look at the woman any more, found himself staring absently at his badge. "Tell him that I will see him."

With a sweet nod, she stepped away from the surrey, raising her maimed hand in a farewell. "Good," she said in guttural English. " 'Bye."

"So long, fair maiden," Caldwell said in wretched sarcasm, and tapped Vaughan Coyne's shoulder. "Let's go home, good man."

Coyne flicked the reins. The lawyer had asked to drive, privately telling Daniel that he couldn't stand sitting in the back with that pompous deputy commissioner any more, and Daniel didn't mind. He sat in the back beside Patty Mullen, thankful when Caldwell quickly drifted off to sleep, and pulled out his notebooks, reading again. In front of Daniel sat Ellenbogen.

It was, he thought when he looked up an hour later, a beautiful day. To his right rose the Wichitas against a blue sky dotted with a few white clouds low in the horizon. Wind blew the tall grass like ocean waves, and trees formed patches of rich green on the brown and tan rocks of the mountains. He wet his lips, and read some more.

"He buries his nose in those tablets like they're Dickens."

Daniel sighed. Jonathan Caldwell had awakened. He tried to ignore him, turned the page, spotted a note he had written back at a campsite south of the Red River.

"You have been poring over those pages," Coyne said easily, trying to make conversation. "Find anything new?"

Daniel started to close the tablet, but looked at the words again. *Don't believe the Police Gazzette!*

"I spelled *Gazette* wrong," Daniel said, and Coyne, Patty, even Ellenbogen laughed.

Looking around again, Daniel frowned.

"You know where you're going?" he asked.

"East," Coyne said. "You think I'm lost?"

Daniel shook his head, closed the tablet, and dropped it at his feet, deciding to give the *Police Gazette* one more try. "No, Dakota, I think you know exactly where you're going."

Patty's head turned sharply. Ellenbogen seemed not to have heard. Caldwell just didn't care, and patted his suit coat in a futile search for one more cigar. Slowly Coyne looked over his shoulder at Daniel, his eyes narrowing.

"Daniel," he said evenly. "I've never been called Dakota." He turned forward, clucking the reins, and saying: "You're barking up the wrong tree, Daniel. Now, let's drop it. I'm your friend. I'm not Dakota."

"Nobody's Dakota," Daniel said. He wet his lips. "It's like Frank Striker said back at the agency. When he called Miss Mullen 'Dallas'. He said it didn't mean anything. Blake Browne didn't mean anything, either. Just a name. Just a place."

Leviticus Ellenbogen turned his big head, suddenly intrigued by Daniel's statement. Jonathan Caldwell sighed, and pulled down his tall silk hat.

"Go on," Patty Mullen spoke in an unsure voice.

"Sure." Coyne chuckled. "Go on. I'm a lawyer. I'll hear your theory, but I'm starting to think you need to hire a new counselor. Your cheap accusations are annoying me."

"First there was Blake Browne's partner," Daniel said. "Ted Smith, but Browne called him 'Uvalde'. Smith came from Uvalde. At least once, Browne called Marshal Noble 'Arkansas'. Just a point of reference. That's all he meant when he mentioned Dakota."

"Interesting." Coyne shook his head. "But not evidence. It doesn't make me this man Dakota."

"But you told me you once worked at the Standing Rock Agency. That's in Dakota Territory."

"I never said I hadn't practiced in Dakota."

"That's where you met Fenn O'Malley. That's where you got O'Malley cleared of a whiskey-running charge. That's what Brink Brinkerhoff wanted to talk to me about." He was guessing now. "Brink recognized you. That's your biggest mistake. A damned foolish mistake. O'Malley wasn't the only soldier from the Seventh transferred to Fort Sill. That's what will hang you."

"Have you proof, Sergeant Killstraight?" Ellenbogen said gruffly.

No, he had no proof. Daniel knew he could be dead wrong. He didn't know what Trooper Brinkerhoff wanted to talk to him about, and Blake Browne's Dakota could very well have been Fenn O'Malley, but he was certain, dead certain, that Vaughan Coyne was not his friend, never had been.

"I have plenty," Daniel lied.

Coyne pulled hard on the reins, stopping the surrey, prompting another curse from Caldwell. He set the brake, wrapped the reins around the lever, and turned, his eyes angry as they locked on Daniel.

"You try my patience, boy. I got you out of that hell hole they call a jail in Wichita Falls. When Blake Browne filed a charge against you, I got the charge dismissed."

"So you could frame me for Browne's murder. Or try to. When that didn't work, you had to kill the other *taibo,* Horace Benson."

"Your marshal pal asked me to defend you. Remember?"

"Did he? I thought so, too, but you didn't seem to recognize Harvey's name when you first visited me. Not that it matters. Maybe he did ask you, but you planned on defending me anyway. To find out how much I really did now about Coursey and Cox, to learn how much Blake Browne had told me.

To find out if you needed to shut Blake Browne up permanently. Which you did. And then you needed to shut me up. Stop me. Somehow."

"I stopped that lynch party," Coyne said. "You'd be dead if not for me."

"You started that lynch mob," Daniel said. "Harvey Noble and Hugh Gunter stopped them. You planted that Old Glory tablet under the body of the second whiskey runner you killed."

"That's an infernal lie."

"I bought that tablet in Wichita Falls. Remember? You walked into the mercantile with me. Nobody else knows my superstition when it comes to pencil tablets." *Except Gunter and Noble,* Daniel thought. *And Patty Mullen. Maybe Ellenbogen. Perhaps a lot of others, but nobody in Wichita Falls.* At least, the theory sounded good to him, and he must have jabbed Vaughan Coyne's nerves.

"My God, Daniel. I'll slap a slander suit on you. I suppose I also killed those two Creeks!"

Daniel said nothing to that. "You murdered Blake Browne," he said. "Slashed his thigh. Made it look Injun. Or O'Malley killed him. But you helped him."

"Daniel . . . ," Patty began.

"Have you forgotten that I warned you

301

about Carl Quantrell?" Coyne's face had paled.

Daniel shook his head. "You were the only person, other than Agent Ellenbogen, who knew I was going to Dallas. You got word to Quantrell, maybe. You told those thugs. . . ."

A scene from that dark night near the Trinity River popped into his head again. He shook his head. "No." He looked at Patty, his mouth open as a new thought came to him. Laughing, he turned back to Coyne. "I'm a damned fool."

"That's the first sensible thing you've said." Coyne pointed above his right eye. "Remember Quantrell cut me with his knife, to keep me from helping you. Threatened my life. He wounded me because I was helping you."

"Over your right eye." Daniel tilted his head toward the deputy commissioner. "You pointed something like this out back in Pittsfield, didn't you, Mister Caldwell?"

"What?" Caldwell, for once, looked uncomfortable. "I am completely lost and struck dumb by this conversation."

"You're left-handed, Vaughan," Daniel said. "You cut yourself. Left hand holding a knife, it's natural to put it over your right eye. And I bet if I asked Major Becker about Blake Browne, he might agree that Browne was brained first. He wasn't shot with those arrows. You stabbed him with them. That explains why one of those pathetically made arrows broke. No Indian would have used such arrows. Indians have pride in their work. Those arrows hadn't been fired from a bow. They were rammed into the body like a spear. I bet the way those wounds were would suggest they came from a left-handed man."

Another wild guess. Browne could have been shot with those arrows. Suddenly he heard the *clopping* of hoofs. Vaughan Coyne swung back to face the road. Daniel lifted his eyes hopefully, wanting to see Marshal Harvey Noble and Hugh Gunter riding hard to save his life, but knew. . . . Cursing himself, he grabbed Patty's hand with his left as Coyne reached inside his coat, and he dived off the surrey, pulling Patty behind him.

Nácutsi, he was thinking as he fell. Nácutsi could have fired those arrows into Browne. He has no pride.

He hit the ground with a grunt, his hat rolling over the rocky ground. Rising, Daniel jerked the Remington from its holster. "Run!" he screamed, and he was pulling Patty to her feet, searching the rocks to his right, shoving her. "Run, Mister Ellenbogen! They mean to kill us!"

Too late. He saw the gun in Vaughan Coyne's hand. Heard the horses bringing Fenn O'Malley and Nácutsi closer.

"What is the meaning of this?" Caldwell cried out.

Standing in the surrey, Coyne thumbed back the hammer, but a giant hand swallowed both pistol and hand. "Run!" Leviticus Ellenbogen yelled. "Get out of here!" The agent shoved Coyne over the wagon's side, turned, standing, reaching for the brake and the reins. "Get Miss Mullen out of here!"

A gunshot sounded like a cannon. Nácutsi shrieked his war cry, jacked another round into his Winchester.

Daniel pushed Patty toward the rocks. "That way!" he said. "Get over that ridge." Not that it was much of a ridge. He looked back. Leviticus Ellenbogen desperately worked at the brake and reins. Jonathan Caldwell had leaped down off the surrey, screaming, fleeing in a wild panic. Underneath the wagon crawled Vaughan Coyne. The lawyer still had his pistol in his hand. He cocked, aimed. Daniel heard the pop, saw the smoke, but the bullet sang off a rock somewhere. He snapped a shot himself, missing, started moving back toward the rocks, toward Patty. The horses charged.

"Get out of there!" Daniel heard himself yelling at the Indian agent. "Take cover!"

Another rifle boomed. Ellenbogen jerked back, releasing the brake, dropping the reins, slamming into the seat, and slumping over, as the wagon lurched forward.

By then Daniel was running, catching up with the confused Patty Mullen, grabbing her hand, jerking her, pulling her roughly over the lichen-covered rocks. He dived, taking her with him, hearing another gunshot, yelling as the bullet tore through his left calf.

They hit the rocks on the other side of the low rise. Blood already soaked his pants, his moccasin. He crawled up, pulled the Remington's trigger, saw Fenn O'Malley dive from the saddle, saw Nácutsi charge his pony after the screaming, terrified deputy commissioner. He saw the surrey, saw Vaughan Coyne, saw Leviticus Ellenbogen.

He closed his eyes, but only briefly, and ducked as O'Malley drew his Colt, and loosened a shot.

"Come on," Daniel told Patty. "This is no good."

Horses screamed. The team jerked the surrey down the road.

A bullet whined off a rock to Daniel's left.

"Gunpowder!" Fenn O'Malley roared at the Comanche scout. "Get your ass back here! Coyne! Coyne!" No answer.

He didn't have much time. Daniel glanced at the Remington. Three shots. If the percussion caps worked — if the cylinder hadn't been shot loose — if the damned relic would fire. The rocky field wouldn't offer much cover, nor could they hide in the grass. Patty Mullen couldn't run far, not with her injured foot, and the bullet that had torn through Daniel's leg would slow him considerably. Quickly Patty loosened a scarf, tying it around Daniel's wound, looked left, right.

"What are we going to do?" she asked.

Daniel had no clue. The mountains were too far, but just north, maybe two hundred yards, rose a dead cottonwood. That was it. One tree, but it was better than where they were.

Crouching, he pulled himself to his feet. "Come on," he told Patty, taking her hand again. Roughly, stumbling painfully, they darted through the grass toward the barren tree in the middle of . . . what had Caldwell called it . . . ? Perdition itself.

Just as the palomino mare carrying Nácutsi rounded the corner, they slid underneath the giant tree. Daniel gasped, shoved Patty hard toward the ground, lying still, watching, trying to control his savage breaths, his pounding heart. Slowly he raised his head just a bit, saw Nácutsi rein in and slide from the saddle, running in a crouch toward the rise, toward the rocks where Daniel and Patty had been hiding.

A miracle, he thought. Nácutsi hadn't seen them. But it didn't matter. The Army hired him as a scout for a good reason, and even a fool would be able to follow the trail through the grass, follow the blood. Nácutsi crawled the last few rods, then stopped.

"Gunpowder!" O'Malley's voice screamed from the other side of the rise. "Where the hell are you?"

Nácutsi sat up, studying the land in silence, then Daniel thought he could see the Comanche grin. He was looking straight at the cottonwood tree, and Daniel dropped his head. A futile gesture. Hopeless. Nácutsi had found them. Again Daniel looked around, tried to find a better place. The Remington felt heavy in his hand. He turned back as Nácutsi shot to his feet, and ran to the top of the ridge, yelling in English. "Here! Here!" Waving. Then slamming backward as the rifle roared from the other side, falling hard, his head smashing on the rocks with a sickening thud Daniel and Patty could hear over the echo, over the distance. The palomino galloped across the field of grass and rocks.

"I got that son-of-a-bitch!" Fenn O'Malley's voice.

Daniel wet his lips, cocked the Remington. "Stay here!" he said, and he was running the dash of a wounded animal, toward Nácutsi, crouching, his leg throbbing.

"I got him!" Fenn O'Malley yelled again. "Gunpowder. I killed the Metal Shirt! Gunpowder! Where the hell are you?"

He knew O'Malley would be running, too. Running up the rise.

They met. O'Malley's eyes fell on Nácutsi's body, absorbing the sight slowly, realizing he had just killed his own man, then seeing Daniel, a few rods away, saw the Remington as the hammer snapped.

Daniel cursed. Misfire. He flung the revolver at O'Malley, kept running, watched the deserter toss the single-shot Springfield rifle to the ground, jerk the Colt from his waistband. O'Malley was cocking the big .45 when Daniel slammed his shoulder into O'Malley's stomach. They fell hard against the rocks. The pistol roared. Daniel's ear rang painfully from the shot. He rolled off, cursing himself for throwing the Remington, realizing he should have tried the other two chambers. Tried to stand, attack, but his leg gave, and he fell, turned over, saw Fenn O'Malley standing over him, bringing the gun barrel down. Then dropping the Colt. Dropping to his knees. Holding the two quivering shafts of arrows in his stomach. O'Malley's eyes began to glaze over, and blood poured from his mouth.

Another arrow slammed into his chest, and the soldier fell beside Nácutsi.

I'm dreaming all this, Daniel thought. *I'm dead.* Yet when his eyes opened, Teepee That Stands Alone was looking down on him.

"All rubbed out," Teepee That Stands Alone said, lowering his bow, then drawing a knife. "You claimed first coup on the Long Knife. His scalp is yours to take."

CHAPTER TWENTY-THREE

He tried to stand, couldn't, looked at the two dead men on the rocks, then down at the road. The surrey was gone, stopping maybe a quarter mile down the path, taking Leviticus Ellenbogen with it, and Vaughan Coyne lay in the dust, not moving. It took a moment before Daniel understood what had happened. When O'Malley had shot Ellenbogen, the agent, probably already dead, had released the brake, and the horses had taken off, running over the Wichita Falls lawyer, breaking his back, or his neck. Remembering Jonathan Caldwell's story of his famous Pittsfield murder case, Daniel shook his head as he said, in English: "There's God's justice for you."

He thought of Patty Mullen, tried to stand again, still couldn't, fell back, and yelled: "Patty! Patty! It's all over." The last sentence was barely a whisper. That practically drained him, and he lay down, staring at the sky.

Roughly Teepee That Stands Alone said: "Then I will take his scalp."

Somewhere deep within him, Daniel gathered the strength to sit up, if not stand. He saw Patty Mullen, slowly limping, uncertain, unsteadily, through the high grass. Teepee That Stands Alone knelt over the dead trooper's body, and Daniel shouted: "No. You will not touch this man!"

The old *puhakat* turned slowly, with disgust. "You are not of The People. You have forgotten our ways."

"You are the one who has forgotten, old man," Daniel said angrily, and he made himself stand, made himself tall, kept himself, somehow, on his feet.

"I do not keep his scalp," Teepee That Stands Alone said. "I keep nothing of the Pale Eyes."

"You lie."

Teepee That Stands Alone straightened, took a wild step toward Daniel, willed himself to stop.

"I found the iron at your brush arbor," Daniel said. "Iron from the hoops for Pale Eyes barrels. The iron you got at ration day when you came for your wife. Iron you used to make the points of the arrows. The arrows that the Cherokee, Hugh Gunter, found in the Creek whiskey runners. You killed those Creeks."

Teepee That Stands Alone shoved the knife into its sheath.

"They brought the whiskey that stole my son from me," the old man said. "They brought the whiskey that stole. . . ." His voice cracked. "My granddaughter. My . . . beautiful . . . granddaughter."

Daniel shook his head. "No. They were bad men, yes, but they did not sell that whiskey to your son who goes to The Land Beyond The Sun." He pointed at Fenn O'Malley. "This was that man." Pointed at Nácutsi. "He helped, too." And tilted his head toward the road. "And that one."

"I have avenged my son," said Teepee That Stands Alone. "I have avenged my granddaughter. It is the way of the Kwahadi."

Patty Mullen gagged at the sight of the two dead man. She swallowed, searched Daniel's eyes. "Where's . . . ?" she began, looking at the road, finding Coyne, gasping. "Mister Ellenbogen?" She struggled with the words. "Mister Caldwell?"

Daniel shook his head. He was certain Nácutsi had killed the deputy commissioner before returning to hunt down Patty and him. "Sit down," he told her, and looked back at the Kwahadi holy man.

"Is it the way of the Kwahadi to make others think that someone else killed those Creeks?" he said, feeling sick, light-headed, maybe even broken-hearted. "My friend Hugh Gunter found the whip you used on those Creeks. The leather was old, but the bone handle was new. A cow bone. I found the buffalo bone, the handle you first made years ago for that whip, in your brush arbor. You changed the handle. You left it behind. Made it seem as if another warrior of The People killed those men. Like me." He looked at Fenn O'Malley's corpse, felt a dry laugh coming, shook his head. "Everybody wanted the Pale Eyes to think I was killing whiskey men." Glaring again at the *puhakat*. "Yes, old man, you learned much from the Pale Eyes."

Teepee That Stands Alone's eyes became slits.

"You always boasted of how you were better than all of The People," Daniel said. "You were no different than Coyote Chaser in that regard. You said you took nothing from the Pale Eyes. But that man standing in line at the last ration day was right. You have no *puha*. What's more, you have no pride."

"I will show you my power," the old man

said defiantly, and reached again for his knife.

"You rode the Iron Horse to Texas, old man. I never thought about it until now. Why would the great Teepee That Stands Alone do that? Ride a Pale Eyes train. Stay in a Pale Eyes hotel. Drink coffee, and eat the hard bread of Long Knives. All would destroy your power. Unless your power was already destroyed."

The hand clenched on the bone handle of the knife.

"You collected rations for your wife." Finally Daniel's words stopped the *puhakat*'s hand. "Rations from the Pale Eyes. Which you used yourself. To make arrows. You also used the bone of a *taibo* cow to make a new handle for your whip. You used these as a Pale Eyes would use them, too, used them as you used your own tongue, as crooked, as false, as many Pale Eyes tongues. The great Teepee That Stands Alone uses nothing from a Pale Eyes. That is your lie. Your wife even has a *taibo* name. Grace, she calls herself." He hated bringing that nice Comanche woman into this, but the result was what he needed. The *puhakat*'s shoulders collapsed, the arms dropped to his sides, his head bowed. "Quanah Parker always sought your counsel. We respected you, Teepee That Stands Alone. We loved you. But you shamed us. You shamed yourself. You destroyed your power."

When the Kwahadi looked up, Daniel was the one who felt shamed, shamed by the tears streaming down the old man's face. "You say what your heart tells you," Teepee That Stands Alone said. "But think of what your heart would have told you to do had your granddaughter been killed as mine died. My power is destroyed. What you say is true. I knew it would be destroyed when I rode this trail."

Daniel hung his head. "I cannot say that I blame you," he said. His head rose. "I will protect you as best as I can. This I will do for Grace Morning Star. My heart could not stand seeing her mourn again. Maybe I will do this for Teepee That Stands Alone, for what he once was. But I cannot do this if you take this man's scalp. I cannot do this if your vengeance does not end. Here."

"It is done." The medicine man's voice sounded like thunder, and he turned away. "I am finished."

Daniel struggled with the tight collar and tie, then gave up, gently crossed his legs, and tried to keep from shaking. He sat in

the judge's quarters at Fort Smith, holding
the cane Major Becker had given him for
his wounded leg. On either side of him sat
Hugh Gunter and Harvey Noble. All three
watched a tall man in a blue suit rolling a
cigar in his fingers, talking in hushed tones
with the judge who oversaw the Western
District of Arkansas, which included Indian
Territory.

A lifetime later, Judge Isaac C. Parker and
the taller man walked toward the sofa, and
settled into chairs across from the three
peace officers from Indian Territory.

"Gentlemen." Judge Parker looked older
than Daniel had imagined, like a man
weighted down with an anvil, but his voice
resonated with strength and dignity. It was
a voice that had reminded him of Teepee
That Stands Alone, before that day in the
Wichitas. "You know Solicitor Bates, I pre-
sume."

Still rolling the cigar in his left hand, Bates
reached across a table with his right, smiling at Daniel. "I haven't had the pleasure,
Sergeant Killstraight."

Daniel set the cane aside. The man had a
brutal grip.

"I wish our meeting could have been
under less somber conditions," Judge Parker said gravely. "A terrible affair, what hap-

pened on the reservation. A deputy Indian commissioner gunned down and scalped. A fine man like Leviticus Ellenbogen assassinated by an Army deserter and whiskey runner."

"Ellenbogen died a hero," Bates reminded the judge.

"He saved my life," Daniel said. Which wasn't a lie.

"A hero." Bates retired the unlit cigar into his breast pocket. "As we speak, his body is on a special train to Albany, to lie in state for a week before being transported to our national cemetery near Washington City."

"He fought in the late war to preserve our Union," Judge Parker said. "Was wounded twice. A fine, bold, and highly principled man with a grand heart, and the mettle of a Hercules."

Daniel wet his lips. He hadn't known that Ellenbogen had been a soldier in the Civil War. Hadn't known anything, really, about Leviticus Ellenbogen.

"Patricia Mullen could not tell us much about the final events in the Wichita Mountains," Bates said, coming to business. "She was hiding for much of this gun battle."

"You are to be commended, Sergeant, for saving her life," the judge interrupted.

"Indeed," Bates agreed.

317

Daniel shifted in his seat, tried to gather enough saliva to swallow.

"There is, however," Bates said, "much we don't understand."

Daniel nodded, hoped Gunter or Noble would say something, but they had become wooden statues. "There is much," Daniel began, "that I do not understand."

"What can you tell us?" Judge Parker said.

"Start with the gun battle, Sergeant," Bates said.

So Daniel began his lie, leaving Teepee That Stands Alone out of the story. He started with the truth, how Ellenbogen had grabbed Vaughan Coyne's gun, saving Daniel's life, then pushed the lawyer off the surrey, but had been shot by O'Malley, releasing the brake, spooking the horses, the wagon running over Coyne, crushing his skull. Commissioner Caldwell had fled, only to be shot down by Nácutsi. Daniel kept Nácutsi's death pretty close to the truth, too, but said he had killed O'Malley, had shot him with the Remington. He only hoped he had persuaded Patty Mullen to say the same thing, to forget about the three arrows she had seen in the dead deserter's chest and stomach. To forget Teepee That Stands Alone had been there.

They had buried the dead whiskey runners near the road, but returned the bodies of Ellenbogen and the commissioner to Fort Sill. Relatives had claimed the remains of Ellenbogen and Caldwell, but he doubted if anyone would dig up Fenn O'Malley and realize the man had been killed with arrows, not bullets.

"I was lucky," Daniel concluded, "but, again, I would not be alive had it not been for Agent Ellenbogen's bravery."

Neither judge nor solicitor said anything for a minute. The clock chimed, and Judge Parker cleared his throat. "This O'Malley and the lawyer were part of a whiskey-running gang?"

"In a dice game, Fenn O'Malley won the Coursey and Cox Bottling Works and ginger beer brewery," Daniel said, a little more comfortable with the truth. "When everything got bogged down in the courts, O'Malley hired Coyne. They had known each other in Dakota Territory."

"Yes," Bates said. "Miss Mullen uncovered the court records in Dallas that connected O'Malley with Coyne, but Coyne was hired before, as you say, things 'got bogged down.' After O'Malley killed the gambler, he hired Coyne as his defense counsel. Coyne got that charge dismissed after a preliminary hearing. Also, I have a statement from a soldier named Brinkerhoff that says he recognized Coyne from Dakota, and that Coyne had indeed served as the late O'Malley's counselor on a whiskey-running charge there."

Daniel nodded. "I remembered something when we were in the Wichita Mountains, when I looked back at my notes. When I first spoke to Vaughan Coyne, I told him about the bottles I had found in Blake Browne's wagon. All Coursey and Cox bottles. He said . . . 'That's a lot of ginger beer.' But I never told him the bottles were ginger beer, just beer. That's something he shouldn't have known, not as a Wichita Falls resident. At least that's how I see it. I just didn't see it until I was looking over my notes."

"Always a smart thing to do." A crooked smile appeared underneath Harvey Noble's giant mustache.

"I don't know when they got the idea to run whiskey," Daniel said. "Probably when they had all these empty bottles, a bankrupt bottling plant and brewery. I suspect it was O'Malley's idea, but I'm not sure. Maybe Vaughan Coyne had helped O'Malley run whiskey in Dakota, too. We do know that O'Malley sold whiskey often."

Bates's head bobbed slightly. "And often

to the Indians."

Daniel paused. Hugh Gunter decided to take over.

"We also know, Judge, that these Wichita Falls boys had gotten word to the Creeks, told them to keep out of the Comanche reservation. Apparently they wanted that country for their own."

"At least till they ran out of ginger beer bottles," Noble added.

"So they killed those two Creek Indians that Mister Gunter discovered in the Choctaw Nation," Judge Parker said. "As warning?"

Gunter nodded. "That appears to be the size of it."

"And Blake Browne?" Bates asked. "And the other murdered whiskey runner . . . um, Horace Benson? They killed those two men as well?"

"Yes, sir," Daniel said. "But it wasn't a warning. We think . . . that is, I think . . . that it was O'Malley, most likely, but it could have been Coyne, killed those two men. I think they wanted to make everyone think I did it." He had dismissed the idea that Nácutsi had shot Browne. A Comanche wouldn't have used arrows with hawk feathers, would not have slashed the thighs. No, that had been the work of a *taibo*. Or *taibos*.

"Daniel wouldn't stop nosing around," Harvey Noble said. "They wanted him dead, one way or the other. But they didn't want to make a martyr out of him, have a bunch of lawdogs like me hunting down his killer. They wanted to make it look like he was a dirty, murdering savage."

"They slashed those men's thighs," Daniel said. "That's Lakota sign."

Gunter added: "O'Malley and Coyne picked that up in Dakota, too. Damned fools figured it was the sign for any Indian."

"But this Blake Browne," Judge Parker said, "he said he had worked for these men."

"That's right," Daniel said. "He said he'd never work for Dakota again, though. They must have had some disagreement. Over their split. Or something."

"Wouldn't be the first time whiskey runners started fighting amongst themselves," Gunter added.

"When I caught him that first time, he thought I was working for this Dakota," Daniel said.

"Your Honor," Noble said, "Browne figured he was being cheated by Coyne and O'Malley, and Coyne and Malley figured they didn't need Browne any more. That's another reason they killed Browne."

"And tried to make Daniel hang for it,"

Gunter added. "Same with Benson. He was running whiskey for them. They killed him, planted the tablet under his body, just to get Daniel strung up."

Bates took a deep breath. "We still have little proof."

"And we ain't likely to get much from a bunch of dead folks," Noble said. "But there's a little more. Browne operated out of Teepee City. Coyne told Daniel he had been up that way, had found nothing, but that didn't strike me as factual, because I've arrested six or seven runners in that disputed chunk of land they call Greer County who come out of Teepee City. I knew that Teepee City was Blake Browne's stronghold. So I rode that way. Not exactly my territory, but, well. . . ."

"And found those ginger beer bottles," Bates said.

"That's right. Only they were full of forty-rod, not Dallas brew. I destroyed the whiskey, and helped jog the memories of a few of Teepee City's finest."

Bates's smile was wicked. "I can imagine how you did that, Marshal."

Harvey Noble had a fairly wicked grin himself. "Well, they recollected Vaughan Coyne and Fenn O'Malley real good after I buffaloed three of 'em. Daniel's right. Best

I figure things, from what I learned in Teepee City, is that Coyne and O'Malley supplied the bottles, which Browne filled with his rotgut. Browne had the still, see. Then Coyne and O'Malley decided, once they found out where the still was, they didn't need Browne no more."

"I can't believe a lawyer as smart as I have been led to believe this Vaughan Coyne was could ever think he could get away with all this," Judge Parker said.

Gunter snorted. "Criminals ain't never smart. Just uppity."

"Very true," Parker said sadly. "Very true."

"Coyne's law practice wasn't making much money," Daniel said. "Whiskey running can be profitable."

"And what became of the Texas Ranger?" Parker said.

Noble's gaze fell on his dirty boots. Daniel stared at the lawman. Quantrell was one part of the puzzle he couldn't quite fit, but he had started a new theory back on that road in the Wichita Mountains.

"Well, reckon I'm partly to blame for all that," Noble began. "Reckon I should have confided in Daniel, told him about our operation." He stroked his mustache before facing Daniel. "It's what we called a joint operation, Daniel. Carl Quantrell was act-

324

ing on the sly, a spy if you will. It was our intention to make folks believe he was crooked as they come, that he was helping transport whiskey into the Nations."

Bates picked up the story. "Quantrell came to Browne, confided in him, earned that nefarious character's trust. The last report Ranger Quantrell sent to Austin was that he was on his way from Dallas to Wichita Falls, then on to Teepee City."

Daniel sighed, and tested his own idea. "Coyne kept pointing to Quantrell, saying he was Dakota, saying he was trying to kill me."

"Blake Browne trusted Carl," Noble said. "Coyne, however, suspicioned him."

"Typical for a miserable, damned *dtyhh*." Gunter spit into the nearest cuspidor.

"When I was beaten up in Dallas," Daniel said, "Quantrell stopped those thugs from hurting me worse than they did. He found Coyne's note on me. I remember him cursing Coyne."

"That's likely when Carl realized Coyne's part in all this," Noble said. "Miss Mullen come along, and Carl took off, still pretending to be a real bad *hombre*. Went off after Vaughan Coyne."

"Has there been any word from him?" Parker asked.

Noble's head shook. "Best guess, Your Honor, is Carl's dead. Reckon he confronted Coyne, and Coyne, or O'Malley, killed him. That's about the time O'Malley deserted."

"Dead?" Bates shook his head.

"If I was a betting man, I'd say they took his body out toward Teepee City, buried or dumped him somewhere. There's a lot of country out yonder to hide a dead Texas Ranger. Maybe they killed him there. We might not never know. They likely flew into a panic once they'd done Carl in. Killing a Ranger in Texas'll put the fear of God in even the coolest criminal. My guess is that they hid the body, then realized they should start some rumor that Daniel was to blame."

"A terrible shame," Parker said, "if it's true. A terrible loss, to us, and to all of Texas."

"Yes, sir," Noble said. "Carl was a fine man. You would have liked him, Daniel. Liked him when he wasn't pretending to be the biggest enemy you ever had."

Daniel didn't know what to say.

"Why murder Ellenbogen and Caldwell?" Bates asked. "Why the ambuscade?"

"Everything was coming apart on them," Noble said. "Likely they decided they had to kill Daniel once and for all. The agent and that Caldwell fellow just showed up at the wrong time."

Gunter added: "They would have killed that newspaper woman, too. That's how rotten those men were."

A Regulator clock chimed. Daniel wet his lips. His leg ached.

Parker spoke again. "And the dead Comanche? The one who took the life of his daughter?"

Sighing, Daniel said: "Suicide. I wanted to believe that Coyne killed him, too, but, from what evidence we have, we believe he took his own life."

"I would have done the same," Gunter said. "But wouldn't have taken so long to do it."

"What about the other Comanche?" Parker asked.

"The one they call Gunpowder?" Noble said. "He ain't the first Comanche to help white men sell whiskey to Indians."

The judge's head shook. "No, not that one. I mean the old man in that place near the Red River. The one with the dead kitten, that died that awful death."

"Seven Beavers," Daniel said.

"Was he poisoned?" Bates asked.

"Bad batch of whiskey," Gunter said. "Just bad luck for that old chief. Ain't that right,

327

Daniel?"

Daniel lied one last time.

CHAPTER
TWENTY-FOUR

It is the way of The People, Daniel explained to the new agent, Joshua Biggers. When a Comanche becomes too old, too much of a burden, he is thrown away.

Biggers's head shook without comprehension. "A life of violence, a life of darkness without Christian compassion, thus ends with neglect," the agent said in a soft Southern drawl.

"I guess you could say that," Daniel said.

The agent sighed. "I do not understand this at all, Daniel," Biggers said. "It will take prayer. It will take time."

Daniel smiled. Biggers was a young man, a Baptist preacher from North Carolina, the third agent in less than two years to try to understand the Comanches, Kiowas, and Apaches on the reservation. The Department of the Interior had tried a Texan hard rock and an Israelite. Now it was Biggers's chance. Daniel offered his hand, and thought of Leviticus Ellenbogen with a great deal of sadness, thought that maybe the previous agent would have been able to help, been able to understand, if Daniel hadn't been so blind, and angry, so distrustful of any white man. "I will help," Daniel said, "if I can." He jutted his jaw at the door. "I will speak to Coyote Chaser. I will see to him, Reverend."

"Thank you, kindly," Biggers said as he shook Daniel's hand, and slowly, Bible in hand, he turned, and walked away.

After taking a deep breath, Daniel limped into an agency cabin that smelled of death. He leaned his hickory cane against the wall, slowly grabbed an oaken barrel, and dragged it over to the cot. He pulled back the damp sheet, and took the frail hand of the dying Yamparika.

The marsh hawk's words rang again in his mind: *Remember Maman-ti.*

In the language of The People, he whispered: "Hear me, Coyote Chaser. I know your heart. I know that your wife, your family have cast you out. I know you asked them to do this. I know you asked them because of your heart. Because of your shame." He looked at the closed, still eyes, hoping for a response.

"I know," Daniel said, "that you killed the

Penateka from Huupi. . . ." Careful not to say Seven Beavers's name. "I know you poisoned him. Like the *dohate* once cast a curse and claimed the life of the great peace chief of our Kiowa friends, you killed the old Penateka. I do not know why."

He stopped, gathering his memories. It had been his first thought, after the death of Seven Beavers. He had ridden south to prove Coyote Chaser had killed Seven Beavers, had murdered him, poisoned him. Later, he started to blame white whiskey runners, but he had been right the first time. He wished he hadn't.

"Maybe you were angry with him as you often were, and your anger led to this wicked deed. Perhaps it was because he was old, and you knew he would be thrown away, too, and you did not wish that upon him, even a man you fought with often. But you killed him, and by killing him, as a great leader of The People, you knew that you must forfeit your own life. This is why you are here, traveling to The Land Beyond The Sun."

The breath was ragged. Still no response.

"I do not understand all," Daniel said. "I am not the bright detective they say I am." He thought of Patty Mullen, wondered if she had reached Omaha yet, having closed

The National Temperance Leader in Dallas, having said good bye to Daniel at the Fort Smith depot. The newspaper folded because of a lack of advertising, she had told him, but he wasn't sure that was the real reason. The real reason might have been seeing the Wichita Mountains stained with blood. Or lying about Fenn O'Malley's death to a federal judge and prosecutor. "I am not the brave warrior The People say I am." He thought of Fenn O'Malley, thought of the warrior's feast Ben Buffalo Bone had thrown last night for Daniel. The People sang of the bravery of the Metal Shirt called Killstraight who had wiped out the whiskey runners. Whiskey kills, both Pale Eyes and Comanche called these deaths. Brave deeds by a brave man. But Daniel knew the truth. He tried to picture Leviticus Ellenbogen's body in a fancy casket in the New York capital.

"I am nothing."

Son of a Kwahadi warrior and a Mescalero Apache woman, Daniel thought, a boy shipped away from his home to travel the white man's road. A sergeant in the tribal police who earned $8 a month. A Comanche in a world that kept changing, most recently with this Dawes Act that Congress had passed. He didn't know what that would bring to The People.

Sighing again, he patted the old man's hand, held it gently. "I don't know why The People do some things. I do not know why we throw our old away. But hear me, Coyote Chaser. You will not be abandoned. You will not begin your journey to The Land Beyond The Sun alone. I will wait with you."

The breath stopped, resumed, hoarse, rattling with death, but there was a flicker beyond those eyelids, and slowly Coyote Chaser's hand squeezed Daniel's, then relaxed.

"I am here," Daniel whispered. "For me, as much as for you."

He heard something, looked up, found Rain Shower standing in the doorway. Tears filled his eyes. He tried to find the words, but could not.

"I will wait with you," Rain Shower said, and she walked toward Daniel.

ABOUT THE AUTHOR

Johnny D. Boggs has worked cattle, shot rapids in a canoe, hiked across mountains and deserts, traipsed around ghost towns, and spent hours poring over microfilm in library archives — all in the name of finding a good story. He's also one of the few Western writers to have won three Spur Awards from Western Writers of America (for his novels, *Camp Ford,* in 2006, and *Doubtful Cañon,* in 2008, and his short story, "A Piano at Dead Man's Crossing", in 2002) and the Western Heritage Wrangler Award from the National Cowboy and Western Heritage Museum (for his novel, *Spark on the Prairie: The Trial of the Kiowa Chiefs,* in 2004). A native of South Carolina, Boggs spent almost fifteen years in Texas as a journalist at the *Dallas Times Herald* and *Fort Worth Star-Telegram* before moving to New Mexico in 1998 to concentrate full time on his novels. Author of dozens of published short stories, he has also written for more than fifty newspapers and magazines, and is a frequent contributor to *Boys' Life, New Mexico Magazine, Persimmon Hill,* and *True West.* His Western novels cover a wide range. *The Lonesome Chisholm Trail* (Five Star Westerns, 2000) is an authentic cattle-drive story, while *Lonely Trumpet* (Five Star Westerns, 2002) is an historical novel about the first black graduate of West Point. *The Despoilers* (Five Star Westerns, 2002) and *Ghost Legion* (Five Star Westerns, 2005) are set in the Carolina backcountry during the Revolutionary War. *The Big Fifty* (Five Star Westerns, 2003) chronicles the slaughter of buffalo on the southern plains in the 1870s, while *East of the Border* (Five Star Westerns, 2004) is a comedy about the theatrical offerings of Buffalo Bill Cody, Wild Bill Hickok, and Texas Jack Omohundro, and *Camp Ford* (Five Star Westerns, 2005) tells about a Civil War baseball game between Union prisoners of war and Confederate guards. "Boggs's narrative voice captures the old-fashioned style of the past," *Publishers Weekly* said, and *Booklist* called him "among the best Western writers at work today." Boggs lives with his wife Lisa and son Jack in Santa Fe. His website is www .johnnydboggs.com.

RS 10-10
TW 1-11
PEP 5·11
MUM 8·11

W M V OCT 2011

FBC 12·1
PC 3-12
K65-12
MCX6-12
WB8-12
~~MME 11·12~~
DGH 11·12
WSC 2·13
MMN 4·13
WHF 8·13
BGD 10·13
PPA 2·14
SmR 6·14
EW 3-14
DGH 7-16
PEP 7·17
WMV 10-17

Horn 6|19